Quest for Eden

A Novel by Sara Drake

Whiteley Publishing

Published by Whiteley Publishing Ltd
First paperback edition 2013

ISBN 978-1-908586-64-3

~~ Dedication ~~

I would like to thank my wonderful husband Ben, for his strong belief in my writing. My six children, Jonathan, Chris, Abbie, Hannah, Ross, Hayden. I am proud of you all and always will be.

A special mention for my brother Marcus, for the idea of doing a soul mate novel in the first place. To my ever supporting family, I love you all. For those no longer with us, you maybe gone, but never forgotten.

A big thank you goes to Leah Hustchinson for the cover design.

I would also like to thank Jae, as without her help I believe getting my story into print would have been much harder.

Finally, I would like to dedicate the book to my mum and dad, as I would not be the person I am without them.

The moon said to the ocean, I have a hole in my soul. I fight to fill it, but it just keeps on spilling. It leaks out my passion, patience and knowledge. Incomplete, I feel nothing more than a reflection. The ocean replied to moon, I can help you fill it. Let my waves wash over you and inspire your imagination. Experience my calmness, to soothe away your doubting tolerance. Slip into my deep abyss and rouse with a new awareness.

~~ *Prologue* ~~

I sit on the railing of this bridge contemplating whether to jump. The devil on one shoulder whispers in my ear to end it all. An angel on the other, begs me to believe there is a higher purpose in my struggles. Either way I've had enough. I am sick and tired, tired of going on and on with no end to my dilemma in sight.

Listening to people discuss soul mates, they often wonder if they really exist. I can confirm they do and that they may cause you tremendous suffering or great happiness, depending on your situation. My name is Eve and yes, I do mean the original Eve, as in Adam and Eve.

Perhaps I should explain the predicament which traps us both. Together, my mate and I were complete, the first ever soul mates, with the idea of being apart unbearable.

Firstly, I never die. No, that isn't entirely correct. I do indeed die and have done thousands of times. I suffer the throes of death, only to be reborn again and again reincarnated. To begin with, I have no memories of my true identity, I exist in total ignorance of the fact I have ever lived before. I live a new life until my eighteenth birthday. On the rebirth of my subconscious, an electric shock of billions of past memories shudders through me. The chaos makes me catatonic for a while. When I rise to full awareness a few days later, I'm able to assign each memory into different categories in my mind. I believe divine intervention grants me the ability to process it all, because my ever faithful guardian angel watches over me.

The greatest agony is not finding my original life's companion by my side yet again. So instantly after I recover from my ordeal, I resume my unstoppable mission to track him down, hoping if I find him to reawaken the love he once felt for me. My search has often ended in failure or tragedy. I then continue in those lives, wallowing in sadness and cursing the idea of soul mates, who can crucify your heart and soul.

On the occasions I have found him and got him to remember, no matter how short lived those are, they are magical times and I wouldn't change one moment. But the only way I can make Adam remember our past, is for him to fall truly in love with me. A difficult task when I'm living in a new body, with a soul he doesn't yet recognize.

The instant when Adam, as the person he currently is, loves the new me, I see a distinctive look on his face as he passes out. The joy I feel though quickly turns to anticipation as I await his recovery. Sometimes I can deal with the disappointment of not finding him, or failing to make him fall in love with me. Other times, I need to lean on the tremendous comfort of Gabriel's presence.

If not for Gabriel, I might have already surrendered to the Devil's influence before now. Compared to him, I look like a hobbit standing next to an elf from Lord of the Rings. In this body, I am a size six and a tad over five feet tall. Gabriel, on the other hand, must be at least seven feet and I can't even estimate the circumference of his chest. He looks almost like an oversized human, with a mop of curly blonde hair and a dimpled smile. Although what truly sets him aside from us, are his large feathered white wings and bright orange eyes. Gabriel's massive size still seems sort of weird for an angel. His muscles bulging underneath a tight, silky white jumpsuit, kind of reminds me of a barefooted Superman with wings.

I truly don't deserve to have him as a guide, especially as I've also developed a bad habit of throwing objects. I once heaved a garden frog statue at his head, knocking him out cold. Suddenly worried what price I'd pay for killing an angel, if even possible to do so. I ran to where he laid on the ground. Much to my relief he came round, then staggered about for a bit, sporting a lovely black eye.

Another time when I woke as a Chinese girl, on seeing Gabriel I freaked out. That was when I discovered kicking a male angel in the balls hurt him the same way it did humans. Guess he didn't want to risk a similar experience, because I believe he has worn some kind of protection down there ever since. For an angel, Gabe isn't preachy and judgemental. Actually, he's pretty cool and has a great sense of humour, which is good because putting up with me must be extremely challenging.

After some atrocious acts on my part, Gabriel often makes himself invisible for a week or so. If he abruptly pops back up, angered and surprised, I screech at him for abandoning me.

~~ *Chapter One* ~~

The lifetime I'm currently living, Gabriel had stayed in the shadows. Just when he thought he could come out reasonably unscathed, he appeared for the first time in the ladies bathroom at my college. I gave him my opinion, punctuated with a shot of hairspray in his eyes.

Squinting because his long eyelashes were stuck together, he said, "Hello Eve."

"Piss off, Gabriel!"

He frowned. "I figured I might get that kind of response."

"So why do you even bother?" I pulled a hair brush from out of my red and black backpack and started brushing my long wavy auburn hair. "Why can't you just leave me alone for once?"

"Come on, Eve, you know I'm really your best friend. Plus, I'm only here until you wake up Adam. You can't deny we've had some good times either. Some of them granted I'd rather forget too, but all in all, we make a good team."

I heaved a sigh.

He winked at me. "We both know you love me."

I steeled myself and tried to sound defiant. "I refuse to go through this bullshit anymore. I quit." To reinforce my charade, I nonchalantly added another layer of black mascara to lashes framing my coral green eyes.

He laid a hand on my shoulder. "Who knows, Eve, this time might be the last life?"

I whirled towards him and stared into his burnt-orange eyes. "How many times have you told me that before?"

"Yes, but this still could be the one."

Before I could protest, he placed me in a bear hug. I attempted to push him away, but it was like trying to push an elephant off me.

"Gabriel?"

"Yes, Eve?"

I wheezed, "Can't breathe."

"Oops, sorry," he said, releasing me. "I forget how delicate you humans are."

Stay by Rihanna, drifted from my bag. I rifled through it and after finding my mobile phone, silenced the loud ring tone. "Can you do me a little favour, please?"

"Sure, anything." He winked.

"Give me another week to get my head together. I need some more time to figure out where to go from here. In the four weeks since I came out of the coma, I haven't detected anything to steer me in his direction. Who knows, he could even be dead like the time he died as a kid. I'm not ready yet to accept enduring another lifetime without him."

"He's not dead, Eve, otherwise I'd already know, but I do understand if you need time to pull yourself together. See you in seven days." He kissed me on the forehead and vanished.

Back at home, I flopped down on my bed and sobbed uncontrollably. My phone ringing again fractured my despair. I snatched it out of my bag. Prepared to throw it against the wall I saw a number pop up on the screen. Not in the mood to talk to anyone, I cast the phone in the direction of my bag, closed my eyes and surrendered to exhaustion.

"Sweetheart, are you okay?" Concern framed Mum's words as she shook me awake. "Dinner will be ready soon."

I stirred and gazed up at her. With shoulder length, rich brown hair, and a trim figure, Mum is pretty for a woman in her forties. People say I inherited my bright green eyes from her and that we looked like sisters. Mum, or Caroline, is a dedicated charge nurse in a trauma unit in London, and commutes there daily. My Mum and Dad, Colin, met when a bus Mum was on, knocked Dad off his bike. Mum jumped off the bus in a flash, assessed his condition and reassured him until the ambulance came. Mum laughs when Dad says he couldn't die before getting acquainted with the angel who comforted him on that day. Mum maintains it was the other way round. Given Dad's crystal blue eyes and sandy blonde hair, I'm sure he caught her fancy. Mum clearly loves Dad and he adores her.

Now, the love for me reflected in her eyes tore open my raw heart.

I sat up and launched myself at her, wrapping my arms around her neck.

She caressed my head. "Honey, what's wrong?"

I longed to tell her who I really was, but she'd never believe me. Anyway, I'd made that mistake in a previous existence and it didn't end well. I spent years in a mental hospital, drugged up to the eyeballs. I wasn't about to make that same mistake again.

I settled for the only part she'd understand. "I've decided to break up with Jack."

Jack is my boyfriend in my current life. I'd barely spoken to him since becoming Eve again.

"I'm so sorry, honey. Maybe it is just a temporary hitch you're going through."

I shook my head. "No, it's over."

She kissed me on the forehead. "Do you want to talk about it?"

I grabbed tissues from the box on my night table and dabbed at tears welling in my eyes. "Not really."

Sounding choked up, she said, "Your father and I love you so much. We're always here for you. You know that, don't you?"

"Yes, Mum. I know and I love you guys too."

She still looked concerned. So I forced a smile. "Really, I'm fine, Mum. I'll be down in a minute."

After she left, I looked at my phone and found six missed calls from Jack. What was I to tell him? I so hated this part. I'd often believed, before I remembered Adam, that I truly cared about the love interests in each of my new lives. Although, instinctively I knew deep within my psyche, that something was amiss in my heart. Having to break their hearts was something I really dreaded. Now I needed to find a kind way to let Jack down.

Mum calling my name broke into my thoughts.

"Jasmine, are you coming down?"

My given name in this life is Jasmine Brown. Unlike some others, I do really like this name.

The idea of breaking up with Jack made me lose my appetite, but I needed to put on a good show to my parents. I broke up from college in two days and intended on using the summer term before I started at Cambridge University, to persuade Mum and Dad to let me go up to Scotland for a day or two. I so wanted to visit my box again.

Wrapped in thought, I sat quietly while Mum dished up the food, my favourite, spaghetti and meatballs. Even the lovely aroma drifting off my plate failed to make me feel at all hungry. If anything, it made me feel quite nauseous.

13

Mum, always over protective, commented on how pale I looked. Being comatose for days, does tend to leave one looking a bit pasty. Despite having fully recovered, Mum still watched me like a hawk.

"Mum, stop stressing," I told her with a fake smile. "I'm just a bit tired and not very hungry."

The worried look remained in her face. Mum wasn't easily fooled; I knew I needed to step it up a notch or two if I wanted her to believe me. I hastily forked half a meatball into my mouth.

Time seemed to stretch endlessly until I escaped back up to my room. The moment I closed the bedroom door, my mobile rang. I knew it would be Jack. I prepared myself for the difficult task ahead, and picked up my iPhone.

"Hello, Jack."

"Hey, babe, you finally answered. I've been worried about you." He sounded genuinely concerned. "Is everything okay... are we still okay?"

"I'm sorry, Jack, I meant to talk to you earlier, but I needed time to clear my head." I paused and gulped, ready to say my piece. "I've made some important decisions, and sadly they don't include us being together anymore."

"Why? What have I done?" Shock filled his voice. "Don't dare give me that it's not you, it's me rubbish!"

Tears begin to run down my freckled cheeks. "I don't want to be i n a serious relationship right now. Also, we have very different ideas of what we want in the future... I'm young and want to travel."

"Look, just tell me the truth." He sounded annoyed, very annoyed. "I just don't do it for you anymore, right?"

"No Jack, it's not that. I do care for you... and you're great... really."

"Whatever," he snarled. "Go find yourself, or whatever

it is you're looking for. Just remember we had something special; something you're unlikely to find again." The line went dead.

I stared at the phone clutched in my hand, thinking Jack had no idea how truthful and painful his warning was. Unless reunited with my Adam, there was little possibility I'd ever experience true love again in this lifetime.

~~ *Chapter Two* ~~

I decided to get some fresh air. Hoping to get out of the house without drama, I grabbed my purse and tiptoed downstairs. Oblivious to anything but her favourite TV show, Mum sat watching Eastenders. Dad was snoozing in his chair. I passed by the living room in stealth mode, slowly opened the door and gently closed it behind me.

I hurried to my blue Fiesta which was parked up the street. Dad had brought the second hand car for my eighteenth birthday. I liked living in Cambridge again because whenever the feeling arose, there were many interesting places you could go to chill out. I enjoyed strolling along the river Cam during summer and watching boats filled with happy people drift by. Luckily, being late June it wasn't dark at this time of the evening. The trip only took me ten minutes and after I parked the car I strolled over to the river.

I plopped down on the grassy riverbank and watched two ducks pruning themselves under a beautiful weeping willow tree. Glancing over in the direction of the water, it surprised me to see a punt boat cruising down it. The last punt trip normally ended at 6pm. I decided the man at the helm must be a punt owner. He waved at me and I responded in kind.

He brought the punt to a stop near my resting place. "Hello there," he said smiling at me. "You look like you have a lot on your mind. Want to jump on here for free?"

Looking at the tall guy, wearing a granddad style cap, I politely declined his offer. In the past, I had loved punting down the river with Mum and Dad but since remembering my identity, I'd developed a phobia of rushing, deep water. Mum blamed it on the trauma of my coma. But naturally, I knew the real reason was some past life experiences with water, had gone terribly awry.

"Come on, I don't bite," the man urged. "I promise it's perfectly safe and I have life jackets." He pointed over to life preservers stacked at the far end of the boat.

I shook my head again. "Thanks, but I just don't do water."

He grinned. "Come on. I promise to save you from your life's dilemmas. You don't need to find redemption in my eyes."

Wondering what he meant, I stood and brushed blades of grass off my clothing. "Thanks again for the offer, but I really should be going now. Have a nice evening." Walking towards my car an eerie chill slid down my spine. I glanced back over my shoulder and saw no sign of the man or his boat. Puzzled, I stopped and scanned the river. "That's weird," I muttered. The current must be flowing very fast to have carried him down river so fast, I thought.

At home, I found Mum still glued to the TV and Dad snoring away. I decided to call it an early night and hit the sack.

Over the next week, I tried to stay busy and keep Mum off my case with her over worrying. I told my parents that due to a project in history, which would be on my course at uni, I wanted to get a head start and travel to Scotland at the weekend. A believable ploy, as I was taking a masters course in the subject, which was ironic, considering it was a subject after turning eighteen, which I knew really well. They both agreed that it was a good idea and my Dad made the arrangements.

Saturday morning I sat on the train, looking out the window as it shot passed different landmarks. My mind wandered to lives past, I would often think of the one that was right after we were first Adam and Eve. It never made sense it was the one and only lifetime, that at age eighteen even I never remembered who we were. Maybe that life held the key to everything? But Gabriel didn't know why either, or if he did he wouldn't tell me. All he would say was it was the following life God assigned him to me.

When I sensed someone sitting by me, it wasn't rocket science to know it was him. Not to mention his size took up all the space in the next chair, so he was snugly close up against me.

"I wondered when you'd show up," I muttered under my breath. In the past I'd forgotten no one else could see or hear Gabriel and I often looked like a crazy person chatting with an imaginary friend.

Gabriel chuckled. "Certainly, because I know if left to your own devices, you'd soon become mired in some sort of disaster."

I glared at him. "Thanks for the vote of confidence."

He smiled and helped himself to a peanut M&M from the open bag in my hand. "You're welcome, my dear."

I rolled my eyes, I never understood angels. For a start, what were they exactly? Did they really feel any pain? Or was it just a ploy on God's part to make them appear more human? They certainly didn't have physical needs and yet I'd seen Gabriel eat and drink a lot but never need a toilet break. I often wondered where all that food and liquid went?

It suddenly struck me how funny it'd be if an angel in the midst of helping someone remarked, 'Hold on a minute I need to take a piss'. The idea made me laugh aloud.

Gabriel directed a puzzled look at me.

I stifled my giggle and told him he really didn't want to know. But he was right. We did make a good team. Sure, in the beginning I wanted to kick his arse back up to heaven. Now, I couldn't imagine life without him. I rested my head on his comfy shoulder and soon fell asleep.

Gabriel woke me when we arrived. I knew exactly where I was going. After all I'd completed this trip many times before. I usually travelled by train, boat or plane. Once when I was luckily reborn in Scotland, I made the journey on a peddle bike.

We made our way through a throng of other passengers and headed to the park. Rain began seeping from dark grey clouds in the sky. Gabriel shielded me from the downpour by holding a wing over my head. Gabriel doesn't mind rain. In fact, he actually enjoys it, often smiling as droplets run off his hair into his handsome face.

Nervousness hovered over me, until I saw my tree in the distance. I sighed with relief. I always feared that it'd been cut down to clear the way for a road or housing.

By the tree, Gabriel lifted me up. I reached inside the deep hole made by a Great Spotted Woodpecker ages earlier. I felt around until I found the worn leather box, with two hands I pulled it out.

Back on the ground, Gabriel wrapped his wings around me hiding me from any possible curious onlookers.

I retrieved a recent photo of myself from out of my handbag and placed it inside the box. All told, there were approximately twenty two photos, or miniature paintings of me from previous lives. Before the invention of cameras, a painted depiction was the only option. Other times, an artist captured my image in stone or metal. The British Museum has an excellent bust of me as Cleopatra, though sadly it won't fit in the box. Then there was a black and white photo of me as a Sioux girl hanging on a museum wall in Iowa, America.

My box is so sentimental, it fills me with peace to remember and keep a sort of record of my journey through time. Even though in each life, I could ask Gabriel to fetch the box for me; it was like a sacred tradition within my soul to travel to its hidden location. I sometimes wondered what people would think if the box was ever discovered. Would they try and piece together all the different people?

I flicked through the photos. It pained me to see only a few photos and paintings of Adam and I together. I gazed fondly at the black and white snapshot of us as an elderly couple, who looked so happy and still in love. Finding Adam that time proved a most difficult task. I'd all but given up hope when quite by accident I found him. Fate or God granted us that time together.

I sighed and pulled out another old photo of me kneeling by Adam's grave. On the day of my eighteenth birthday when memories of Adam came flooding back, I'd instinctively knew something was wrong. Gabriel confirmed after I'd recovered from that coma, that Adam had died as a child. I wept and screamed about the injustice of it to no avail. Gabriel never left my side until that life ended for me. My fingers, moving things in the box, pulled out a picture of when I found Adam quickly and things had been going great. That was until I caught a deadly form of meningitis and died soon after, leaving poor Adam all alone. Unlike me, Adam has never had a guardian angel, for reasons I am still unsure off.

Gabriel looking at another photograph I had taken from the box, said, "I admired your courage and unselfishness in that life, Eve."

"It hurt to walk away so Adam wouldn't remember who I truly was, but I had little choice. He needed to carry on with his important work; I didn't want to be a distraction. I was already dying and I could never have him put through watching me waste away."

Gabriel gave me a gentle hug. I placed all the pictures back in the box and closed the lid, praying I could add another photo of Adam and myself soon.

The rain had now stopped, so Gabriel let down his wings and returned the box to its hiding place. Wrapped in silent meditation, we strolled through the park for a while. Gabriel was a good judge of when I needed to be alone in my thoughts.

After a time I broke the silence. "Do you ever wish you were assigned to someone else?"

I knew by Gabriel's big grin that some wisecrack was on the way. "Everyday, as you're a complete pain in the butt."

My stunned look, made him quickly correct it. "I'm joking, silly; I see it as an honour to help guide you. Not to mention things with you are never boring and sometimes, it seems like we're running our very own, little circus."

"Gabriel, bend down for a second, please," I requested soberly.

When he did, I smacked him ever so lightly on the head. "You're not so easy to put up with either," I told him with a half laugh.

Gabriel smoothed his ruffled hair back into place. "Who me? Hard to deal with? No way! I'm far too divinely witty, charming and good looking."

We both giggled and trudged back towards the station.

Back on the train, I grabbed a drink from the onboard refreshments and chose another window seat. Gabriel sat next to me. A slurping sound filled the air. I looked at Gabriel and found him drinking an ice bucket of red wine.

"Gabriel?"

He smiled at me with a big cheeky grin. "Yes, Eve?"

"Don't you think they may miss the ice bucket?"

He shrugged. "It's not my fault they serve everything in such puny, silly plastic cups. The whole contents are nothing more but a mouthful to me." He smirked, before returning to happily drinking.

Unlike me, Gabriel didn't have to worry about sucking down a gallon of wine. With my bladder, I'd be living in the loo for a week after drinking that amount.

Racked with thoughts of Adam, I heaved a heavy sigh.

Gabriel stopped staring at a kid who had picked his nose and wiped it on the leg of a gentleman sitting next to him. Instead he fixed full attention on me. "What's wrong, Eve?"

"I wonder what's in store. I can't stop thinking about Adam. Where he is? Who he is and what he's doing right now?"

"You always wonder and say that in every life."

Frowning I said "I'm sure I do, but reminding me of that isn't actually helping, Gabe!"

"Think positively, Eve. As each life is a journey of discovery and if things work out in your favour, then the rewards are great."

"Always, with the philosophy Gabriel... blah, blah, blah! You say the same old rubbish in every lifetime."

"Ha ha!" He was in the midst of adding another comeback, when a sudden impact threw both of us forward.

"What the hell," I screeched as Gabriel helped me up off the floor.

Concern furrowed his brow. "I don't know what happened, but I intend to find out. Stay here while I check things out."

Within moments, he reappeared.

The distressed look on his face alarmed me more. "What's happened?"

"A motorcar stalled on the tracks. The engineer managed to slow the train, but it still hit the vehicle. The car's driver is in a bad way. I don't think he'll make it."

"Any passengers on the train injured?"

"A few, but I don't believe seriously."

A sudden foreboding hit me, setting my heart to race. I clutched Gabriel's arm tight. "No, please don't let it be true!"

"Eve, what is it?"

Tears threatening my eyes begin to overflow. "I can suddenly sense Adam's possible location."

Gabriel patted my hand. "Okay, but that doesn't mean he is the guy on the tracks. Most likely, the train has stopped near his current location. Don't always assume the worst, Eve."

Trembling with rising dread, I snapped, "Why not; the worst case scenario describes most of my lives."

"Perhaps seeing the man will settle your nerves. I'll take you to him and we'll know for sure."

I nodded and filled with rising dread, I followed Gabriel through fellow passengers assessing their injuries. Outside, I saw the fire brigade cutting the man from a mangled car welded to the train engine. The moment they freed him, paramedics gently placed him on the stretcher and begin working on him. Gabriel curved a wing around me, cloaking me with invisibility and we edged closer.

Adrenaline pumping, I forced myself to look as paramedics transported the man lying on a gurney to a waiting ambulance.

Gabriel, his tone edged in nervousness, asked, "Well?"

I tried twice before finding my voice. "It's not him, but I'm certain he's linked to Adam in some way."

Under Gabriel's directions, I put my arms around his neck. His wings fluttered effortlessly and cloaked from view, we followed the ambulance to the hospital. Inside, we watched doctors struggle to save the injured man. Certain he was connected to Adam I prayed he'd pull through for his family sake and selfishly my own. The doctors finally managed to stabilize him, but his condition remained critical.

After assessing the situation, Gabriel suggested I return home to rest. Realising no good would come of alarming my parents, I permitted Gabriel to fly me back to my car parked outside my local train station.

Mum and Dad were beside themselves when I walked in the house. The last time I called them, I was on the train. A breaking news report had alerted them to the wreck and they had been trying in vain to call me.

Spurred by the fact angels often fiddled with modern technology, a lie of convenience slid out of my mouth. "I'm sorry, but my phone battery died."

They both hugged me, Mum wiping tears from her red eyes.

"What happened? The report just said that the train had been involved in an accident and they would update us soon as they knew more." Dad said.

"It was a guy; he deliberately drove his car onto the tracks. I don't think he will make it. Other than that, there weren't many other injures." I replied back weary.

Mum hugging me again said, "That's so sad, but the main thing is that you're okay. We couldn't imagine losing you."

Her eyes still moist with tears, she asked if I wanted a hot coco drink.

I nodded and she released me from her tight grip and went

24

off to the kitchen. After I had drunk the hot drink, I took myself off to bed. I was exhausted and had so many thoughts turning over in my head.

The next morning I poured cereal in a breakfast bowl, splashed milk on top and switched on the TV. The news was on. I stood there spooning cereal into my mouth, watching the tail end of a story about some poor bugger stabbed in London. A photo of the train crash then flashed across the screen. I watched intrigued as the news reporter said the injured man was the brother of famous movie star, Malcolm Dice. Another photo appeared on the screen. The spoon heading to my mouth slipped from my hand and clanged against the floor. I stood there dumbstruck staring at the television.

With a hundred thoughts racing through my mind like spooked antelopes, I grabbed the remote and hit pause. Staring at the image on the screen, I attempted to shove the possibility away. Frozen in place, I hardly noticed Mum entering the room.

"What's the matter, honey," she said, putting on her jacket to go to work.

"Err... nothing, Mum; just watching news reports about the train accident." My hand began trembling so violently soggy cereal splashed on my bare toes.

"Jasmine, your cereal!"

I levelled the bowl. "Sorry, Mum, I'll clear it up." I raced to the kitchen, set the near empty bowl on the counter and grabbed a dishcloth. I sped back to the living room and started sopping up the mess.

Lost in thought, I didn't respond when Mum shouted, "Bye; love you," as she left.

Intent on containing the spilt cereal gathered inside the soaked towel, I headed back to the kitchen and ran smack dab into Gabriel. I routed around him, tossed the whole mess into the sink then faced him. "Have you seen the news? I'm a complete nervous wreck."

He nodded. "It would be an interesting development."

His clam tone irked me to no end. "Interesting? One of Britain's biggest movie stars and interesting is all you can say? That's bloody absurd, God or whoever in charge of deciding my many lives has a warped sense of humour. Perhaps it provides them with a bit of fun to erect impossible barriers for me to conquer."

Gabriel rubbed his chin. "You've overcome greater obstacles many times before."

"Oh yeah, well I'm not sure I have." I stormed back in to the living room and pointed to the photo of Malcolm Dice paused on the TV screen. "Look at him! Women faint at the sight of him. To them, he's a god."

He frowned. "Have you forgotten the time when Adam was a priest in Poland?"

I glared at him. "How could I? Even though I was a Hindu girl from India, I stupidly allowed you to persuade me to convert to Catholicism. Wow, that turned out so well. My parents carted me back to India and forced me to marry a local man with no teeth. It required all my willpower to survive endless hours of submitting to the disgusting lout before you rescued me. Then what did you do? You immediately left me with monks at a monastery for safekeeping."

Gabriel chuckled. "Come on, Eve. Your groom didn't look that bad, unless he opened his mouth."

I jerked open a drawer and grabbed the rolling pin inside.

Gabriel, stumbling backwards, yelled, "Okay, okay, he was a disgusting lout."

Gabe was such a git and if not careful, he'd experience painful redundancy upside his head. Wondering if one could fire a guardian angel, I placed the rolling pin back in the drawer. Smothering a smile caused by the idea, I met Gabriel's gaze straight on. "Come on, wise guy, what's our first move to solve the current mystery?"

Gabriel began pacing. "Well, first we need to establish if it's really him."

I signed, "Okay, Einstein and exactly how do you suggest we do that?"

He shrugged his shoulders "Haven't figured out that part yet."

I shook my head in disgust. "Awesome, you're so reassuring."

Instantly, I thought, wait a minute. Only almighty God has infinite knowledge and wisdom, so that ruled out Gabriel. "Bend down, Gabriel, please?"

He took a couple of hesitate steps backwards. "Why, are you going to hit me again?"

"Do I look like someone who abuses angels?"

He grinned, "Sure you want me to answer that?"

"On second thoughts, don't." I smiled and gestured for him to bend down. "Why do angels have to be so tall? It makes things so inconvenient at times."

He reluctantly did as I requested.

I kissed him on one cheek and patted the other. "You know, I'd be lost without you."

He winked at me. "As I would be without you."

I got rid of Gabriel using the excuse I should finish my daily chores. Truth told, I needed alone time to gather my thoughts. With Gabriel around, we'd most likely waste precious time bantering with each other. He agreed and vanished.

I bathed, dressed and did some chores. Intent on finding everything I could on Malcolm Dice, I logged on to my laptop. Waiting for my the ice age internet connection to boot up, my mind wandered to a lifetime neither Gabriel nor I liked to remember.

The time when Adam killed me!

~~ *Chapter Three* ~~

I was a Jewish girl in wartime Germany, when Nazis rousted my whole family from bed in the middle of the night. Terrified, we were transported to a concentration camp. Adam in that life was one of the camp guards. I tried everything possible to make him feel something for me. Occasionally, I saw a small spark of recognition in his eyes, but it quickly died. Defeated and starving from lack of food, I worked from sun up to sunset. With the odds stacked against me and time running out, I resigned myself to the fact there would be no miracle.

One day, the soldier I knew to be my Adam escorted my work group to a field. Instead of facing the usual backbreaking work, my fellow prisoners and I found ourselves staring at a line of Nazi executioners. My beloved pointed his gun barrel at me but hesitated. When a superior officer ordered him to pull the trigger, he still faltered. The bark of his superior echoed again. This time he shot me in the head.

Poor Adam, I made the terrible mistake in the next life of telling him it was me he had killed. I can almost see the memory of the horrific moment flash through his sad eyes. I know he's racked with such guilt and sorrow. But luckily he had not reawakened to his true self that life so I try and reassure him he had no choice, he'd have faced execution instead otherwise if he hadn't have pulled the trigger.

The internet's welcome tone on my laptop jarred me out of the past.

I keyed Malcolm Dice into the browser and a list of search results loaded. Immediately an announcement that Malcolm had recently proposed to his long time girlfriend, captured my attention. Holy crap! Malcolm's newly announced fiancée was gorgeous model and actress, Lily Olsen.

Scrolling down, I saw a report about Malcolm's brother James Dice. It stated Malcolm was flying in from the states to see the injured man. That didn't spur any hope. With Malcolm's brother critically injured in a hospital, it wasn't exactly the right circumstance to introduce myself to him. What was I thinking? Odds were I couldn't even get close to Malcolm in the first place. My thoughts were spinning at cataclysmic speeds. I wished I could forget all about him and enjoy a normal life for a change. If only it was that easy.

A noise rattled from the kitchen. Curious about the source, I went to investigate. When I rounded the corner, I saw the fridge door half open, with huge white wings sticking out behind it.

"What the hell, Gabriel, at least give me fair warning before raiding my fridge." Annoyed to no end, I grabbed the fridge door and jerked it open further.

It wasn't Gabriel!

I stared at the dark haired angel devouring Mum's homemade apple pie reserved for our dinner. "Who the heck are you?"

He swallowed the mammoth bite stuffed in his mouth. "Who am I? Well, like you, Eve, I've had many names and we have met before."

A sinister chill ran right down my spine.

He grinned. "A few of my favourite names are Satan, Judas or Legion and not forgetting my given name; Lucifer! But my all time favourite is The Devil. Has such a classy ring to it, don't ya think? Plus, it's a title that designates I'm the one and only."

Facing the evil grin on his face, control over my mind vanished. I tried to form a response but holy shit, crap, fuck and Jesus, were the only words left in my head.

His grin widened.

Shaking like a leaf, I managed, "Get out!"

"That isn't very hospitable, Eve." He used a long fingernail to spear an apple slice from the half eaten pie he held. "Would you like a bite, Eve?"

I stood frozen, hypnotized by his glowing almost reddish eyes. It took all my strength to shake my head.

He chuckled. "Yeah, probably not. Still, after what happened the first time, I do find it amusing that you still even eat apples."

Grinning he sucked the apple into his mouth. "I really should give my personal appreciation to your mother for this delicious pie."

A loud voice vibrated from just behind me. "She said get out!"

Gabriel's presence filled me with relief. I backed away from the damnable foe who had helped put me in this situation of eternal no rest.

The dark one directed a charming smile at my guardian angel. "Gabriel. What a pleasant surprise." He offered the pie to him. "What about you? Would you like a slice of this delicious pie? The apples are divine. One might say, they're even worth damnation." His demonic cackle reverberated off the kitchen walls and rattled the windowpanes.

Gabriel moved me aside. "She refused you and told you to leave. Last time I checked, that means that you have no power over her." Gabriel stepped forward and stood nose to nose with him. "Unless you want a cross engraved on your forehead and then doused with holy water, you best go!"

He shrugged and tossed the rest of the pie into the sink. "I was about to leave." He stared at me and hissed, "Got what I came for anyway," then disappeared.

My knees buckled. Gabriel caught me before I hit the floor and helped me over to a chair.

I looked up a Gabe. "What did he mean by that?"

"Don't worry; as you know he's a notorious liar. He's trying to mess with your mind. Don't let him succeed, Eve."

I leaned my throbbing head against the chair back. "Why does he have to show himself now?"

Gabe massaged my temples. "Oh he's popped up many times before, just not in his true form. He has tried pulling your strings a lot in the past, but I interceded. Don't worry; I've got your back."

I turned and looked shocked up at him. "Why didn't you ever tell me any of this before now?"

"There was no need. I can handle him. You see, I have the one thing he craves."

"What's that?"

He grinned down at me. "God's power behind me."

I smiled. "Thanks for the reminder, Gabe."

He patted the top of my head. "No problem. Now, I really must go."

Frustrated, I yelled, "I hate it when you go poof without letting me respond more first."

No answer came.

I threw the mangled remains of the pie from out of the sink into the bin. That evening, I told Mum I'd accidentally dropped it while getting myself a slice. She was not overly pleased, but let me off pretty lightly. With my head fogged by confusion, the day seemed endless.

Later on, my mind working overtime, I lay in bed staring up at the ceiling.

Gabriel earlier confirmed Lucifer had appeared in many of my lives, but just not in his true form. So I begin reviewing the particular bad ones in my head. The one when I was the Sioux squaw and Adam was an American soldier, could Lucifer have been one of my tribesmen? No, surely the dark one would never make his presence that easy to detect. Maybe he also was one of the American soldiers who visited my tribe. The images of that life burst in my troubled mind.

~~ *Chapter Four* ~~

It had been in the middle of a harsh winter when the troop of soldiers arrived in my small village. They had visited only a few months previously, offering us a peace treaty that dictated certain rules that we should follow. To show good faith, they gave us supplies, pots, pans and warm blankets to help us through the bitter winter. Our chief, Chief Chayton was unhappy with restrictions the whites laid out but he told the council what happened to a neighbouring tribe who refused to cooperate with the soldiers. In the end, the council agreed to accept the demands made upon them.

To commemorate the treaty, a photographer took pictures of our chief and others. Unaware of what lay ahead back then, I smiled happily in the one taken of me, just a week before my eighteenth birthday.

Although it soon became obvious this time around, when the US soldiers arrived without any warning, that their intentions were hostile. On this occasion most of the braves had formed a hunting party, leaving women, children and the elderly alone in the village. My world was then turned upside down as the US soldiers began shooting every Indian in sight.

I watched in horror as a solider gunned down the chief's wife trying to protect her third born son. The soldier bashed the injured child's skull with his musket butt. The screams of women and children filled the air. Pure hatred for the all whites filled my heart as I raced towards the river. I heard the thunder of horse hooves behind me. Running like the wind, I lost my footing and tumbled down the high riverbank.

From the corner of my eye, I saw a soldier pursuing me slide off his chestnut coloured horse. I scrambled to my feet and dived into the water. At the exact time as my fingertips met ice cold water, the solider grabbed my waist. I struggled, but he held fast. The raging river current carried us downstream. In that awful moment, the soldier's gasping breath on the nape of my neck parted the curtain of remembrance. I knew instinctively he was my Adam.

I felt his grip on my waist slip away. I saw him begin to drift past me. I clutched his shirtsleeve and desperately reached out for a tree branch dangling over the water.

A saviour suddenly appeared and grabbed hold of my arm.

Gabriel dragged him and me out the water and onto the bank. The soldier lay lifeless on the frozen ground.

Through chattering teeth, I asked Gabe. "Is he dead?"

Gabriel shook his head. "He's breathing, but just barely." He flung him quickly over a shoulder and curved an arm around my waist. "I need to get both of you to someplace warm immediately."

The sound of hooves echoed. Soldiers on horseback were speeding in our direction.

Gabriel cloaking us sprinted like a cheetah across the ground and took flight. Within seconds, we landed on one of the mountains surrounding my village.

Gabriel carried us inside a cave and laid us both on the floor. He vanished and instantly reappeared carrying an armload of wood. He dumped it nearby and snapped his fingers. Fire leaped from the woodpile. "Eve, get those wet clothes off both of you and quick. I'll be back with some blankets shortly"

I crawled to where he lay and began to swiftly undress him. His skin looked so pale and he felt so cold, I doubted that he would survive. Appraising the man before me, I struggled to accept an enemy who wanted to wipe out my entire village, could be my original soul mate.

By the time Gabriel returned, which was only minutes, I lay snuggled against him trying to keep him warm. Gabriel covered us with several blankets and a thick buffalo robe. Still trembling from cold and shock, I cradled his frozen body against my naked skin. Warmth from the fire sent tingling needles of pain through my body as it warmed. I looked at him in hope of seeing some signs of life, but he lay eerily still in my arms. My heart sank and I surrendered to fatigue.

When I awoke, it shocked me to find him sitting up and staring at me with a look of confusion on his face. His eyes met mine and he blinked like a man coming out of a stupor. You could see that he may have recognized me from the village, but clearly he didn't remember I was his soul mate. It was a start, so I smiled sweetly at him. Looking puzzled by his current surroundings, he grinned back.

As usual, with him still not having yet remembered his true self or me, he couldn't see Gabriel standing guard near the cave entrance. Even though I knew his language because of my past lives, he would think it more than a little strange if I started talking fluently in English. So Gabe suggested I use signing to talk with him.

I sat up and patted my bosom. "Ayasha."

He then patted his hairy, muscular chest. "Henry."

Trying to avoid looking at my bare breasts, he sighed,

"Thanks for saving my life."

Several attempts to talk more failed miserably. Frustrated, I sized up the situation. I didn't like to use my feminine charms to awaken him, but unable yet to communicate any other way, I thought why not. After all, to me he is my Adam, who I love with all my heart and soul. What do I have to lose? With the idea of physical talking in mind, I slowly pulled the blanket completely off my naked body.

Gabriel decided this was his cue to leave and flew promptly out of the cave.

Henry couldn't take his eyes off me. Careful not to make any sudden moves that might remind him of the gulf between Indians and the white man, I crept towards him on my hands and knees. I smiled seductively up at him and brushed my lips across his. For a moment, I thought he would strike me; but then he leaned forward and kissed me back. I slid my hand around his neck and returned his kiss with all my desire. His kiss deepened and I parted my lips to receive his tongue. I pressed my body against his for a moment. Then pulling away, I lay on the ground and held out my hand. No verbal words were needed, as he in a flash launched himself between my legs before you could say, jack rabbit!

What rabbits we were. After making love at least four more times, exhausted, he lay beside me, caressing my nipples. Hoping our repeated bonding had stirred some real feelings other than just lust in him, I fell asleep in his arms.

Upon awakening, I found myself wrapped in his arms, he was soundly sleeping. Smiling, I caressed his cheek. It felt so good to be with him even if he did not yet remember our past.

Without warning, a terrible feeling of dread flooded over me. My village and people what had become of them? Tears streaming from my eyes, I bolted upright. He opened his eyes and mumbled something. I didn't bother trying to respond and reached for my clothes laid over a rock nearby. But he grabbed my hand and cupping my chin, tilted my face up. He stared into my eyes. Seeing the sudden sadness on my face, he kissed me gently and then passed me my dry clothes.

We both dressed and he taking my hand led me out of the cave. We made our way down rocky cliffs then weaved around brushes and trees in the forest. As we approached my village, I saw thick black smoke rising into sky. I begin wailing.

He stroked my face, putting his finger to his lips. "Shh... they might still be searching for anyone who got away."

Unable to stem the tears, I cried harder. He clamped a hand over my mouth.

Gabriel appeared beside me, "Eve, you must be quiet!"

At the village, the scene that lay before us was horrendous. Everything was burnt and charred bodies littered the ground. The stench of death was indescribable. When I reached my home Tepee, I devastatingly saw the burnt remains of my mother and younger sister. I was sure that my father and brother's bodies would be somewhere near by, but had no heart left to try and find them. Unable to contain my grief, I sank to my knees and screamed. Henry pulled me into his arms and held me tight. At the sound of horses in the distance, he grabbed my hand and sprinted towards the woods, half dragging me along.

Deep within the forest, certain we were safe, I sighed with relief and looked up at him. He pulled me into his arms and kissed me gently.

Suddenly, a soldier on horseback crashed through the bushes. "They're over here!" Wearing a bright grin, he spurred the horse forward. His eyes almost shone like dark fire in the sunlight. His companions answered his alert.

Others were on their way!

We began running. Heart churning with fear, I stumbled and my hand slipped from his. In the same moment, a musket bellowed. Pain seared into me. Henry whirled and tried to help me stand. A second gunshot echoed. He suddenly looked so surprised, his face contorted then he hit the ground with a dull thud.

Blood oozing from a gaping hole in his chest, he stretched out a hand and gasped, "Eve." Then his eyes closed.

After the soldiers had left me for dead, time crawled forward in agonizing slow motion.

Gabriel tried everything in his power to make me comfortable. "The pain will soon be over, Eve, but I'll stay by your side like always."

I managed to whisper, "He remembered Gabriel. I saw it in his eyes and he called me by my original name just before he died."

Tears rolling down his cheeks, Gabriel nodded. "I know, Eve... I know."

After what felt like an eternity, death released me from that body.

After reviewing this former life, I realised the horseman who had appeared out of nowhere and alerted the others was the Devil. The bastard had helped them kill us. One question though remained. What did he have to gain from it? There must be an ultimate plan in his evil mind.

I begin counting the other unsavoury characters, which Adam and I had encountered in our past lives.

The Nazi officer who ordered Adam to shoot me was another that came to mind. The officer had glared at me on more than one occasion as he patrolled the outer fence where I and the others were imprisoned. Each time, he wore a strange smile and an aura of pure evil radiated from him, which made the tiny hairs on the back of my neck stand up. A comment he once made to me, then ran through my thoughts. "Your faith will finally cease and your soul will make the perfect weapon."

At the time, I didn't understand the baffling statement, but now it was clear. He was sending me a message. I thought again about all the other bastards who appeared in my different lives. Yes, that was it! The Devil had made special guest appearances quite often. Why didn't I fit the links together before? Although an old soul, obviously, I hadn't learned much over the years, but then foresight wasn't one of my stronger attributes.

My life as Cleopatra proved that point. Taken as a whole, I enjoyed that time, especially when I discovered Adam was Mark Anthony. Our fruitful escapades led to the birth of twins. But before becoming entangled with Mark Anthony, I was the consort of a man who had most of the world at that time, kneeling at his feet, Julius Caesar.

Oh no! A sudden rush of nausea afflicted me. Before awakening to my true identity, I'd slept with Julius Caesar and bore him a son. Oh my god! Was he the Devil? Had I given birth to the Anti Christ?

I yelled, "Gabriel."

He immediately appeared. "Is everything okay, Eve?"

"Tell me, he wasn't... please, tell me I never slept with the bloody Devil and birthed his spawn."

Gabriel, seeming amused by my question, smiled. "No, Eve, you've never slept with the Devil or gave birth to his child. For a start, angels including Lucifer, cannot sire a child. Also, when Lucifer appears to you in a form, other than his true self, he's not exactly of flesh and blood. In modern terms, he's what you'd maybe call a sophisticated hologram."

Although grateful for the insightful news, I inquired, "So the Devil wasn't ever Julius Caesar?"

"Definitely not, although Julius Caesar was one of his minions, as was Judas, Hitler and many other evildoers."

"Do you know who the Devil was when in my lifetime as Cleopatra?"

"Yes."

I raised one eyebrow. "Well?"

Tone a bit sharp, he said, "Does it really matter?"

I folded my arms and stared him. "What are you not telling me, Gabriel?"

He heaved a sigh. "Why do you want to know? What good could it possibly do you now?"

"Gabriel, I'm trying to form a picture of what he has been responsible for in our lives."

Gabriel avoided meeting my eyes. "If you must know, on that occasion he appeared to be you."

"What!"

Gabriel muttered, "Sometimes when you weren't present, he pretended to be you."

I knew there was more. "Gabriel, you're hiding something else from me; come on, spill the beans."

He remained silent as a stone.

Growing more impatient by the second, I snapped, "I won't stop bugging you until I know!"

"Okay, okay!" He took a deep breath. "I knew it would come to light one day. You remember the tragedy of Adam as Mark Anthony, but there are facts surrounding his death you don't know."

Intrigued, I urged, "Go on."

"Well, the day you found him dead, you were the only one that would not believe he'd killed himself. And as you know, in the next life that you found Adam again, he confirmed to you that he had been assassinated. Although, he did not know who had sanctioned his death. Well, I do, because it was Lucifer impersonating you, who ordered him to be killed and instructed it should look like he committed suicide."

I suddenly felt queasy to my stomach. "Err... what the hell?"

Gabriel took my hand. "I am so sorry, I didn't know until it was too late. To my knowledge, it was one of the few times that he has escaped my detection. It was a cunning plan on Lucifer's part to be you. But although history believes you killed yourself too, we both know differently."

Tears in my eyes blurred Gabriel's image. "I considered taking my life, but you stopped me. Why didn't you tell me the truth back then?"

He averted his eyes. "I failed you and Adam and my failure resulted in your grief. In some ways, I was relieved when someone planted the Asp in your bed, because you got a fresh new life." He pulled me close and embraced me tenderly.

"It's okay, I don't blame you," I whispered. "You maybe a divine being, but you're not God. I doubt if God permitted you the foresight to prevent what happened. Who knows, it may have started a domino effect that would've ended badly." I pulled free of his arms.

"After all, you keep telling me God works in mysterious ways."

"But, Eve, I should have —"

I interrupted his regret. "Instead of reliving unpleasantness, tell me who else the arsehole has been, I have been trying to establish exactly which ones he's been in?"

"Eve, he's been in every single one of your lives. When he is not in his original form, he's weak and I have the power to send him packing. Most of the time I banished him back to Hell, before he even got a chance to screw things up. But the thing is today, he came to you in his original form, which doesn't bode well for you."

My Mum called to me from downstairs.

The realization it was morning hit me.

I had promised Mum I'd go shopping with her. I told Gabriel we'd have to finish the conversation later. I then got washed, dressed and rushed downstairs.

~~ *Chapter Five* ~~

The entire time Mum and I were out shopping, my mind never strayed far from everything going on. I rubbed my blurry eyes, and strained to focus on numerous outfits mum kept insisting I try on for my cousin's wedding.

"You look tired, darling," she said, handing me another dress. "Didn't you sleep well?"

I appraised the selected black dress with a low cut neckline, although thinking it was not really a suitable wedding outfit. "No, not great, Mum."

Looking at me suspiciously, she asked, "Anything to do with Jack? You still haven't said why you guys broke up."

"No, Mum, it's nothing about Jack. We were just going in different directions in life, that's all. I felt it was best we parted. Hopefully we can still be friends."

She put an arm around me and squeezed my shoulder. "That's a real shame. Though to be completely honest, I've been concerned ever since you came out of the coma. You seem different somehow. I'm worried that you may be suffering from some unknown side effects."

I raised an eyebrow and looked at her. "Why do you think that?"

"You seem distant at times, detached." Staring at me straight on, she said, "Your father and I have also overheard you talking aloud to yourself."

"Mum, believe me I am fine!" Realizing my tone was too sharp, I quickly added. "If I wasn't, you're the first person I'd tell."

Mum's phone rang in her handbag and she answered it. From what I gathered, it was the hospital where she worked, a rare occurrence. After hanging up, she apologised for having to cut our shopping trip short. An important patient was being transferred to the hospital and she needed to report to work. Thinking the patient must be a government dignitary, I reassured mum I'd be okay. I decided to buy the sexy black dress, although not to wear at the wedding. I then drove mum to the train station.

Thirty six hours later Mum finally returned home. Clearly exhausted and looking upset, she plopped down on the sofa and kicked her shoes off.

Assuming things hadn't gone well I made her a coffee and passed it to her. "How did it go, Mum? Did the patient make it?"

"We did everything possible, but sadly, he didn't. His brother was so distraught at the news I didn't even recognise him at first."

"Why, Mum, do you know the brother?"

She took a sip of coffee before answering. "It was Malcolm Dice. His brother was the man in the car that the train you were in, hit. The poor man should have never been transferred to our hospital. His head injuries were too severe to be moving him, but I guess the family wanted him to have the best care available."

A knot formed in my gut, but I managed to keep my voice nice and level. "That's too bad, Mum, but don't beat yourself up. I'm sure your team did the very best they could for him."

Although truly sorry Malcolm's brother had died, I prayed it would open up the right opportunity for me. Maybe I was a step closer to discovering if Malcolm Dice and Adam were one and the same. Wondering though didn't get me anywhere and irritated me even more.

A few days later, I sat in a chair on the patio drinking a cold glass of cola while Mum tended to her rose bushes in the garden.

Dad raced out of the house, nearly tripping over our beagle, Bonnie. Wearing a huge grin, he shouted, "Guys, you're never going to believe this!"

After Mum grabbed hold of Bonnie, dad told us, "I just got off the phone with a client who recently buried her husband in one of my elite models."

Dad was extremely good at his trade of woodworking and made coffins. Business had picked up for him of late.

Dad's eyes lit up. "Wait for it! Turns out she's the cousin of Malcolm Dice's Mum." He paused, rubbing his nearly bald head. "Guess what? They want me to provide the coffin for Malcolm Dice's brother."

I jumped to my feet. "Holy Jesus!" Talking, while trying to swallow cola nearly choked me to death, but Mum came to the rescue and began patting my back.

"You haven't heard the very best part yet," Dad continued. "The Dice family, including Malcolm, is coming to my shop to select what they want. I luckily have one that I'm sure they'll like."

I sank into the chair, staring into space. As usual I imagined God playing chess up in heaven, manipulating the game, moving one of his hapless pawns closer to her goal.

Mum directed a weird glance at me and then gave Dad a congratulatory hug. "Wow; that's unbelievable, honey."

Dad gave her a quick kiss, saying he needed to make a few calls as he rushed back inside the house. I smiled, as Dad would undoubtedly spend half the night on the phone, sharing the news with everyone on his contact list.

I gave Mum an excuse and went up to my bedroom. There I whispered Gabriel's name and he swiftly appeared.

"You once told me, that it was random coincidences when Adam and I found each other so easily. Well, I feel like such an idiot because it's shockingly clear that we've been manipulated in each life."

In the tone of someone certain of what he spoke, he said, "Eve, the concept of how one's fate is decided, is beyond yours and even my full comprehension. Not everything you assume stands up to time, space, or heavenly truth. However, I cannot deny that unseen hands have helped certain events in your lives. Many things were predestined before God created you and Adam. You are on a divine path, Eve, but free will always prevails. Be careful though, that you don't stray too far from that path."

I stared at Gabriel in awe. It was as if he'd read my mind and answered all my unsaid questions. "Okay; on that note I'll shut up, go with the flow and hope I don't steer my arse off in the wrong direction."

He nodded, grinned, and vanished.

"Hey," I said aloud. "I wasn't finished talking yet."

"Got places to go, people to save," said a bodiless voice. "You'll be fine for the time being."

Perched on the large window sill seat in my bedroom, I gazed up at the night sky sprinkled with stars. Regardless of what life I'm in, twinkling sequins against a dark backdrop never ceases to amaze me. Even in the Garden of Eden, I wondered what secrets lay just beyond them. With the Almighty determined to teach me a lesson, I feared I may never get to know.

After a restless night, I squeezed a lump of toothpaste on my brush and looked in the mirror. I gasped at the sight of my reflection. Dark circles under my eyes accented my sallow complexion. If Malcolm Dice was Adam, how could I compete with his model, actress girlfriend? Only one thing to do and that was to get Susan to come over here pronto!

Susan, a friend who I admired for her daring and confidence, expertly perfected her best features and those of others. I glanced at myself again and cringed. To help me, Susan's talents would be sorely tested.

Hours later, I looked in the mirror and did a double take. The radiant beauty that stared back at me at me, had lush red lips, sparkling green eyes and ringlet curled auburn hair, held in a stunning up do style by a jewelled butterfly clip. "I don't know how you do it, but you're a magician," I told Susan. "Is that really me?"

Stuffing her potions and makeup in a tote, Susan smiled. "No silly, it's Cinderella and she shall go to the ball."

"Wow; thanks, Susan. I owe you big time."

"No prob, but don't forget I want a signed photo of hunky Malcolm." She laughed. "I prefer the photo where he's wearing next to nothing."

I giggled. "I know the one you mean."

After she left, I pulled the new sexy black dress over my head, trying not to damage the work of art Susan had created. I studied the final results in the mirror.

"You have never looked more beautiful."

I turned and found Gabriel beaming at me. Face heating up, I mumbled, "Thanks, but I'm not sure if I am ready for this. Besides, Malcolm has a fiancée already, remember?"

He rested a gentle hand on my shoulder. "Don't believe everything you read in the tabloids. The last six months have strained their relationship. It's possible she may even be cheating on him."

Relieved things in Malcolm's life wasn't as perfect as they seemed, I smiled. "I'm always grateful for some info from a higher power."

Gabriel smiling pushed me towards the door. "Now go. He won't be able to take his eyes off you."

Mum and Dad were ready and waiting for me. They gasped when I walked down the staircase.

Mum cooed. "Oh, sweetheart, you look so lovely I could almost cry."

"Jasmine, you're stunning," Dad added "But you do know we're going to my shop and not a movie premiere, don't you?"

I feigned surprise. "Oh no! And here I was thinking we were going to the Oscars."

Dad laughed and kissed me on the forehead.

Mum, wondering if Malcolm and his family would recognize her from the hospital, decided to check her hairdo in the bathroom mirror.

Dad shook his head. "That's the fourth time she's checked her hair."

I laughed. After Mum did one final mirror check, at long last we walked out to the car.

The fifteen minute journey to Dad's shop seemed to take hours. By the time we arrived, my hands shook, my lips quivered, and I had an annoying eye twitch going on. I was always a nervous wreck when facing the first introduction to a possible Adam candidate, but even more so now.

Dad insisted we get to the shop half an hour early to prepare for the Dice family's arrival. My assignment was to act as waitress and offer them refreshments that my auntie Grace, had provided.

At the shop, watching dad and mum rush around attending to last minute details, it struck me how ironic it was to meet Malcolm, under such unfortunate circumstances. Adam, candidates and I often met in the middle of such unpleasant situations.

In 1907, I was the first female surgeon charged with saving the life of a teenage girl who suffered a terrible fall. She was transported to the hospital with internal bleeding. I stood by the child's bed assessing her condition when her father, a widower bringing his kids up alone, rushed into the room. I'll never forget the shock when I realised the girl's father was actually Adam. If she hadn't pulled through, I wondered to myself whether the happy outcome that followed for Adam and I, might not have happened. Although, that happiness was short lived, as I was unfortunately murdered, by a mentally disturbed patient.

Now, placing sandwiches on a serving tray, I speculated what lay ahead, what if Malcolm wasn't Adam.

The shop bell ringing when Mum opened the door for dad's guests splintered my thoughts. A middle aged couple entered.

I stood like a frozen mannequin, hardly even breathing.

Malcolm strolled in behind his parents. He looked tired, but still drop dead gorgeous. With black hair slightly ruffled looking, his piercing eyes sparkled like aquamarine coloured pools of water.

"Jasmine?" Mum repeated the third time before I finally snapped out of it.

I told myself okay you can do this, after all it wasn't surgery. Although thinking about it, I'd probably mess that up too as it had been so long since I'd last preformed one. Another thought instantly followed. Who am I trying to fool? My lipstick kisses covered a poster of Malcolm Dice

50

that had decorated my bedroom wall since I was fifteen. I was so going to screw this up.

Mum glared at me. I grabbed a silver tray holding glasses of wine from the service table and offered drinks to our guests. Dad introduced me as his daughter, Jasmine.

When introduced to Malcolm, I squeaked, "It's nice to meet you." Crap! I sounded like a damn mouse. The great Malcolm Dice, would never notice a woman whose voice sounded like fingernails scraping a blackboard.

He directed a dazzling smile at me. "Relax, please. Even though I played a vampire in my last movie, I don't bite. I'm really quite harmless."

My heart nearly pounded out my chest as I realised he was in fact without doubt my Adam. Struck mute, I froze staring at him like a dummy. We then both stood looking strangely into each other eyes.

His brow furrowed. "I know you from somewhere. We must have met before?"

I found my normal voice. "I don't believe so."

He quirked an eyebrow and grinned slightly. "No. I never forget a face. It's one of my many special talents. Soon as I saw your mother, I recognized her instantly from the hospital."

I felt my face blushing like a ripe tomato. "Sorry, I'd certainly remember if we had met."

Awkward silence hung between us until Mum, having decided to express her condolences to him, butted in. I could have strangled her.

Malcolm/Adam, as I now viewed him, thanked her. He looked at his parents standing nearby. "Speaking on behalf of my Mum and Dad, we're grateful for the effort you and the doctors put forth trying to save him."

His mother grabbed a tissue from her bag and started

crying. Mum lost interest in Malcolm and tried to console her. His father, clearly uncomfortable, stood with both hands in his pockets, staring at the floor. Dad asked them if they were ready to choose a casket. Malcolm's father nodded and Dad led him toward the showroom. Mum, with an arm around Malcolm's mother, gently coaxed her to follow along.

Malcolm kept glancing my way as we trailed towards the showroom. At the doorway, he said "After you."

When I walked past him, I suddenly felt his hand rub and squeeze my arse. Stunned, I quickly edged around him. Appearing like nothing of consequence had happened, he focused on helping to choose a casket for his brother. Face heating, I excused myself and headed to the ladies' room. Inside, intending to splash cold water on my red face, I turned on the tap.

Suddenly an arm curved around my waist and pulled me back against a man's body. Shocked, I demanded that he let me go.

The moment he released me; I turned and glared at him.

A smirk curled his lips. "Come on, baby, over the sink would be perfect. I know how to make you say my name over and over. Only yesterday, a fan begged me for more."

Dumfounded by such behaviour, I backed away. "Err... I don't think so."

He followed. "Now, I remember. I've done you before haven't I?"

I took another step towards the door.

He matched it. "Considering the circumstances, I can understand if you're a bit put off." With a half laugh, he reached for me. "Well don't be, baby, view it as grief counselling."

Wow, I realised Adam, or Malcolm in this life was a self-centred arsehole, one whose massive ego overshadowed his true soul.

Unimpressed and revolted, I jerked the bathroom door open. "I've never had the misfortune to be one of your conquests."

I stormed down the corridor and back to the showroom. Mum, staring at my backside, raised her eyebrows. Wondering why, I ran a hand down the back of my dress and discovered my skirt hitched up, revealing my underwear. Flustered, I quickly pulled it down. If looks could kill, I'd died from the one Mum gave me.

Malcolm strolled into the room, looking like a cat fresh off having enjoyed a bowl of cream.

Anger reflected in Mum's eyes reached atomic level when she fully connected my dress problem and the pleased smirk Malcolm wore.

Bloody hell, I thought. She is never going to believe me.

Luckily, Dad and Malcolm's parents were unaware of the looks my Mum kept sending me. Malcolm's smug expression confirmed this was just a game to him. Well, no way on earth would I be just a tawdry prize to feed his massive ego.

After deciding on the coffin, Malcolm and his parents shook hands with Mum and Dad, then me. As Malcolm took my hand, he leaned down and whispered, "I'll be in touch."

His seductive tone sent a shiver of excitement down my spine and yet, stunned that he was a chauvinist pig, it freaked me out.

Mum was quiet on the trip back home, too quiet. Dad didn't notice the hard set to Mum's jaw, but I sure did. When we arrived at the house, I rushed upstairs, undressed and put on my pyjamas.

Mum soon followed.

Sitting on the bed, I stared at my hands while she stared at me.

Finally, she said, "I'm very disappointed in you, Jasmine. Have you no respect? How could you let your father and me down like that? Shame on Malcolm Dice too, but in his defence, grief does do strange things to some."

I sighed, wondering if I should try to convince her nothing happened, the evidence though certainly wasn't in my favour. Might as well give it a go, I decided. "Mum, if you're going to assume the worst, then I see little point in trying to defend myself, but for the record, nothing happened. Malcolm Dice is a womanizer with very poor morals. You can blame it on his grief if you like, but it's my opinion fame has thoroughly blighted his personality."

Mum's face softened and she hugged me. "I'm sorry, sweetheart; I do know you, but honestly, I was not sure what to think."

"Oh, it's okay, Mum. I understand because you didn't see the full picture. I hope the jerk behaves better at the funeral."

Mum agreed and left me to go to bed.

The moment the sound of her footsteps faded down the hallway, I summoned Gabe.

When he popped up in front of me, I said, "I assume you witnessed everything that happened at the shop?"

Gabriel nodded. "Sadly, I did. I must say in previous lives, before he remembers, Adam has generally retained some part of his original character. In this case, the adoration of fans has influenced his persona in extremely negative ways. I blame the current society. Far too many people are fame addicts. In the world today, people don't focus on living in harmony with others. It's all about who you know, the wealth you have, and power. I'm sorry, Eve, but it's a sad reality."

I shook my head. "Has it not crossed your mind that there may be other forces at work?"

Gabriel scratched his head. "An interesting concept,

Eve. Ummm... his actions do indicate he has a god like complex. Lucifer does certainly encourage such behaviours in mankind."

The painful emotion of memories rippled over my soul. "No need to remind me of that fact. If surrendering to temptation was a tournament, I would have received the first ever gold medal."

Gabriel's, voice hard with authority, said. "Don't beat yourself up about something you can't change. Choices you make now influence your future."

Weary beyond belief, I lay down on the bed. "I know, but it doesn't make my regret easier to bare."

"You've learned from your mistakes and that's the important thing. Knowledge you've gained over the ages will help light the path to complete peace." He bent down and kissed my cheek "I'll help you in any way I can." A light breeze filled the room and he vanished.

I hugged my oversized pillow and wishing I'd discover it was only a dream in the morning, I closed my heavy eyes.

~~ *Chapter Six* ~~

Two days after our meeting, the news reported the funeral of James Dice being a small private ceremony. A photo of Malcolm looking grief stricken flashed across the TV screen. Maybe Mum was right. Grief did do strange things to people. Perhaps I should have considered that before reacting.

The next day as Dad tried to assemble a new oak coffee table in the living room, he asked me to fetch another screwdriver from his work shed. I nodded, grabbed the key hanging on a hook in the kitchen and headed to the shed. Unlocking the door, I stepped inside the dark structure and hunted for the string pull to the light. Dad's workshop was the length of four garages and the main reason we had moved here when I was little. In Dad's line of work, he needed a large outside shed. Dad also had a passion for hoarding things he believed might come in handy someday. Mum didn't share his viewpoint. An ultimate neat freak, Mum carefully assessed whether each piece of furniture or accent fit her chosen décor style. If an item failed to measure up, she'd demand Dad remove it from the house immediately, which made the work shed even more cluttered.

Trying to evade accumulated junk, I bumped into something

covered by a brown tarp. Curious, I lifted the dusty sheeting and found it concealed an intricately carved piano that had seen better days. I recognized it as one Dad had picked up for a few quid several years earlier. He'd purchased it from an elderly woman who bought a coffin for her departed husband. Needless to say, Mum was not impressed when she came home and found the piano standing next to her expensive Tiffany lamp. My ever practical father argued the piano still worked beautifully. Mum countered with none of us could even play. Dad insisted if restored to its former glory the piano would be a priceless treasure. Mum's dour face revealed there was no point in arguing. Dad sighed, shrugged his shoulders and moved it out to the shed.

After I turned eighteen and regained all my memories again, I recalled being a professional pianist in one life. Now, staring at the neglected piano, I couldn't resist trailing my fingers across the dusty keys. The resulting tinkling sound began to sweep me into another time and place. With Dad waiting, I shook off faded memories and continued searching for the requested screwdriver.

I took the tool to Dad and returned to the shed. Pulling a wooden crate over to the piano, I sat on it and began to play. Dad was right; the old piano possessed beautiful tone and resonance. Engrossed in playing a tricky piece by Mozart, The Requiem, I suddenly sensed someone's presence. Fear swept over me and my fingers halted in mid-movement. I slowly turned and found Mum staring at me with dumbfounded eyes.

I giggled nervously. "Surprise!"

"This is way more than a surprise, Jasmine. I'm bloody flabbergasted. I started to hang the washing out when I heard a piano being played as if it by a pianist at the Royal Albert hall. For a moment, I though the piano was haunted or something and playing itself. She paused and stared at me. "Where and when did you learn to play?"

"Err... ever since Dad brought it home, I've secretly been taking lessons. I hoped Dad would fix it up in time for your twenty fifth wedding anniversary at the end of the year." In the midst of mentally congratulating myself on a good come back, I noticed Mum seemed like she was going to cry. I went over and hugged her.

Unshed tears in her eyes, she wrapped both arms around me. "Oh, Jasmine, that's such a lovely thing for you to do for us. Can't believe I've gone and ruined the surprise."

Feeling guilty, I muttered. "Don't fret about it, Mum. It's really my fault. I got lost in practicing and forgot you'd be home soon."

To distract Mum, I offered to help finish hanging out the wash and quickly pulled the tarp back over the piano. With wet bed linens drying on the clothesline, we went back inside the house. Dad stood admiring the new coffee table.

Mum said to him, "Now you've finished with the table, you can get straight to work on fixing up that old piano."

Dad gave her a bewildered look and then glanced at me. Standing behind Mum, I mugged surprise and shrugged my shoulders.

As usual, Dad went with the flow, grabbed his tools and went out to look at the piano. Over the next week, Mum worked overtime at the hospital and Dad kept busy with his new project. Left on my own, I tried to catch up on some reading, but as usual, the urge to reunite with my original soul mate proved the bane of my existence. I found it impossible to block out reoccurring thoughts of overconfident Malcolm Dice, but dignity forbade me to throw myself at his feet. Something in me wanted to prove I didn't need a man to complete me, but my heart knew otherwise.

A few mornings later I started up my pink dell laptop, which I had got for Christmas. After checking my emails, I logged on to Facebook. I saw a few friend requests. Though one really stood out above the rest, Malcolm Dice. I muttered, "You arrogant ass." With a wry smile, I clicked the accept button.

He soon popped up in chat. "Jasmine, I sincerely apologise for my atrocious behaviour last week. On reflection, I'm utterly disgusted with myself. In my defence, I can only plead temporary insanity caused by the circumstances under which we met. To make it up to you, I'd be honoured if you would have dinner with me tonight."

I laughed while typing my reply. "You have mistaken me for one of your starry eyed groupies, who fall at your feet at any given whim. Considering the loss of your brother, I'm not cold hearted, so I accept your invitation. I stress though any funny business on your part and I'll remove myself from your company immediately."

"I assure you that there will be no shenanigans. I'll endeavour to be a perfect gentleman. I make only one request. Please wear the black dress you had on when first we met. You wouldn't believe the fantasies I've had about you and me getting our groove on."

My eyes widen and I felt myself blush. I quickly typed my response. "Wow, you are clearly suffering from a condition known as egotistical mania, accompanied by delusions you are God's gift to women. If I decide to come, which is now highly unlikely, I'll be wearing a black bin liner, or maybe a Nun's habit."

I giggled waiting for his reply. Ten minutes passed without an answer. Maybe I actually hurt his feelings. I suddenly felt guilty. I was in the midst of composing an apology, when the doorbell rang. Probably the post with something Mum ordered from eBay. I raced to the door and flung it open. But it wasn't the postman; it was Malcolm. I tried to say hello. My mouth moved, at least my lips did something, but nothing came out.

Malcolm grinned and handed me a black bin liner. "Your corner shop doesn't stock nun outfits. You should have seen the bizarre look the shopkeeper gave me when I asked him if he did. I'm afraid you'll have to settle for a bin liner."

Stunned and embarrassed, I tried to gather my wits about me. "Err... thank you, this will do very nicely."

His grin widened. "What say I pick you up around seven this evening? Does that suit you?"

Dazed from staring into his electric blue eyes, I nodded.

He winked. "Seven it is." Whistling, he strode back to a chauffeured car, parked outside my house.

Physically trembling, I set the bin liner down on the chair. I heard a notification alert on my laptop and saw another message on the screen from Malcolm!

His message read, "It doesn't matter what you wear, as you'll be hot regardless."

I smiled and thought, cheeky bugger.

Gabriel appeared in front of me and glanced at my laptop. "Oh, the wonders of technology these days. You could have done with the internet and social networks in your past lifetimes."

"I don't know, Gabe; I don't think it would have helped much before now. It is not like I could pick up a potential Adam, from talking to him over the net. Nothing can replace the good old face to face getting to know someone. Anyhow this way of communicating with him, still doesn't change the fact that he's fame and money addicted, just like so many other people in the world."

"Things are changing though," Gabriel replied. "I've seen

60

positive developments in the last few years."

"Perhaps, but as you often remind me, the driving force in man's nature is power and greed."

Gabriel insisted, "I still believe God's essence stored in each human soul will manifest itself."

I heaved a sigh. "It's too early in the morning to decipher exactly what you mean by that, Gabe." I walked into the bathroom and closed the door. I turned on the shower tap, undressed and got into the shower closing the blue striped curtain.

Gabriel suddenly yanked it back.

I screeched, "Gabriel, some privacy please," and jerked the curtain back closed.

He chuckled. "Are you really going to wear a bin liner?"

I shouted, "No, silly, now get out of here."

I sensed his presence leave. Pouring sweet pea scented shower gel on a sponge I thought, bloody angels. How can one keep any dignity with them appearing willy nilly whenever they like.

I dried off and rifled through my wardrobe looking for something nice, but not overly sexy. After trying on twenty different outfits throughout the day, I decided on a tartan red dress that ended slightly above the knee, paired with mid-heel black pumps. I tamed my auburn hair into a fishtail plait and highlighted my face with a little colour. The freshwater, pearl necklace my nana had left me provided the perfect accent for my outfit. Judging the results in the mirror, I looked sophisticated with a hint of sexy. I glanced at the clock, an hour to go. Riddled with sudden nervousness, I checked myself in the mirror repeatedly. A knock on the door interrupted straightening my necklace yet again. "Come in."

Mum walked into my bedroom. "You look lovely; are you off somewhere nice?"

"Yes Mum, as a peace offering Malcolm Dice invited me to dinner." Nibbling my lips painted dark ruby, I wondered what her response might be.

Her tone sounded a little off. "In the olden days, a young man wanting to take someone's daughter to dinner needed permission from the girl's father."

"Yeah, yeah, I remember that time only too well, Mum." Realizing I was thinking about another life, I quickly corrected the error. "I meant that I've read about it many times."

Mum frowned. "You know, I have a can of pepper spray for when I work late at the hospital. Do you want to put it in your handbag?"

I kissed her on the cheek. "Mum, stop; I can take care of myself, really I can."

"Okay; well have a nice time, but don't stay out too late. You know how I worry, sweetheart."

"I'll phone if I am going to be late." Thinking she'd never view me as an adult, I added, "I do have my own key, remember."

At the sound of a car pulling up outside, I grabbed my black handbag and rushed downstairs. Waiting for the doorbell to ring, my heartbeat felt like it was keeping time to the rhythm of a drummer on drugs. When the bell finally buzzed, I opened the door and found Malcolm holding a dozen red roses.

Nice touch, I thought.

He handed the flowers to me, and complimented my appearance. I thanked him, passed the roses to Mum, bid her goodbye and said she shouldn't worry.

Malcolm guided me to the car and opened the door. Inside the limo, I glanced over at the chauffeur and swore worriedly that his eyes had a slight red glow to them. I considered making up an excuse and getting the hell out. Then I remembered what Gabriel said, tried to relax and ignore the devilish chauffeur. Malcolm got in and scooted close to me, but not too near. As the car cruised down the street, I avoided looking again at the driver, which wasn't difficult as Malcolm was a great distraction. The man oozed with overwhelming sex appeal. His hand brushing my arm lightly when he reached to the drink compartment, sent shivers over me.

He handed me a crystal goblet of white wine and smiled a dazzling smile. "So the bin liner was over doing it for the occasion?"

I took a sip of my drink. "On the cutting edge of the designer fashion, I didn't want to put other ladies dining at the restaurant to shame."

He grinned. "To be honest, I was looking forward to seeing you wear it tonight; guess I'm kinky like that."

Trying to keep a blush at bay, I didn't answer.

"I hope you like Indian food? I made reservations at Indian Dreams; they serve an awesome Koldil Duck. The place is like stepping inside India and the exterior design is stunning." He raked his eyes over me. "Not quite as stunning as you though"

I smiled, as a blush this time escaped. "Thank you. I love Indian food, not so sure my hips do, but it sounds like a great place."

The twenty-minute trip seemed unusually long, with us glancing back and forth at each other, not saying much.

From the outside Indian Dreams resembled the Taj Mahal. The doorman had a small Capuchin monkey on his shoulder, who wore a cute red hat. The decor inside Indian Dreams confirmed Malcolm's review. The restaurant emitted the tropical richness of India. The waiters wore jewel encrusted turbans. Female entertainers, wearing bright coloured Bharathatya costumes danced to music played by men in traditional clothing. It swept me back to my past life as an Indian girl forced into an arranged marriage.

While being escorted to our table, I noticed large bronze statues of different gods lined the back wall. Malcolm pulled out my chair. Thanking him, I eased down in the ornately carved, silk upholstered chair.

"What do you think?" he asked. "Amazing, isn't it?"

Staring at a water fountain with three marble elephants, their raised trucks, pouring blue tinted water into the centre, I nodded. "It's a lovely presentation of Indian culture."

"Wait until you taste the food, it's like a party going on inside your mouth."

The waiter seemed impressed Malcolm chose to dine at the establishment again. He welcomed Malcolm and told him a complementary bottle of wine would arrive at our table shortly.

Malcolm acknowledged the greeting with a slight nod and then focused his sea blue eyes on me. "Permit me to order for you, unless there's something you don't like?"

"Please do. I love all Indian cuisine." I smiled.

The waiter opened the bottle for us and poured wine into our glasses.

Surveying the menu, he smiled. "Enjoying Indian food is something we have in common." He gave our order to the waiter.

My eye brow rose and the wine I was sipping suddenly made me cough at that very comment.

While we waited, a pretty girl handed me a long stemmed pink musk rose. "Wow, thank you," I told her.

A musician playing a pulluvan pattu strolled over to our table and serenaded us with an exotic tune.

When our food arrived, the tabletop looked like a small buffet. The colours and aroma lit up my taste buds.

"Here, you must try this divine duck." Malcolm said, heading a spoonful towards my mouth.

I chewed the meat he put in my mouth. "Yum, tender and delicious."

He appeared pleased I liked the duck. "So, Jasmine, tell me about yourself."

The thought of telling him about the real me, and my lives made me giggle inwardly, but I said, "Not much to tell really, I'm pretty boring."

He grinned. "Okay, if you won't tell me anything, I'll have to hire a private detective to dish the dirt on your scandalous life."

I smiled, "Fine, but it'll be a waste of money."

"Come on, meet me half way here." He took my hand and gently caressed it with his fingertips. "For example; what's your favourite music? Other than mine, what films do you like?"

"Well, pop mostly, Rihanna, Cold Play and All Angels. Film wise, Avatar rocks, as do the Lord of the Rings movies. Strangely, I also enjoy retro black and white films, something my friends find quite amusing."

"While sweet, I agree it's unusual for someone your age." He paused. "Speaking of age, how old are you, twenty... twenty one?"

"Eighteen."

He chuckled. "A ten year gap between our ages, eyebrows will rise upon hearing that number."

Suddenly I felt young, too young. "What about you; what music and movies do you like?"

"I'm a heavy metal guy myself, but I know good music when I hear it. As for movies, I'm a fan of anything I appear in." He winked.

I grinned and continued eating. The waiter refilled our wine glasses.

Music playing in the background suddenly got louder and more dancing girls arrived. I couldn't help but jig along as I took a sip of the sweet wine. Malcolm, grinning, got up from his chair and held out his hand. I frowned but placed my hand in his. He led me through the maze of tables to the dance floor.

"Don't look so worried, Jasmine, it really isn't difficult, just follow my lead." He started to mimic the dance movements of the performers.

I smiled and tried to copy him, but soon memories of my past life in India and the dance instruction I received there flowed from my body. Lost in the hypnotic music, I pulled my hair loose from the fish plait and begin to swirl and sway in the cosmic dance of Shiva. Malcolm looked stunned as I rolled my hips side to side and twisted my arms like a snake. We both giggled and after the song finished we made our way back over to our table. Malcolm, his face flushed and a little out of breath, ordered us some water.

"You are full of surprises, Jasmine. Where did you learn to dance like that? I think you were better than some of the dancers."

Stalling for time to think of an explanation, I slowly sipped from the glass of ice water a waiter placed before me. I settled on a half truth to satisfy his curiosity. "When I was younger, I had a friend whose mother taught Indian dancing. After school, I often accompanied my friend to her mum's small dance studio."

"Well, you certainly impressed me that's for sure."

"What about you? It's clear you are familiar with traditional dance of India, so where did you learn?"

"I did a Bollywood style film a few years back. A low budget affair, but the director employed great dance instructors. I'm still good mates with one of them. He's working on a new movie." Malcolm's eyes lit up. "Hey! Maybe I could get you a part in the movie?"

Laughing, I shook my head. "I'll pass. Don't think I'm cut out for acting."

"If you change your mind let me know. I wouldn't mind seeing you gyrate your hips again." He winked.

My face flushing hotly, I focused attention on drinking my water.

A waiter then brought the tea and dessert, Kherr garnished with dried fruits and cashews. The basmati rice pudding spiced with cardamom and saffron, nutmeg and cinnamon proved sumptuous.

The waiter asked if he could get us anything else. Malcolm looked to me

"I couldn't eat another morsel." I replied, slightly rubbing my full stomach.

"Another bottle of your finest, please." Malcolm smiled.

The waiter bowed and walked away.

After the waiter returned with a bottle of Champagne, Malcolm refilled my glass.

"I do insist you taste this excellent Champagne though."

"I hope you're not trying to get me drunk, Mister Dice?"

Eyes sparkling, he said, "Of course not, whatever would give you that idea?"

I smiled. "I can't imagine." Watching him pour one for himself, I said, "May I ask you a personal question?"

"Fire away."

"Are you still dating Lily Olson?"

He replied after a slight pause. "No."

"Oh, may I ask why, or would you rather not talk about

it?"

He appeared uneasy. "She wanted a commitment. I'm not ready to settle down yet, not when I feel there's a missing connection. I can't fully commit to someone, until I feel it."

"That's interesting, so you are looking for a soul mate?"

"Oh heavens no, I don't believe in such nonsense, just some spark I haven't experienced with anyone."

"I see." Disappointed, I adjusted the napkin on my lap and then readjusted it. I felt him staring at me, but I couldn't meet his gaze. I fingered the stem on my wine glass.

Heavy silence stretched.

He took a sip of his wine, "A penny for your thoughts?"

I forced myself to look at him. "Oh, it's nothing really."

"I believe we were discussing personal matters. So tell me, what side of the bed do you sleep on and what would you like for breakfast?" He smirked.

I sighed, "Really? Here I thought we were getting to know each other, but all you want is to get in my pants. That's all this dinner is about, isn't it?"

He grinned. "If it helps, I only bring ladies here who really stir my fancy."

Before I could reply, one of the entertainers approached our table.

The stunningly beautiful woman with long black hair, looking distraught, glared at Malcolm. "You said you'd call, but it's been two weeks. You made me believe our relationship was going somewhere."

"Sorry, love, I apologise if I left you with that impression. I often forget how naive women can be. I would highly recommend you to some mates, as you were a good lay though, but I've since moved on." He sneered, as he glanced over at me.

Tears begin running down her cheeks. "But you said I

was so special and you wanted me to live with you in your penthouse."

Malcolm shrugged.

Voice edged in panic, she cried, "You took my virginity! Because of you, I've disgraced my whole family. No decent man will ever touch me now." Dissolving into hysteria, she ran away.

Malcolm turned his attention back to me. "Awkward."

Face burning, not from embarrassment, but anger, I jumped to my feet. "I'm leaving."

"Come on, Jasmine, we both bloody well know the reason you came tonight. You want me nearly as much I want to see what's underneath that sexy dress of yours." He chuckled. "Otherwise, after what happened in the loo, you wouldn't have accepted my invitation."

"Like a fool, I laid your disgusting behaviour on the loss of your brother and wanted to give your sorry arse another chance. It's clear now though, that you're the arrogant bastard I put you down for at our first meeting." I threw my napkin down on the table and stormed towards the exit.

"Jasmine, wait please," he called, trying to catch up with me. "At least let me take you back home."

I yelled back, "And trust you won't try something, I think not!"

As I jerked the restaurant door open, he shouted, "You know what they say about redheads, don't ya. They're fiery damn bitches. Well now, isn't that the truth!"

Outside, tears blurred my vision. The evening had started out so good. At one point, I even thought I saw a glimmer of my Adam there inside Malcolm. I grabbed my phone from inside my bag. In the middle of calling dad to pick me up, I felt someone touch my shoulder, I pressed end call. Boiling over with hurt and anger, I whirled around. "Malcolm, I told you..."

It wasn't Malcolm.

Gabriel's eyes were soft with understanding. "I'll take you home."

Sobbing, I threw my arms around him. He lifted me into his arms and whispered soothing reassurances until we landed.

At home, I pulled myself together and dried my tears before going inside. Mum and Dad had gone to bed early. I knocked on their bedroom door and after a moment, Mum opened it. "You're back; did you have fun, honey?"

I half smiled. "Yeah, up to a point. I'll tell you more tomorrow."

Mum kissed my cheek. "Okay, goodnight, sweetheart."

"Night, Mum."

Gabe waited inside my room. Fighting back tears, I sat on my bed.

Gabriel, sounding smug, told me, "At the moment, Malcolm is paying for more than dinner. After you stormed out, he punched one of the restaurant pillars. He might have a broken knuckle or two."

Puzzled, I thought for a minute, and then it dawned on me. "That implies he was upset I stormed off."

"It appears tonight wasn't such a waste after all. You might be breaking down his defences."

"Did you see the chauffeur, Lucifer, right?"

"Oh yeah, since he wasn't in his true form, I banished him. Surely, you must have sensed I was close by." He laughed. "I couldn't resist spicy curry and poppadoms."

I quickly dragged a brush through my hair and removed my makeup. "What do you think I should do now?"

"Nothing, you played the right card tonight. Since Malcolm became famous, not one woman has walked out on him. You're a whole new experience for him." Gabriel kissed my forehead and said, "He'll be in touch," then he vanished.

After changing into a pink nightshirt, I laid on the bed. Staring at the ceiling, I wondered whether Gabriel was right. Would Malcolm call? The way Malcolm treated that poor girl confirmed he didn't have one ounce of respect for women. If not my Adam, I'd wash my hands of Malcolm completely. How could I ever make such a callous, self-centred man fall in love with me? Would I be destined to spend another lifetime without the comfort of my soul mate?

~~ *Chapter Seven* ~~

Next morning with bleary eyes and constant yawning, I shuffled into the kitchen and plopped down in a chair at the pine breakfast table. Mum's colour scheme for the kitchen lay in stark contrast to my mood. The bright red cupboards by themselves could give you a headache after a rough night and I already had a mind splitting one.

Dad, dressed for work, stood in front of the kettle. Smoke hovering over a red toaster and charred bread in the red polka dot bin, confirmed he'd burned the toast yet again. Mum repeatedly warned him to stay out of her territory. The kitchen was Mum's pride and joy. Royal Doulton collectible plates and teapots filled every nook and cranny. Mum would be on pins if she knew Dad was mucking up her domain.

I watched Dad pour the hot water and a splash of milk into one of Mum's brand new collectable cups. Smiling I shook my head; it was a good thing she'd left for an early shift at the hospital. Handing me the fragile cup brimming with hot coffee, he said. "So what are this Malcolm Dice's intentions towards you?"

I took a sip. "Dad, it was only a dinner, nothing more. Don't put too much into it."

The doorbell buzzing pulled him through the living room to the hall. I heard voices. Curious, I followed, and saw people pouring into the house. Several carried huge bouquets of brightly coloured flowers, asking where they should put them. Dumbstruck, I tried twice before finding enough voice to mutter, "Put them anywhere."

A man in a waiter's uniform lugged in a hamper filled with gourmet foods, boxes of chocolates and bottles of champagnes. A girl holding a pink wicker basket containing white Persian kittens trailed him. Bonnie, our dog, trying to inspect the basket, reared up on the girl's dress. The girl shoved the basket of kittens at me and hurried out of the room. Her companions followed.

Dad closed the front door and stared at me. "Just a dinner huh, nothing more?"

I rolled my eyes. "Maybe I misread the evening."

"You think? Where do you plan on putting all this stuff?" He moaned, as a kitten scrambled out of the basket and clawed its way up Mum's new blue drapes.

Dad glared at me. "They are certainly not staying here and you know I'm no fan of cats."

I gently pried the kitten's claws out of the expensive fabric. "Don't worry, Dad, everything is going right back to him."

He sighed and glanced at his watch. "I should get to my shop, so I'll leave you to deal with it."

The second he left, I grabbed my laptop and logged onto to Facebook.

Malcolm immediately popped up on chat, as if he was waiting for me. "I'm incredibly sorry for last night."

"You think sending me all this stuff will make me fall at your feet?"

"Well, it was worth a try."

I could practically see him grinning. "Wrong!"

His rely posted immediately. "Seriously, I wanted to make up for my bad behaviour, yet again."

"A single rose would have gotten your message across. Now, thanks to you my living room resembles a bloody garden centre. Plus my poor dog is hiding under a table scared shitless of two devil spawned kittens that are attacking her."

"Oh you have a dog? Sorry about that, but shouldn't it be the other way round?"

I quickly typed. "Bonnie is a special kind of dog."

"I love dogs. I'd have one if I were home more often. What say we take Bonnie for a walk later?"

"Absolutely not! You hold the record for being the worst arse in the shortest amount of time."

"Please, I'll be good promise. Scout's honour!"

I considered how to reply. I wanted naturally to make him remember our past. At the same time, I didn't want to seem too easy. Only one person could help me decide what to do. I called, "Gabe, are you here?"

Gabriel popped up by me. He grinned. Go, but take your Mum's pepper spray with you."

"Seriously, please!" I pleaded.

"I do think you should go. As I told you last night, that in his own strange way, Malcolm is showing you that he cares. He just hasn't learned how to express himself, without messing up. Moreover, Lucifer hasn't been helping. Which is why, I think you need to watch for signs of his involvement."

"Okay, quickly, what should I reply back then?"

"Whatever you want to."

I sighed. Tone dripping sarcasm, I said, "Thanks, Gabriel; you're always such a big help."

He chuckled. "Glad to be of service." Like many other times, he disappeared, leaving me to my own devices.

I thought of something and my fingers flew over the keys.

"I asked my seven year old cousin, Claire to come with me today when I take Bonnie for a walk." Hoping suddenly that Claire wasn't busy later, I added, "But I suppose you could tag along?"

"Give me a time and I'll be there."

I told him two in the afternoon. I then quickly logged off, grabbed the phone and punched in Aunt Grace's number. Aunt Grace is a touch wacky and that's putting it lightly. I'll never understand how she and my Dad came out of the same gene pool. When she answered my call, I asked if Claire could come along. I told her a male friend from school would be escorting us. If I'd mentioned Malcolm Dice by name, Aunt Grace would have demanded to come too. By sheer luck, she agreed. Relieved, I hung up.

Cursing, I discovered one of the kitties had made a nasty mess on the rug. What to do with them suddenly became my number one priority. An idea suddenly struck me. Tom and Thomas, fondly nicknamed the two Ts, were our neighbours. Tom and Thomas were to be married in a few months. They loved cute and fluffy animals, especially cats. Two marshmallow looking kittens would make an ideal early wedding gift. I chased the little hellcats down, shoved them in the pink basket, and raced next door. Thomas, standing at nearly six foot tall, with blonde short hair, was the one who answered my knock.

On seeing me, his sapphire coloured eyes sparkled. "Jasmine, sweetie, do come in."

"Sorry, Thomas, don't have time to chat today, just wanted to give you guys an early wedding gift." I held up the basket.

A huge smile spread right across his face. "Oh my god, they're just adorable. Thank you so much." He cried, "Tom, come see what Jasmine has given us."

Tom slightly shorter, more bulked out with dark hair

appeared at the door, his rich, coffee coloured eyes, widened upon seeing the kittens. "Wow, what little cuties. You shouldn't have Jasmine."

I passed the basket to Thomas. "No worries, guys; glad you like them."

I left them cooing over the kittens and rushed back to my house. I cleaned up kitty poop, stored what gifts I could, and divided the flower arrangements among all different rooms. To help Dad out, I cleaned up the kitchen and carefully returned Mum's collectable cup to its assigned place. A glance up at the wall clock sent me running upstairs.

I paired jeans with a black t shirt bearing a Hollister logo, pinned my hair up in a bun and slapped on some makeup. Racing around like a headless chicken, I went to Mum and Dad's room, sprayed on her Chanel No. 5 perfume, flew downstairs and grabbed my keys. When I arrived at Aunt Grace's, little Claire was ready and waiting. I then quickly drove back to my house, tried to coax Bonnie from underneath the table and failed.

I mumbled, "Crazy dog believes the kittens are still here."

Crawling under the table, I dragged Bonnie out by the scruff of her neck and held her while Claire attached the leash.

The doorbell rang.

Suddenly quite flustered, I told Claire, "He's here; he's here."

I took Bonnie holding onto her leash and placed her on the floor. The bell buzzed again and she practically dragged me to the door. The second I opened it, Bonnie reared up on Malcolm.

Malcolm laughed, squatted down and patted her. "She's friendly."

Bonnie, tail wagging madly, began licking his face.

I jerked on the leash. "Bonnie, get off him!" Frowning, I told Malcolm, "I don't know what's got into her, she's normally nervous around strangers."

"She knows underneath all the fakery I'm a nice guy."

Thinking that's somewhat ironic, I smiled.

I called Claire and after locking the door, we walked to my car. I put Bonnie in the back with Claire. Malcolm removed a baseball hat from the back pocket of his jeans and put it on before getting into the passenger seat. Inside the car, I saw Malcolm now also wore sunglasses.

He grinned. "It's a disguise to keep the fans off my back."

Starting the car, smiling I asked. "Does it work?"

"Sometimes, if I'm where fans least expect to see me."

At the park, Malcolm opened my door, then Claire's. When I took the leash off Bonnie, she ran in crazy circles like a puppy again. We took turns throwing a rubber ball for her to chase. Claire, growing tired of the game, began to run around and Bonnie followed.

It was a beautiful day with fluffy white clouds drifting across blue skies. Left alone, Malcolm and I walked along for bit, not saying anything.

I finally broke the silence. "How are you and the family doing since the funeral?"

He avoided meeting my eyes. "Not great. Mum is in a bad way and Dad is quiet, keeping to himself mostly. I intend to stick around for a while. I was supposed to start filming a new movie in Canada, but the studio agreed to delay the start." Looking down at the ground, he said, "I can't understand why James drove onto the rail tracks."

Hoping I wasn't prying I softly said, "Was he unhappy?"

"Minor work and relationship issues, but nothing that'd make him do something so totally out of character. With only a fifteen month age gap between us, James and I have always been so close. Lately, he'd been acting a bit strange. I received an odd phone call from him the night before he died."

"Oh yeah, what did he say?"

"Told me he'd seen terrible stuff and something was making him do crazy things."

"Like what?"

"He didn't go into much detail. Claimed voices were whispering to him, saying people were out to get him." Malcolm paused. "I couldn't really talk at the time, so I told him that I'd call back the next day." He swiped at tears in his eyes. "By then, it was too late."

I gently rubbed his arm. "I'm so sorry."

Malcolm's eyes locked with mine then leaning closer, his lips touched mine. Bonnie broke the magical moment by jumping up at us. Laughing we carried on walking until Claire called to me. "Can I go on the swings, please?" She pointed to play equipment in the distance.

I smiled. "Sure."

At the play area, Malcolm asked Claire if she wanted him to push her swing and she happily agreed. Sitting on a nearby wooden bench, I watched other kids running around. A boy about five years old, with thick curly brown hair came and sat on the bench beside me. I smiled sweetly at him.

He grinned. "Was your mother pissed off about the apple pie?"

Shocked, I stared down at the boy's angelic face. "I beg your pardon?"

"You're stupid, Eve, not deaf."

Him! A thousand thoughts raced through my mind and I begin trembling. Instinct screamed to summon Gabriel, but I decided to bluff it through. "What do you want?"

"Your soul, but your fear will do for now."

His cackle in a child's voice sent chills down my spine, but I told him, "You're not very frightening as a small child."

"Personally, I can't think of anything scarier. The creepy, little, bastards suck the life out of everyone."

"Well, you succeeded and scared me, so you can now leave."

"Not yet. I plan to have some personal playtime with your little cousin. Claire, isn't it? And see how scared that makes you." He grinned.

"Don't you dare go near her!"

"What would you do, Eve, sic your dog on me, the one cowering underneath this bench?"

"No, I'll let my bodyguard punt your puny arse back to hell."

Cringing like a frightened child, he smiled. "Yikes, I'm so scared. The blonde bombshell is going to spank my naughty bottom."

I quickly stood up and walked towards Malcolm pushing Claire on a swing.

He followed. "You know, his brother James was a useless tool, and way too easy, that it was almost boring."

I stopped and stood frozen in place. Malcolm waved to me, and somehow, I still managed to wave back.

Gabriel appeared in front of me. He glared at the monster just behind me.

The devil cackled. "Ah, the cavalry has arrived."

Gabriel's, attention locked on his foe, "Eve, please distract Malcolm and Claire for a moment."

Worried about what Gabriel might do, I walked toward the play area. An invisible Gabriel hurting a sweet looking child in front of other people would raise quite a stink. What I didn't count on was Gabriel having backup. As I then saw another angel I once met, behind the steering wheel of an ice cream van that was zooming across the ground. Thinking this is a bit comical, I distracted Malcolm and Claire by pointing out two boys scuffling in the distance. Out of the corner of my eye, I saw the van stop, blocking anyone's view of the demon kid from the play area. A loud pop sounded and a puff of bluish smoke rose into the air.

Claire wanted to get off the swing, so Malcolm lifted her off. To my horror, she ran towards the ice cream van. "Jasmine, may I have an ice cream?"

Worried I thought to myself either the van would be empty or worse she might see a charred devil child lying by it, so I lied. "Sorry Claire, I don't have any change."

"I have some," Malcolm told me. "I'll get her one. Do you want one too?"

"No thank you." Though looking at numerous children and their parents heading for the van, I quickly changed my mind. "On second thoughts, if you'll give me the change, I'll go and choose something and one for Claire."

Malcolm nodded and dropped several coins into my hand. Malcolm and Claire waited to the side while I stood in line behind the other customers. I tried to see the ice cream vendor and couldn't. Then I did. Gabriel in human form stood inside the van, serving up treats to people.

Wearing a perky white hat on his head, he smiled at me as I got to the front of the queue. "And what would you like, miss?"

I whispered, "I've never seen you in human form."

He winked. "Lucifer isn't the only changeling, although I can't morph into different people like he can."

I pretended to study the menu painted on the van. "Is he gone?"

"For the time being, but unfortunately, he'll be back."

I pointed to my selection.

He smiled as he passed three cones filled with chocolate ice cream. "On the house."

"Thanks, see you around no doubt."

He nodded and as I turned around I noticed that Claire and Malcolm had decided to come closer and met me as I handed Claire an ice cream.

Claire began devouring her cone, but Malcolm glanced at the van and then looked at me. "There's something odd about that ice cream vendor."

I stopped licking my ice cream. "What do you mean?"

"Can't quite put my finger on it, but I know him from somewhere."

"Maybe you do, it is a small world after all."

He laughed, "Or in another life maybe?"

I shrugged and smiled. "Perhaps?"

"Don't tell me you believe in the foolish notion of reincarnation?"

I grinned and strolled toward a wooded area where Bonnie was chasing after some poor squirrel.

Malcolm, watching the squirrel scrambling up a tree, chuckled. "I gather Bonnie isn't afraid of squirrels?"

"No just cats. Thanks to my Dad Bonnie thinks they are evil monsters. Dad hates cats. If one ever invades his prized flower and vegetable patch, he runs screaming like a lunatic into the house and gets a water pistol."

Malcolm stared at me. "Oh dear, I gave you kittens; bet I'm not in your Dad's good book."

Suddenly aware of how Malcolm's eyes seemed to look right into my soul, I felt my face heating. "It's okay. I gave them to my neighbours. But they best keep them inside, or they'll end up soaked little kitties."

Claire ran up to me, saying she was hungry. "Oh, Claire," I said, "In the mad rush to get out the house, I forgot to pack anything."

Malcolm pulled out his phone. He punched in a number, said something and hung up. Gesturing to picnic benches near a play area, he said, "Lunch is this way, ladies."

Within minutes, I saw Malcolm's chauffeur striding our way, carrying a wicker basket.

Oh no, I thought to myself, I hoped it wasn't Lucifer again. I prepared myself for anything, but it wasn't and the chauffeur placed the basket on our table, and walked back to the car.

Malcolm pulled out an assortment of deli meats, cheeses and breads from the basket. Spying a tray of chocolate chip cookies, Claire's brown eyes widened and she pleaded for one. Malcolm ignored my objections and handed Claire a cookie, which she shared with Bonnie. After we ate, Malcolm and I chatted while Claire and Bonnie shared the leftover cookies. The afternoon flowed into early evening.

Malcolm told me, "I promised to have dinner with the parents, feel I owe it to poor mum. So I best be leaving."

"Of course, I completely understand."

He embraced me, kissed my cheek and then playfully rubbed Claire's head. Watching Malcolm walk to his limo, I smiled.

I dropped off Claire and drove home. Relaxing on the sofa, I looked at a picture of Claire and Malcolm, which I'd taken with my phone. Apart from my brush with mini Lucifer, the afternoon was extremely pleasant and Malcolm was the perfect gentleman. Dad was glad the kittens were gone when he arrived home. Mum loved the flower arrangements and looking at poor Dad, remarked how she rarely got flowers anymore.

After dinner, I bid Mum and Dad goodnight and went upstairs. Lying on my bed, I stared at vases of roses filling the room with their delicate fragrance. My mobile suddenly beeped.

It was a text from Malcolm. Smiling I read it. "I had a really nice time today. I don't want to jump the gun, but would you consider risking another date with me?"

Not wanting to appear too eager, I waited a minute or two before accepting the invitation. Hearing the beep of another text, I smiled at the reply of a smiley face. Closing my eyes still grinning to myself, the phone sipped from my hand as I drifted off to a distant memory.

~~ *Chapter Eight* ~~

In 19th century England as the daughter of the Mayor of Alcester in Warwickshire, I received a letter one early spring morning, delivered by a man on horseback, one that wrecked my world.

At the time, I was in love with Jonathan, youngest son of the vicar. Jonathan and I had met at a dance and after other social encounters, I found myself enchanted by him. I felt certain it was only a matter of time until we would become engaged. Jonathan's brother, Robert suddenly arrived in town and made it clear he disliked the idea of the possible union. Strangely though, Robert privately confirmed his own desire for me. My younger sister, Daisy, thought Robert charismatic with his blonde hair and sapphire blue eyes, but I viewed him a pompous braggart. I preferred Jonathan's dark smouldering looks and his wittingly cleaver charm.

After receiving yet another annoying letter from Robert, I sent back an immediate reply. I politely, but firmly informed him I did not return his sentiments, adding Jonathan owned my heart. Three days before my eighteenth birthday, I fell ill. For days, I lay unconscious, burning up with a fever. Both Jonathan and Robert inquired daily about my condition.

When I came round briefly once, now being eighteen, all my past lives came flooding back sending me into the coma. When I then recovered from that and awoke again, I begged Mother to allow Jonathan to pay me a visit. It took days to convince her and the doctor that I was strong enough to entertain visitors.

With Mother acting as chaperone, I received Jonathan in the sitting room. I sadly realised straight away, even before Jonathan kissed my hand that he wasn't my soul mate. Shocked and disappointed, I didn't notice Robert enter the room until he cleared his throat. My eyes then swiftly met those of my true love. He was my Adam!

Gabriel made a sudden appearance. From the corner of my eye, I saw Gabriel raise his eyebrows.

"So not good," I muttered under my breath.

Robert handed me a nosegay of white violets. "I'm sorry, Lady Rose, but I didn't catch that?"

"Tis nothing." I accepted the violets, sampled their fragrance, and smiled sweetly up at Robert. "I'm afraid I'm still not quite myself yet."

Robert bowed. "I shall take my leave and allow you to rest."

Jonathan stepped forward and nudging Robert aside, took my hand and pressed a kiss on the back. "Yes, my dear Rose, do rest. I'll return back when you're feeling better."

I nodded and they both took their leave. Mother showed them to the door.

My face worried I asked Gabriel, "What am I to do?"

"Caught between the affections of brothers you may spark a family feud. Still, Robert is Adam. You would do them both an injustice, if you don't follow your true path. At least Robert is taken with you and won't require much effort on your part before he remembers."

Thinking about the day when Robert would remember he was my Adam, I smiled. It had rarely been this easy. I received a letter from Robert the next day. I replied immediately, telling Robert my illness caused me to realize that I had affections more for him than Jonathan.

Two mornings later, Mother rushed into my room. Face flushed, she stammered out the latest gossip. Jonathan had gone into Robert's bedroom and found my last letter. In a fit of jealous rage, he stormed downstairs and confronted Robert. The quarrel escalated and according to a letter he left, Robert trying to defend himself had hit Jonathan over the head with a statue. Mother's rendition painted a graphic picture of Jonathan lying motionless in a pool of blood, an image that forever scarred my heart.

Later that day, I received a letter from Robert that was posted the night before. I ripped it open.

My dearest, Rose,

I do not have much time. Something appalling has occurred. Jonathan discovered letters containing my true intentions towards you and your recent reply. In self defence, I have killed Jonathan. I fear trying to prove it wasn't done in malice will end in my death by hanging. To save myself I have no alternative but to set sail for the New World immediately. I am truly sorry for any distress that this may cause you and wish with all my heart that things could be different. Please forget all about me and get on with your life.

Love, Robert

My knees buckled and wailing, I sank to the floor. While mother tried to comfort me, Daisy grabbed the letter from my hand, and read it out aloud.

That evening, law enforcement tracked Robert down and

shot him dead, after he refused to be detained. I sobbed for weeks; wondering to myself if I could have possibly stopped him from running away.

I then myself drifted into another illness not long after and due to having no heart in wanting to fight it, I passed away only a month later.

Suddenly waking haunted by the painful memories, I saw another unopened text message on my phone screen.

It was from Malcolm again. "Are you free on Wednesday?"

"I am."

Ghosts of the past urged me to add, "I'm looking forward to seeing you again."

Unable to sleep anymore, I decided to get up. Mum, already dressed for work, stood in the kitchen. Her eyebrows rose at the sound of the doorbell ringing. "Who on earth can that be? It is only 6 a.m." She walked towards the hallway. I heard her say, "What a lovely surprise." And laughter drifted from living room.

I went to the living room and found mum hugging her sister Jane who lived in Wales. Mum looked at me. "Jasmine, look who's here for a few days?"

"Hi ya, Aunt Jane," I said giving her a smile.

She kissed my cheek. "Jasmine, lovely to see you."

"Jasmine honey, why don't you make some tea for us," Mum told me.

"Sure." In the kitchen, I filled the electric kettle and switched it on. Waiting for the tea to steep, I heard Mum say, "Wish I could take a sick day, Jane, but due to a breakout of Rotavirus the hospital is understaffed."

I served the tea and after downing hers, Mum gave us both a quick hug before popping out to Dad's shed to let him know about our visitor and then headed off to work.

Aunt Jane patted the sofa cushion beside her. "This will

give us a chance to catch up."

I sat beside her.

"Jasmine, when I phoned your Mum last week, she said you'd gone on a picnic date with a famous movie actor. Is that right?"

I grinned. "Yep"

She smiled, "From all reports Malcolm Dice believes he's god's gift to women. I wouldn't have thought someone like you would have fallen for his charms so easily."

I frowned. "What do you mean?"

"As you know, I was present when your Mum gave birth to you." She paused and stared into her teacup. "I'm surprised she has never mentioned it before."

"Never mentioned what?"

"You didn't cry like most babies at birth, just cooed and sucked on your finger. It amazed the midwife how you supported your head and looked around the room like a three month old. The midwife, who claimed to be psychic, insisted you were an old soul. After a couple of hours, you abruptly begin acting like a newborn."

I stared at my aunt in disbelief. Could it be possible that my past life briefly clung to me after I was born? Did this happen in every life? Was it a good sign or a bad one? I shook off the idea. "Mum doesn't believe in the malarkey of reincarnation, guess that's why she never said anything like that about my birth."

Aunt Jane took a sip of her tea. "I didn't either at the time, but I've since had two children of my own and both acted like newborns from the start." She studied my face. "Perhaps the midwife was right. You do have a certain aura about you."

"Who knows, maybe I have been here before," I said quietly.

She shrugged. "I guess, just one of the many mysteries of

life. Maybe all will be revealed in time."

I stifled a laugh. If only she knew the truth.

She set her teacup aside. "So, anyway, let's talk more about this Malcolm Dice. What's he actually like? Is he really the heartthrob portrayed on screen or is that just a product of Hollywood publicity?"

I blushed. "Oh he's everything you see on screen and much more."

She leaned closer and whispered. "So he's hot, huh?"

"Yeah, too hot sometimes." We both giggled.

The back door opened and Dad walked in from the garden. "What's so funny?"

Still giggling, I sputtered, "Nothing you'd want to hear about, Dad."

Dad rolled his eyes and headed for the fridge. "Your mother made an apple pie. You guys want a slice?"

Aunt Jane shook her head.

Thinking apples were a Lucifer magnet and I didn't need him showing up, I stammered, "Err... no thanks, dad, I've gone off apple pie recently. Besides it's too early in morning for pie."

Dad grinned. "It's never ever too early for pie." He cut himself a large portion.

"If you two don't want any, it leaves all the more for me."

Unable to watch Dad or anyone else eat apple pie, I excused myself and went to my room. I took a quick shower, ran a comb through my wet hair and left it to dry naturally. I wiggled into jet black skinny jeans and put on my pink Hello Kitty top. I jumped when Gabriel popped up beside me.

"So what's going on?" He asked. "Anything interesting?"

"Nah; come to think of it, my Aunt Jane turned up out the blue and told me something fascinating."

The grin on his face widened. "Oh, really?"

I heaved a big sigh. "Assuming you're present every time I'm born, it's a good guess you know what it is." "Of course, but I must say you were a particularly beautiful newborn in this life."

Wondering if he meant I was normally an ugly baby, I frowned at him. Hands on hips, I demanded, "Do I act the same way after each rebirth?"

"I guess so, but no mortal noticed until this life. The midwife who delivered you has the gift."

I pondered if this new information could aid me in the future and ended up more confused than ever. "I don't understand why I'd act like an older baby and suddenly revert to a newborn?"

The corners of his mouth curled, "There must be a reason."

"By your answer, I assume you don't have a clue either."

He winked. "You assume right."

"Sometimes, Gabe, you drive me insane."

He grinned and vanished.

I heard Aunt Jane calling my name and I shouted back, "I'm coming," and slipped on my socks and shoes. Aunt Jane was waiting at the bottom of the staircase. "What are your plans for today, Jasmine?"

"Not much. I'm going to take Bonnie for a walk. Would you like to come along?"

She smiled. "Yeah, sounds good."

When Bonnie saw me collecting her leash, she ran to my side and reared up on my leg. Bonnie tugged excitedly against the leash as we strolled towards a nearby field. The sun parted lingering morning clouds and washed the sky in brilliant watercolours. The day seemed rich with endless possibilities. When we arrived at our destination, I un-snapped the leash and Bonnie curried across the field. Aunt Jane watched Bonnie sniffing the ground for a moment, then turned to me.

"I considered accepting your Dad's offer of pie. Your Mum makes the best apple pie I've ever tasted... but I told you that the last time I had a slice... or should I say half a pie."

It took a couple of minutes before my brain kicked into gear. A hint of red in my auntie's eyes confirmed Lucifer had fooled me again. "Bollocks; just bloody well leave me alone, okay!"

Chilling laughter echoed across the field. "Not likely."

Chasing after Bonnie, I yelled, "Gabriel."

I grabbed up Bonnie and turned. A whirlpool began to form beneath Lucifer's feet and grew, sucking my tormentor down into the ground.

Gabriel appeared. "That'll give him a nasty headache."

I glared at Gabe. "What the hell am I going to tell Mum? She'll expect Aunt Jane to be at the house when she gets off work. But never bloody mind that; what can I tell Dad when I return without her?"

Gabe rubbed his chin. "This is going to be tricky."

Pacing back and forth across dew covered grass, I screamed, "You think!"

"I can't morph myself into a person Lucifer is impersonating, but I might be able to mimic your aunt's voice."

"Okay and then what?"

"I'll pretend to be Aunt Jane and leave a voice message on your Mum's mobile, saying she needed to return to Wales because her son and daughter in law are having their first child."

"But my cousin's wife isn't even due yet?"

"She's only a few weeks away from giving birth, so it could be a false alarm."

"Mum will phone Aunt Jane to find out about the baby...

then what?"

He shrugged. "Yeah, I didn't think of that."

"Clearly not!" I heaved a sigh. "Guess we'll start with the phone message and go from there."

I dialled Mum's number and handed Gabe my phone. He cleared his throat and his deep bass voice took on a soprano tone. I listened in surprise as he left the message for Mum. When he hung up, I told him, "Now we need to think of an excuse to get around Dad." I thought for a moment. "I've got it! Go in the house and grab my car keys for me. I'll tell Dad he was in the work shed when Aunt Jane received an urgent message from her son and I drove her straight to the train station."

"Okay," Gabe said, "hope it works."

I picked up Bonnie and passed her to him, "Take her back inside the house." He vanished and returned with my keys. I needed to pull myself together before facing Dad, so I decided to go for a drive. Gabriel hopped in the passenger seat and I floored the gas pedal. Listening to Evanescence's Swimming Home, blaring on the car stereo, I glanced at Gabe. Concern etched his face. "What's the matter?"

"I normally know when Lucifer has morphed into someone. Why didn't I detect he was your aunt?"

"Beats me. Isn't there an angel handbook where you can look up the answer?"

"Doesn't work that way, and besides that would be cheating."

"Guess asking God is totally out of the question also."

He grinned, "Naturally."

"Why?"

"God comes to us. One can't go to him and ask these things. If he wants us to know, then it shall be. Still, there is always a reason, but it's usually up to us to figure it out."

I sighed. "Not that again. I've lived way too many lives trying to uncover the answer to my dilemma, so if you don't mind, I'd like some alone time before I lose what's left of my sanity."

Gabe laughed heartily. "Okay, but I won't be far away."

I drove around for a while before turning the car homeward. When I opened the front door, Bonnie scampered across the ground and greeted me. I found Dad working in his shed and I told him about Aunt Jane returning to Wales. After Mum finished her shift at the hospital, she walked into the living room.

Her eyes filled with sadness. "I was so looking forward to spending some time with Jane. Think I'll call and see if the baby has arrived."

"Mum, she phoned just before you got home. Seems it was a false alarm. She said she'd let us know when the baby was born."

Dad looked at me. "I didn't hear the phone ring."

Drowning in the lies I'd told, I quickly spoke up. "She called my iPhone and I had it set on vibrate."

Mum's brow wrinkled. "Nevertheless, I should return her call."

"But, Mum..." Too late, as she'd began dialling the landline. I nibbled on a fingernail while Mum tried repeatedly to reach her sister.

"That's strange," she said, "I can't get a connection." Certain Gabe had fiddled with the phone, I told her, "A line might be down somewhere."

She sighed. "I suppose. Well, I guess I'll take a bath."

~~ *Chapter Nine* ~~

Over the next two days, my mind hardly strayed from Malcolm and our upcoming date. Wednesday morning, I received a text from him, saying I should pack a bag for a couple of night's stays and my passport. Not too sure about this, I informed Mum I wouldn't be back until Friday. Her eyebrows rose and folding her arms, she stared at me. To relieve her anxiety, I said she shouldn't worry because it was my time of the month.

Malcolm turned up looking as handsome as ever, wearing black jeans and a white and black striped tight tailored shirt. Whatever his aftershave was, it was gorgeous as inhaling the smell; I sat up closer to him in the car as we set off towards the airport.

"Where are we going," I asked, smiling at him.

Looking pleased with himself, he said, "And spoil the surprise, never!"

The next thing I knew, we were aboard a private jet and flying over the ocean. Malcolm made what he called his specialty cocktail, and handed it me. He looked at me with his smouldering eyes. "There's something remarkable about you, Jasmine Brown. It truly does feel like I've known you all my life."

I only smiled and sipped my drink.

In little more than just an hour later, the Eiffel tower appeared in the distance. I should have guessed that Malcolm would whisk me to the most romantic city in the world. The pilot instructed us to fasten our seatbelts. A chauffeur driven car waited for us just outside the terminal. The sleek black limo then transported us through beautiful Paris and across the countryside to the hotel Chateau d'Esclimont. A moat edged the magnificent building and enchanting gardens lay in the background. Entering the grand foyer of the former castle felt like stepping back into the Renaissance period. I half expected Cinderella to suddenly appear and run down the steps. I was reminded of a past life, but could not drift off into it and remember just yet.

We followed a bellboy to our rooms. Mine lay across the hall from Malcolm's. Alone inside my room, I stared at the opulence spread before me. Wondering what one night must cost, I lay on an intricately carved four poster bed fit for a queen.

A little later I dressed for dinner in a light-blue cocktail dress, one borrowed from out of Mum's closet. I riffled through my overnight case and sadly discovered I had forgotten my pearl necklace.

Feeling a bit underdressed, I rubbed my bare neck several times as Malcolm and I had cocktails at the bar while waiting on our table. Malcolm excused himself and walked towards what I believed to be the bathroom area. He returned not long later, carrying a small red gift bag. Settling on his bar stool, he removed a black box from the bag and handed it to me smiling.

"What's this?"

"It's hard for me to carry on a conversation when I can't

think of anything else except kissing your neck. So I thought covering it up with something might help."

I opened the box. Inside, a white gold necklace with a large, oval shaped, blue Topaz glittered. I gasped and shoved the box back towards Malcolm. "I can't accept this."

"Don't you like it?"

"It's beautiful, but it must have cost a small fortune."

"I'll be offended if you don't accept it." He lifted the necklace from the case, stood, and placed it gently around my neck. "Besides, it matches your dress perfectly." He smiled.

"But... I can't... I shouldn't..."

He grinned. "When someone gives you a gift, it's customary to say thank you."

Fingering the stone resting on my neck, I looked up at him. "Thank you, it's so lovely."

Staring at me, Malcolm's eyes glazed over. Was he on the edge of full remembrance? Was this to be the magical moment? A shiver of expectation slid over me.

But the fog clouding Malcolm's eyes cleared. "You're welcome." Brushing a wayward strand of hair off my face, he asked, "Why are you shivering?"

"A passing chill, but I'm fine now."

Our table was ready, and we were escorted to one with a candlelit chandelier above it. French onion soup preceded tender mussels swimming in a red wine sauce, followed by a heavenly crème brûlée and Champagne.

I smiled at the sweet old couple sitting at the table across from us. It was so nice seeing them still obviously in love. Although I did suddenly wonder why, in most of our past lives whether I got Adam to remember or not, we rarely got to old age alone or together.

After dinner, we strolled through the gardens. A full moon

watched over twinkling stars and a breeze sweetened the air with the fragrance of roses. Malcolm picked a pink one and tucked it into my hair.

"The necklace didn't solve my dilemma. I still want to kiss your neck."

I smiled. "I've become attached to the necklace, so I'm afraid you can't have it back."

"Then a proper thank you is called for." His mouth gently covered mine. His kiss deepened and passion burned through me, but I forced myself to pull away. It was not like I could even surrender to him right now. But would he still view me as just another easy conquest if I could have? With his unfortunate history of being a ladies man, I really needed him to connect with me spiritually first.

Malcolm, looking a bit puzzled, stared at me for a moment then said he had a busy day planned for us tomorrow, and suggested I get some sleep. He left me at my door with only a light kiss.

Looking out of my hotel window, I had to double take as I saw Gabriel leaning against a mermaid statue, which overlooked a fish pond. He waved at me. I smiled and waved back.

That night, dreaming, I returned to a random past life.

I was Christina Shamel, the daughter of a plantation owner in New Orleans and just the awful sound of my father's voice made me cringe. A ruthless man, my father terrified everyone in the household, including my mother and younger brother Zach. He treated my mother appalling, even striking her in front of the servants on many occasions. I never understood why she stayed with him. My father, against my wishes, had promised my hand to Claude Mauston. Claude was the only son of father's best friend, who owned the adjoining plantation. Claude and I were childhood playmates before he went away to school in Virginia, but I had not seen him for years since.

The week before my eighteenth birthday, one of our slaves who practiced voodoo gave me the evil eye and chuckled. Pointing a gnarled finger at me, she said, "The dark one owns your soul."

Within days, I fell into the ritual coma and awoke with the full knowledge of all my lives.

The very next month Claude returned home. To celebrate Claude's homecoming, every family of quality received an invitation to a dinner party held in his honour. Upon our arrival at Mauston House, Claude greeted me warmly and kissed me on my hand. With light brown hair and emerald green eyes, Claude was handsome enough and demonstrated perfect manners. During the evening, he entertained us by playing a beautiful piece on the piano.

Aware sadly that Claude wasn't my soul mate, Adam; I wanted to sever our engagement but feared my father's wrath. To escape the intimidating stares of my father, I accepted Claude's invitation for a moonlight stroll.

The night was humid and we walked silently for a spell, then Claude broke the silence, "Tell me, Christina, are you still pure?"

"Why, Sir, that's a very impropriate question!"

"By your answer, I take it that you are not."

"I most certainly am!"

He sniggered. "Good." Abruptly gripping my arms, he dragged me behind a slave shack and threw me hard down on to the ground. "Raping a virgin is much more exciting." He grinned. I tried to scream, but he clamped a hand over my mouth. "If you make a sound, I'll gut your whole family in their sleep." He barked his face twisted.

Sobbing, I thought of my small brother and tried to block

out the horrendous pain and humiliation. From the corner of my eye, I saw Gabriel looking on. He couldn't intervene because it was forbidden for other humans to see him. However, shockingly an old slave woman was staring right at him, and tutting away.

Gabriel, anguish carving his face, told the woman, "What can I do? I'm not allowed to intervene. No one else can know of my presence."

The woman hissed, "I see ya."

"Likely, I guess because you're spiritually connected."

The old woman cackled. "Angel! For heaven's sake, yer in New Orleans, the birthplace place of witchcraft and voodoo. Ya could help and still remain unseen."

Gabriel nodded and then wasting no time grabbed Claude and flung him across the ground. A thud echoed as Claude's head hit a large rock. Gabriel still cloaked to all others went to pick me up, when a male slave ran to where I lay.

Kneeling beside me, the man whispered, "Is ya okay, mistress?"

I stared up at his warm brown eyes and knew instantly that I was staring up at my original soul mate again. "I'll be all right. Let me be or you'll be blamed."

He lifted me into his strong muscular arms "I ain't leavin' ya here!"

The old woman nudged him. "No, Leon, put her down. Ya wanna get us both killed."

Leon nodded towards the spot where Claude lay motionless. "What if he comes round?" Frowning, he asked, "Who cold cocked him?"

The woman grinned and held up balled hands. "I still have some power in these old fists of mine."

"Ya damn witches and your black magic," Leon declared. "Yer sure to get all of us hanged." Keeping an eye out for the overseer, Leon carried me and as he hurried I could see that look in his eyes, that he felt something strange for me. We then reached his family's hut.

Inside his mother glanced at me and gasped. "Lord a mercy, son, whataya done? Ya done doomed us all."

"Mama, I didn't do nothing.' She was attacked by the master's son."

His mother nodded. "I knew that Claude was a bad seed... ya can see it in his eyes."

Leon laid me on a worn mattress on the dirt floor.

"Thank you," I told him. "You're risking everything to help me."

He looked shocked, as if no white person ever spoke a kind word to him. "Thank ya, mistress, for treatin' me like a man, not a slave."

His mother shooed Leon, his daddy and brother outside. While she bathed me and applied a soothing lotion, she asked me what happened.

I stammered out the whole sordid mess, leaving out Gabriel as the one who jerked Claude off me. I claimed not to have seen who hit him.

Tears begin streaming down her face. "None of 'em will believe ya, let alone Leon. My boy will die for helpin' ya. Just last week, they whipped a ten year old boy for stealing an apple. Can ya imagine what they'll do to Leon for this?"

I placed my hand over hers. "I won't let them. Don't worry I'll think of something."

Leon's daddy, evidently eavesdropping, stormed into the shack. "I'll be takin' blame for this. Leon is young and I'm the age when they don't see me as much use."

Leon tried to persuade him otherwise.

His daddy waved him away. "Hush up, my mind's made up. Now I need to get this gal back ta the house before someone misses her." He hefted me into his arms and strode towards the main house. I saw a crowd gathered on the veranda.

My mother, spying us, cried, "There's my baby," and ran towards us, followed by a slew of others.

Later after Claude regained consciousness, head bloodied, he staggered back to the house and claimed slaves attacked us. Someone wrenched me from the arms of Leon's daddy and several men seized hold of him.

I screamed out the true story to anyone who would listen.

My father rewarded my efforts with the back of his hand, sending me flying onto the ground. Standing over me with clenched fists, he screamed, "You lying whore! Claude didn't rape you. You're covering for that black buck, Leon. You're no longer my daughter."

Blood from my nose mixed with tears streaking my face. A white hot rage seized hold of me, and snatching up a nearby heavy stone; I jumped up and hit my father upside his head. He fell to the ground dead!

Watching blood pool around my father, I knew I'd sealed my fate, but I didn't care. Though being forced to watch the overseer whip Leon's daddy and his whole family broke my spirit. Gabriel, more distraught than I'd ever seen him, claimed it was his entire fault, saying he should have never intervened. I told him Leon would have come to my rescue anyway. Resigned to the inevitable, I wept and pleaded with God to show mercy and let me hang alongside Leon, his daddy and brother. Once again, the path of my soul mate and mine parted.

I watched through my cell window as guards escorted Leon through a crowd on the appointed day. I strangely noticed the old slave woman from before wore a gap toothed grin. Gabriel, staring at the woman, angrily punched my cell wall then disappeared. As the overseer placed a noose around Leon's neck, Gabriel reappeared. Leon's eyes met mine through the bars. The bang of the trap door dropping seared across my soul.

With a scream frozen in my throat, I bolted upright in bed.

If I had known the old slave woman was one of Lucifer's disciples, things might have ended differently. Now as I stared up at the ceiling I suddenly wished my dad Colin were here, I wanted to give him a hug so he knew how much he meant to me. I had been lucky in this life with the wonderful parents I had been given, and wished it had always been that way.

Cursing my eternal punishment, I scooted out of bed and padded to the bathroom. I opened the door, and slammed it hard shut again. Wondering if I was fully awake, I slowly cracked it and peeked around the door.

Lucifer, in his original form, stood in front of the mirror flossing his teeth. I closed it quickly for a second time.

I screeched, "Gabriel! Lucifer is bloody well in my bathroom."

Lucifer laughed from behind the door. "Poor, Eve. I'm sorry, but Gabriel is unavailable at the moment. Your guardian isn't as powerful as you believe."

Dread filled my throat, being in Lucifer's presence without backup scared the crap out of me. Trembling, I demanded, "What have you done to him?"

I then watched terrified, as the door handle slowly went down and his evil face slowly appeared around the door.

Eyes glowing like a mini-supernova, Lucifer sneered. "Oh he's somewhere in Peru. Things are extremely hot for my little bro. But don't worry about him; I assure you it's not entirely unpleasant lying under a mountain of lava. Though, it's a bastard to get out of wings."

I took a couple of steps backwards.

He matched me step for step. "Aww... Come on, Eve, you weren't always so wary of me. We could be such great friends."

I screamed, "Leave me alone, you have no power over me."

Spreading his massive wings, he edged so close that the rotten stench of his breath enveloped me. "That's where you're wrong, my dear Eve. As I hold the key to everything your heart desires and more. Give up this quest to make Malcolm Dice remember he's Adam. You'll never succeed. I hold him and his every thought regarding women in my hand. However, I could offer you a sweet deal?"

"Nothing you could possibly offer would convince me to trust you again." Spying the only weapon at my disposal, I raced across the room and snatched the hotel Bible off the bedside table.

Lucifer laughed so loudly, that I thought the entire hotel would hear. "What do you propose to do with that?"

He barely finished the last word before I smacked him upside the head with the Book. Moving with lightning speed, I raced to Malcolm's door and pounded on it with my fists. The door finally swung open and a bedraggled Malcolm stared at me.

Wearing only Calvin Klein boxers, he asked, "Jasmine sweetheart, whatever is wrong?"

Too frightened to speak, sobbing, I flung my arms around his neck.

He pulled me inside and closed the door. "Jasmine, please tell me what has you so upset?"

Clinging to him, I sobbed, "Someone... something is in my room." Realisation hit me; I swiped at my tears with the back of my hand, and covered the blunder with a half lie. "Nightmare... I had a nightmare."

Malcolm hugged me tight. "It's okay, I've got you. The boogie man won't dare touch you while I'm around."

Wishing he was right, I pulled free of his embrace. "Thanks, I'm okay now?"

He tilted my chin up, looked into my eyes and grinned. "Good to know the famous Malcolm Dice charm still works."

I managed to smile, but dreading what might be waiting in my room, I muttered, "Could you escort me back to my room?"

"Okay, but just to ensure I don't get the wrong idea, why? Is it to check for monsters lurking in the closet?"

Almost wanting to cry again, I nodded. "Only one monster and it's in the bathroom."

"Let me grab my robe and slippers and we'll check it out together."

Nervously glancing towards my room, I waited while he retrieved them.

With me clinging to Malcolm's arm, we walked across the corridor. I waited in the doorway while Malcolm checked every nook and cranny of the bathroom, under the bed and in closets.

With a big grin on his face, Malcolm motioned for me to come inside. "No monster, but I found several dust bunnies under the bed."

I entered the room and glanced around. An eerie chill slid down my spine. I couldn't see Lucifer, but I sensed a presence. Someone or something was watching us.

"Can you smell that Jasmine? Smells like something burning."

"Err… Yeah but I don't see any smoke."

Looking around the room, from the corner of my eye I glimpsed something move. Quickly I grabbed my hair curlers, "Oh that's what the smell is, I left them on. Silly me.

Thanks, Malcolm." I smiled, "I'm fine now. You can return to your room."

Something akin to hurt flashed through his eyes. "Sure you're all right?"

Suddenly I felt bad. In hopes of redeeming myself, I covered with another lie. "Sorry, but I need to use the bathroom."

Malcolm muttered something I couldn't make out and walked out of the room.

I closed and locked the door. "You can come out now, Gabriel."

Gabriel fully manifested. Black soot covered Gabe's feathers and his skin was red and peeling. The stench of fire and brimstone hovered around him.

Tears brimmed in my eyes. "Oh, Gabe! I'm so sorry he did this to you."

Wings shedding charred feathers onto the carpet, he walked across the room and sank down on the bed. "I'll be fine. I was more worried about you."

I embraced him gingerly. "I thought I might never see you again. I don't know what I'd do if something ever happens to you."

"Oh ye of little faith! I'm indestructible; at least I think I am?" He chuckled, but suddenly winced in obvious pain. I tried to smile, but tears begin to roll down my cheeks.

Gabriel hugged me tighter. "Oh Eve, what am I to do with you?"

"Trade me in for someone less high maintenance."

He smiled "Never."

After Gabriel confirmed Lucifer wasn't around for the time being, I showered and dressed. Hoping Malcolm wouldn't be put out with me, I went to his room. I knocked on the door. No answer; I knocked again with the same results. I pressed my ear against the door, but didn't hear anything.

Someone tapped my shoulder. I whirled around and much to my relief found Malcolm grinning at me. "Still a bit jumpy, eh? Thought I'd go down and check if breakfast was still being served. Are you hungry?"

"I could eat a horse."

Taking my arm he escorted me to the lift.

~~ *Chapter Ten* ~~

In the beautiful dining room, Malcolm pulled a chair from under a table for me. Thanking him, I sat down. After we had finished French pressed coffee, warm croissants and fruit topped with crème fresh, Malcolm glanced at his watch. "The car is scheduled to arrive any moment."

Although I'd lived in a France in a previous life, I was excited to see the sights again. Without warning, Lucifer's acclaimed hold on Malcolm swept through my mind. Staring into Malcolm's heavenly-blue eyes I managed to keep my fears at bay.

When the car arrived, it whisked us to Giverny between Paris and Rouen situated in the Normandy countryside. The gardens of Giverny had inspired many of Claude Monet's paintings. In superb condition at the end of July, the flowerbeds were spectacular. Neatly trimmed Japanese gardens with their quaint bridges over serenely flowing water, made me feel as if I was in Japan.

The sun broke through an overcast sky, giving the crisp morning air a golden hue. Malcolm and I walked around arm in arm. In the near distance, beneath a willow tree, a stone statue depicted two lovers embracing. We walked towards the couple from the Tudor era. The exquisitely detailed statue made me gasp. It reminded me when I was a lady in waiting to Queen Elizabeth and witnessed her coronation.

Malcolm noticed my fascination. "It's really something isn't it?"

I whispered, "It's beautiful."

"I forgot my camera. It's back in the car," Malcolm told me. "Do you mind if I run back and get it? I'd ask my chauffeur to bring it round but I need to visit the bathroom anyway."

"Don't mind at all. I could stand here admiring this statue all day."

Saying he would be back soon, he kissed my cheek, and walked back down the path.

Memories flooding my mind, I inspected the statue closer.

My name in 1564 England was Joanna Grey; my Father was Earl of Kent, Henry Grey. Shortly after I turned eighteen, I was one of three pretty girls chosen to attend to Queen Elizabeth I. On the lookout for Adam, I'd hoped working in Windsor Castle would present an ideal opportunity to be able to find him.

The Queen though was a highly strung individual, who had me run off my feet tending to her many, some would say eccentric, needs. She always demanded complete perfection and god forbid if her hair was not as she desired, or all hell would break loose. This naturally put me at a disadvantage with seeking my Adam out. But although she was notoriously bad tempered, I still could see a deep pain showing in her chocolate brown eyes. At times, myself and the other girls would hear her weep in her chamber when she thought no one else could hear her. Something seriously troubled her which she was unwilling to share with anyone.

As one of the Queen's handmaidens, I attended lavish

banquets and other affairs that allowed me to socialize with royal guests or other members of the household.

I hoped that these opportunities would aid me in my quest for Adam. The hall where the banquets were often held, was lit up with many candle chandeliers and the long, wooden rectangular tables were bursting at the seams with carcasses of meat, bread and wine. Street musicians were often employed to play at such occasions, with the lute and virginal being some of the Queen's favourite instruments. I wore gorgeous gowns specially made for ladies in waiting of the queen, embroidered in such delicate detail and covered in small glistening, fresh water pearls. With my sun kissed blonde hair and light blue eyes, I caught the eye of Thomas Howard, 4th Duke of Norfolk and a cousin of the Queen. He wasn't my Adam, so I paid him no attention, which vexed the Duke greatly.

Shortly thereafter, while I brushed Queen Elizabeth's red hair, she issued a royal edict. His Grace had declared his desire for my hand. Unless I presented her with a suitable husband within six months, the Queen would announce my betrothal to the Duke of Norfolk.

Desperation then to find Adam filled my every waking moment. Months ticked away. At every royal occasion, Lord Howard's rakish eyes and smirk filled me with rising dread. He made my flesh crawl, as to me he resembled an ugly toad. He was short and plump in his early forties. His long light brown, balding hair, looked as if it hadn't been washed in years, along with pretty much the rest of him. But I think that it was his slimy grin, which made me sick the most, along with his flat but slightly hooked at the end nose.

Most days I would just walk the castle grounds, asking for any kind of sign of my beloved's presence, praying that I would be saved from this dreadful marriage. Gabriel, always a comfort, said he would spirit me away if need be so I didn't have to marry him. Though, the idea of abandoning my homeland and family who lived near the castle was unthinkable. I also loved it here, not to mention I helped my poor mother by often sending her and my two younger sisters money. My late father, had been a well to do Earl, but after he had died my mother had painfully discovered he had many debts. I really wanted my sisters to have a good life and hoped that if they were well provided for, that I would be able in the future to get them work in the castle too.

Restless, unable to settle my mind I took an evening stroll. Near a lake, I noticed something floating in the water. I walked closer up to the lake. Focused on the object floating in the murky pool, I tripped over a rock and fell headlong into the cold murky water. Caught up in reeds and algae, the more I struggled the more entangled I became.

I awoke in my bed surrounded by a doctor and other ladies in waiting, who were alternately chattering and tut-tutting. I tried to talk but found my voice too weak.

The doctor checking my pulse cautioned, "Don't exert yourself, child; you nearly drowned."

I suddenly remembered being unable to breathe and sinking into the water as the reeds pulled me down under. I whispered to him, "The reeds pulled me down, so how is it that I'm alive?"

"Someone coming to seek an audience with the Queen saw you fall into the lake and rescued you. Rest now child and no more talking." The doctor assigned Mary, who entered the Queen's service when I did, to care for my needs. He then shooed the other ladies from out of the room.

I closed my eyes, but rest evaded me. I desired to thank my saviour. Upon hearing the door close, I opened my eyes and asked Mary if she would find out the identity of my hero.

I assured Mary I'd be fine in her absence and she agreed.

After Mary left Gabriel appeared. He knelt by my bed. "I was all prepared to save you when I saw someone come to your aid."

"Do you know who it was?"

He shook his head. "Only that he wore armour. To my mind, it seemed to take him forever to remove it and dive into the lake."

"Oh, he was a Knight then?"

"I believe so." Gabriel lightly caressed my cheek with the back of his hand. "Now rest."

I lay there wondering if my rescuer might be the one I sought. With hope in my heart, I smiled and drifted asleep. A handsome Knight filled my dreams.

The next morning, Mary, face flushed, rushed into my room. "It was Sir Fredrick de Burns who saved you."

The name seemed familiar and then I remembered Sir Fredrick was one of the kingdoms most stalwart Knights. I had never personally met Sir Fredrick before, but surely, he was too old to be my Adam. I suddenly felt ashamed. Did age really matter if Sir Fredrick was my original soul mate?

After a few days recovering, I went in search of Sir Fredrick. I asked several people and one of them directed me to his house. Quite nervous, I gently rapped on the door. When it opened, I found myself face to face with my Adam. But it wasn't Sir Fredrick, but his squire.

Shoulder length ginger hair framed his handsome face, the squire bowed. "My Lady, may I help you?"

Balanced on rising excitement, it felt as though I would sprout wings of happiness and fly. "I believe you already have."

He looked confused, but then a flicker of partial recognition flashed through his own brown eyes. It was a mesmerizing moment until Sir Fredrick broke it.

Sir Fredrick jerked the squire away from the doorway. "Boy! No time for talking, you have my armour to polish. "

I peeked around Sir Fredrick and saw the boy, who I knew to be my Adam smile at me.

The Knight asked, "Can I be of assistance, my Lady?"

I tried to get another glimpse of my true love and could not. Disappointed, I met the Knight's piercing gaze. "Sir, I'm told you rescued me from drowning and I wanted to thank you."

"No need, my Lady. I serve and protect the kingdom."

Though quite fearful, I spoke a lie. "As a reward, the Queen said I should invite you and your squire to dinner tonight."

He bowed deeply. "If the Queen so desires, we shall be honoured to attend my lady."

I stated an appointed time and ran back quickly to the castle. Wrapped in panic, I burst into the Queen's chamber and dipped a quick curtsy.

"Goodness, girl, what is it," she demanded. "Is there a fire?"

"No, your Majesty... please forgive me," I stammered, "but if you please, may I ask a great favour of you?"

"Speak up, girl, and I may consider your request."

Trembling like a leaf, I said, "I wondered if the knight who saved me from drowning and his squire could be invited to sup with us tonight?"

The Queen stared at me. After what felt like ages, she spoke.

"It's only courteous that we should express our pleasure, so I will agree. However, in the future, remember your position and do not submit requests directly to me. Take them to someone above you and they shall put forth the matter before me. Now fetch me some water and be quick!"

I dipped a low curtsy and bowed my head. "Yes of course, your Majesty. Thank you." I rose and hurried out of the room. Once out of Queen's presence, I sighed in great relief as I pressed both hands to my bosom, feeling my heart beating like crazy.

I flinched when Gabriel appeared beside me.

"That was tense," he told me.

Hurrying to fetch water for the Queen, I said, "I don't know what I would have done if she had refused."

"Now that you know who Adam is, hopefully he will fall in love with you immediately and you won't have to marry creepy Howard."

I smiled, "I do hope so, Gabriel."

I fetched the water and careful not to spill it, I rushed down the stone corridor leading to the Queen's chamber. As I rounded a corner, someone reached out from the shadows and smacked my hand, causing water in the cup to spill to the floor.

Lord Howard suddenly stepped from out of the darkness. "I'm growing tired of waiting to have you as my wife. I shall ask Queen Elizabeth to declare our union immediately"

"But that is unfair, my Grace, as I still have two months time remaining."

He moved even closer to me that his foul breath in my face made me nauseated. "What you think is of no concern to me woman! It's what I want that only matters, and soon you'll be lying on your back in my bed." He glared at me threateningly before striding away.

I ran and fetched another cup and filled it with water. I tried not to spill it, but trembling from the encounter with Lord Howard, several drops splashed on the floor. By the time I entered the Queen's quarters, tears blurred my vision.

Queen Elizabeth, noting my obvious distress, demanded,

"Girl, whatever is wrong?"

I sobbed, "I ran into your cousin the Duke of Norfolk, your Highness. He told me that he is going to request my six month search to find a husband be ended now."

"Do not worry yourself, child, for I have no intention of doing such a thing. Still, you do not have much time, so I suggest you find someone suitable fast." She wore a slight smile, which I hoped meant she wasn't too fond of her cousin either.

"Yes, thank you your Majesty, you're too kind."

She waved me away. I curtsied and rushed to the kitchen, declaring that two additionally guests would be attending tonight's supper.

In my bath scented with rose petals, I scrubbed myself with perfumed soap from France until my skin seemed to glow. Mary plaited my long hair and fashioned it into a bun. I donned my most stunning gown and fastened a gold chain with an engraved cross around my neck. My stomach fluttered like a butterfly picturing the squire's handsome face in my mind.

When Sir Fredrick and his squire arrived, they both greeted the Queen. I felt weak in the knees as they approached me. I smiled sweetly when Sir Fredrick introduced me to his young squire. My soul mate's name in this lifetime was Jacob Hurst.

Squire Hurst bowed low. I bobbed a curtsy. Queen Elizabeth cleared her throat loudly. I looked at her. Tone harsh, she whispered, "Joanna, remember your position. Your social standing is above the squire, just nod."

Face heating, I nodded. I suddenly begin to worry that the Queen would not view Squire Hurst as a worthy match for me.

While dining, I often sensed the squire staring at me,

but whenever I glanced at him, he quickly looked away. I noticed Gabriel perched on a beam at the end of the room was happily devouring a roasted piglet. From the corner of my eye, I saw the squire focused on me once again. I met his gaze and he smiled. Things were going well until the Queen's cousin the Duke entered the hall.

He swept a deep bow before Queen Elizabeth. "Your Majesty." After the queen acknowledged him, he chose to sit beside me. My appetite soured immediately and I pushed my plate away.

I could see a strange look on Jacob's face, as he watched me try to shift my chair slightly away from the Duke. But my attempts were foiled as I felt his hand from beneath the table grab the leg and abruptly pull it back even closer up to him.

Voice too loud, he demanded a goblet of wine and a servant swiftly poured him one. Staring at Sir Fredrick straight on, he quipped. "So then, this is the Knight I owe my gratitude for saving by betrothed, Lady Joanna."

Eyes filled with utter contempt, I glared at Lord Howard.

The Queen, sounding annoyed, injected, "Lord Howard, Lady Joanna has two months remaining before I agree to her becoming your wife. I have no intention of confirming the betrothal any sooner."

The Duke chuckled. "I am aware of that, your Majesty, but each hour that passes brings me a day closer when she will be my wife."

Bile boiled up in my throat and beginning to retch, I asked the Queen for permission to leave. The Queen noting my obvious distress, granted permission and I sped from the room. I barely made it outside before rejecting the contents of my stomach. Hearing footsteps approaching and worried it might be the Duke, I gathered up my skirt and rushed down a small dirt path that led to a wooded area near the castle.

Just as I ran into the dense forest, someone reached from behind me and grabbed my arm.

I turned and found myself face to face with Squire Hurst. "Are you okay, my Lady?"

Relief flooded me, and beginning to sob, I instinctively threw my arms around his neck. He wrapped me in his strong arms and held me. After I regained myself, I raised my head and looked into his rich walnut coloured eyes. He abruptly covered my lips with his. I surrendered to desire threading me and returned his kiss in full. He scooped me up and carried me deeper into the forest and laid me on the mossy ground. I welcomed his weight as it descended on me. His mouth covered mine passionately and his hand slid under my dress. In the throes of passion, I undid his breeches and exposing his manhood, caressed it until it throbbed. He moaned and entered me. I met each thrust with wild abandon.

Afterwards, as I lay in his arms, he kissed me gently. "You are the most beautiful woman I've ever seen."

Heart full of hope our union would induce full remembrance in him I smiled. "Thank you, kind Sir. You are the most handsome man I have ever laid eyes on."

He caressed my cheek. "I'll make sure that smirking weasel, Lord Howard never touches you."

We agreed to meet again and quickly dressed. When he gave me a parting kiss, I clung to him wishing it would never end, but knowing it must. I managed to scurry to my room without anyone noticing my state of disarray. Relieved, I sat on my bed.

Gabriel popped up wearing a grin. "Things are going well. Now we have to wait for him to remember. I do believe the Duke will be thwarted."

"I'm not sure, Gabriel. The Queen may not approve of the squire."

"I think she will. Besides, I have important news."

"Pray tell."

"Today's encounter has left you with child."

Shocked, I stared at him. "How... do you know... are you certain?"

"Eve, I am an angel. The moment you conceived, I sensed the birth of a new soul."

I bounded to my feet. "What am I to do? If the Queen learns of my secret, she shall throw me in the dungeon.

"Queen Elizabeth is much more compassionate than you think. Confide in her and I'm certain all will be fine."

Sometimes Gabriel's advice was sound and other times it led to disastrous results. I shook my head. "I shan't speak to the Queen yet. Squire Jacob should know first, but I need to wait a while. After all, I can't tell Jacob an angel informed me we're to be parents!"

Gabriel shrugged and disappeared.

Jacob and I met in secret many times, each filled with passionate lovemaking. Once, when Sir Fredrick returned home earlier than expected, he almost caught us in the act. With Jacob laughing, I scrambled out the window just in time, falling right into a pen filled with squealing pigs.

Thinking if caught by the Queen, it was going to be tricky to explain I hurried to the castle and snuck inside. Luckily, Mary was the only one who saw me. My friend and confidant helped me to bathe. Two months pregnant, I knew it wouldn't be long before my condition became obvious. With barely a month to present a future husband to the Queen, I decided to tell Jacob when next we met.

He waited for me in the usual spot, underneath a willow tree. His face beamed as I rushed into his arms. He embraced me, trailing breathy kisses down my neck. I pulled away, "Jacob, I must tell you..."

Before I could finish, royal guards surrounded us. Lord Howard, clutching Mary's arm walked out from among them. Mary, clearly terrified with tears streaming down her face stammered how sorry she was. The evil Duke had threatened to slaughter Mary's family if she didn't tell him all.

Panic rising in my throat I looked terrified to Jacob. He stepped in front of me and looking fiercely at him. "How is it a crime for me to love her?"

Jacob suddenly glanced back at me. Shock filled his eyes as full remembrance hit him. Reeling under the weight of memories, he staggered. He whispered, "Eve," and passed out, hitting the ground with a thud.

The Duke ordered a guard to arrest me. I struggled and shouted asking if the Queen was aware of this, as two of them grabbed me forcefully by the arms. But the toad of a man just wickedly grinned, Jacob was then picked up off the floor and dragged behind me as they pulled me, still kicking towards the castle

It puzzled me when the guard took us to the Tower used to contain only certain people of nobility. The guard shoved me in a cell. Certain I would be transferred to dungeons in the bowels of the castle at any moment; I waited until the guards left before whispering, "Gabriel, are you here?"

Gabriel materialised.

"Gabriel, check on where and how Jacob is please." Nibbling on my lip, I watched Gabriel vanish.

Soon he reappeared. "Where is he? Is he okay?"

Gabe nodded. "Yes for the moment he is being held in the next room to yours."

Heaving a sigh of relief, I sank down on a bed of mouldy straw in a corner. One part of me was happy Jacob had remembered our life as Adam and Eve, but the other half worried about what lay ahead for us.

The prison cell door opened and Royal Guards escorted the Queen inside. Skirts swaying vigorously, she walked over to me. "Joanna, I can't believe you have been so stupid. Surely, you knew I would never agree to such foolish union. Mary revealed everything, even the fact that you are with child. I'm afraid my hands are tied. I have no option but to punish both you and Squire Jacob severely. Your trial begins tomorrow."

I bowed my head, and muttered, "But I love him, your Majesty."

"That may be, but it changes nothing." She then stepped closer to me and offered her hand. Surprised, I clasped it and placed a kiss on the back. When I did so, something slipped into my palm. I curtsied and the Queen smiled slightly, nodded, and left.

After the door clanged shut, I opened my hand and found a tightly folded piece of paper. I undid it and read the note.

Joanna,

I have enjoyed your service to me, and I know without a doubt that you are a good person. I understand the pain of loving someone you should not. Because of this, I intend to help both of you escape. Two guards loyal to only me will be on duty tonight. They shall provide you with clothes, a small purse of money and some bread. A guard will guide you to a waiting cart and horse. The cart will be full of bags of flour. Hide Jacob within them. To make it appear you escaped with outside help, after you change clothes, you must hit the guards on the head with a branding iron. Do not hesitate to do so. I've assured them that they shall be well compensated. Tell the guards at the main gates to the castle that you are going to sell flour in the town. They expect a shipment of flour to leave the castle today. Destroy this letter immediately and God bless you both.

Done reading, I quickly ripped up the note, stuffed the pieces into my mouth and ate them.

The change of guards happened just as the queen predicted. A guard unlocked our cell doors and with the other ones help lug Jacob to the cart. We hid Jacob between the bags and covered all with a burlap tarp. I changed clothes and tucked the money purse into a pocket. The guards led me back inside the prison; one of them fetched an iron and then hit the second guard with it knocking him out cold. The guard with the iron then instructed me to hit him too. I lost my nerve as I gripped it. He urged me to do it and quickly. I raised it above my head but I just couldn't strike him. Gabriel cloaked in invisibility, snatched the iron away and banged it soundly against the guard's head. The guard slumped onto the floor next to the other one.

Gabriel grabbed my hand and we raced to the tied up cart. I undid the rope the horse was tethered too and slid on the driver bench, whipping the reins the horse surged forward. Near the main gate, my heart pounding, I turned panicky eyes to Gabriel.

Gabe patted my arm. "All will be fine." He grinned. "If not, I have a spare branding iron back of your seat."

I reined up the horse at the gate.

One of the guards approached the cart. "State your business?"

"I'm to sell flour in the town."

"We expected the old man who usually does it. Where is he?"

I forced fear from my voice. "My father is sick so the task fell to me."

He stared at me for a moment that seemed endless, then strode to the back of the cart and lifted the cover. A deep lump formed in my throat, making it hard to swallow. Gabriel reached for the branding iron. Relief swept over me when the guard replaced the cover. He waved to his companions and shouted to open the gate.

I flicked the reins; the horse strained, and the cart rolled through the gateway. A good distance away from the castle, I heaved a sigh and looked at Gabriel. The sight of Gabe still clutching the iron made me laugh.

I pushed ahead for as long as possible before stopping to check on Adam.

My original soul mate lay locked in the coma that always befell him upon remembering.

Gabriel studied him then looked at me. "You're exhausted. Let me fly you far away from danger. If you sit between my wings and I can carry Adam."

"I've never ridden on your back. Sure I won't fall off?"

He smiled, "Not if you hold onto my neck."

I glanced back toward the castle. "At first light, the Duke of Norfolk and the royal guards will be scouring the countryside."

Gabriel bent down "Then climb on my back and let's get out of this cursed place."

Without a better choice, I climbed aboard Gabe and locked my arms tightly around his neck. He picked up Adam, flapped his wings and streaked like a bullet through the sky. When Gabriel negotiated a wobbly turn, I panicked thinking what would happen to my unborn child if I fell. I closed my eyes and tightened my grip. After a bumpy flight through storm clouds, we landed in the moors of Scotland near an abandoned rock hut.

For days, I dripped water into Adam mouth, praying he'd awake from the coma. One morning while lying next to him still half-asleep, I felt his arm go around my waist. I opened my eyes and found the other half of my soul smiling at me. Overjoyed, I hugged then kissed him repeatedly. He asked what happened and where we were, so I filled him in. He too laughed about Gabriel and the branding iron. Gabriel, hearing the laughter, poked his head into the hut. Adam stood and thanked him for aiding our escape. Gabe renewed his promise to be available if we needed him. He kissed my cheek then wished us both a long lifetime. My eyes brimmed with tears when watching Gabe soar into the clouds. The years blessed Adam and me with many children and grandchildren and much happiness.

The sudden sound of approaching footsteps snapped my mind from out of the past.

I turned and saw Malcolm striding towards me. Trembling with leftover emotion, I wanted, needed someone to hold me. Malcolm must have seen that in my eyes, because at the first available moment, he reached out, pulled me into his arms, and kissed me passionately. I wanted nothing more than to unleash the desire I felt, but I held back.

He grinned down at me. "Maybe we should go somewhere a bit more private?"

"I'm sorry, I can't"

He released me, looking hurt, "So, it is still like that then?"

"Malcolm, you don't understand."

His eyes hardened. "I understand perfectly. You're not the first woman to play me."

"It's... well...it isn't." I averted my eyes and blushing, mumbled, "the right time of the month, if you know what I mean?"

He chuckled. "Oh I see; the woman's curse and all that. Blast that bloody Eve for damning us all to hell."

I didn't laugh, instead tears formed in my eyes.

His brow furrowed. "You look mortified. Did I say something wrong?"

Unable to respond, I ran toward the main entrance. Burdened by guilt over my original sin in the Garden of Eden, I had trouble catching a full breath. Winded, I walked to a bench near a waterfall flowing into a pond edged in purple lavender. I sagged down on the wooden bench dedicated to a Josephine Montello and sobbed. Unknowingly, Malcolm gave voice to the horrible truth sealed inside my heart. As Eve, I had indeed dammed the whole of mankind.

Malcolm jogged up and sat next to me. "Jasmine, I can be an insensitive arsehole, but I truly don't know what I said that hurt you so."

Sniffling, I grabbed a tissue from my handbag and wiped my eyes. "I'm sorry, Malcolm, it's not your fault. I had a close friend called Eve." I paused. "Who recently died."

I felt so bad for lying, especially after he had just lost his brother James.

"Oh no, I'm extremely sorry, Jasmine. I wished I'd known." He took me in his arms and held me tightly.

I muttered, "That's okay," and laid my head on his shoulder. We sat there, listening to the peaceful sound of running water.

After awhile, Malcolm asked, "Hungry? I know this quaint little bistro not far from here. It has a friendly atmosphere and does a pretty decent lunch."

I gazed into his amazing blue eyes and smiled. "Yeah, that sounds really nice."

He stood and offered his hand. I placed my hand in his and he pulled me up from the bench. He retrieved his cell phone from inside of his jacket and told the chauffeur to pick us up at the gate.

~~ *Chapter Eleven* ~~

The bistro was picturesque, with wicker baskets of colourful flowers hanging from wooden hooks on the facade. Le Bistrot Monique lay scrawled in bold orange letters on a weathered sign over the entrance. The decor inside was shabby chic. Muted yellow paint covered the walls. Red and white chequered tablecloths adorned a dozen small, round tables. A black vase filled with red and yellow tulips sat atop each table. The aroma of baking bread and freshly brewed coffee made my taste buds water.

Malcolm led me to a table and pulled out my chair. A petite waitress with a thick French accent took our order. We were soon enjoying more freshly brewed coffee. The wait staff and other customers seemed so friendly I managed to relax.

After we finished savoury meats and cheeses on crusty baguettes and rich coffee, Malcolm asked if I would like to tour the Louvre.

"Could we? I've always dreamed of visiting there."

At the Palais du Louvre, which began as a fortress in the late 12th Century, Malcolm helped me from the car. A sparkling, twenty one metre high glass pyramid designed by a Chinese American architect covered the main entrance.

The sheer size of the place amazed me. It would take months, perhaps years to view every piece of art. My eyes couldn't get enough. Clutching Malcolm's hand, I pulled him from one piece of artwork to another. He laughed at my eagerness. In Salle de la Joconde, known as the Mona Lisa room, we stood admiring Leonardo De Vinci's greatest masterpiece.

Malcolm looking at the painting said, "This wall is missing something?"

Puzzled, I looked at him. "What would that be?"

Hugging me, he said, "A portrait of you?"

I laughed. "One of us together would be nicer."

"Okay," he said, leading me fast towards the entrance.

Half a block from the Louve sat an old French guy sitting with an easel, paint and brushes.

Noticing us walking his way, the man nodded. "Bonjour, Monsieur Dice."

"Bonjour, Max."

"What may I do for you today, monsieur?"

"Max, will you paint a picture of us both, please?"

"I would be honoured." He picked up two folding chair from the sidewalk and set them up beside each other. He gestured to one. "Please, mademoiselle, sit here."

I did as he requested.

"Très bien, mademoiselle, perfect," Max told me. "Now, Monsieur Dice, sit here next to the mademoiselle."

Malcolm placed his arm around me. I sat there smiling while Max began applying paint to a canvas.

I tried not to move; something I'd grown accustomed to in the past when having my portrait painted.

Max paused painting to study me. "You possess great beauty, mademoiselle." When done, he turned the easel towards us.

I gasped. The likeness was uncanny. Much too large for

my memory box, but I could take a photo of the painting, and put with others detailing my many lives. I smiled at Max. "It's amazing."

"Merci, mademoiselle"

Malcolm handed the artist some money. "Max, you have outdone yourself,"

"Merci, Monsieur Dice, my pleasure." Max offered me the painting but Malcolm chose to carry the wet painting to the limo.

On the trip back to the hotel, Malcolm indicated a formal dinner lay ahead. I immediately begin fretting because I hadn't packed anything suitable for such an occasion. In fact, not one formal dress hung in my closet at home. Malcolm instructed the chauffeur to re-route to 30 Avenue Montaigne. I looked at him intrigued. When the limo stopped, the chauffeur jumped out and opened the car door. We were in front of The House of Dior! Malcolm laughed at the surprise on my face when helping me exit the car.

Holding his arm, I stared like a kid going to Disney world for the very first time. The world famous store was immaculate. The aroma of expensive perfume filled the air and extravagant paintings covered the lofty ceilings. A smartly dressed salesman recognised Malcolm. Malcolm said something to the man. The man guided us to a gilded antique settee and then said he'd be back in a moment. I watched the man chat with several other salespersons. A young lady in an understated, but chic dress instructed me to follow her. Trailing after her, I glanced back at Malcolm. He grinned.

The women seated me in a grand salon and served me a glass of champagne. "Monsieur Dice said you should to choose whatever you want." She clapped her hands and beautiful models, each wearing a breathtaking dress, paraded before me.

Such a large selection of designer dresses left me dizzy with uncertainty. Another line of models entered the showroom. One dress caught my eye, a silky, lilac coloured, backless evening gown.

I nodded to the dress and the saleswoman escorted me to a fitting room.

I tried on the gown and judged myself in the mirror. Staring at my reflection transported me back through time.

In all of our many lives across the centuries, only once had Adam been the first to remember our past

In 1945, my name was Carla Spencer, a pretty and popular junior in a Birmingham, Alabama high school. Josh Redmond, a senior fancied me and my friends often teased me about him. Josh was clumsy and geeky, which fuelled others taunting him. I didn't fancy Josh at all, but I felt bad about my friends and how others treated him.

One rainy day, my car wouldn't start after school and Josh offered me a lift home. Buckets of cold rain were falling on my head, so I got inside his car.

Josh passed me a blanket from the backseat.

Teeth chattering, I mumbled. "Thanks," and wrapped it around myself. Awkward silence filled the car on the journey to my place.

When the car cruised to a stop in front of my house, Josh broke the tension. "Would you like to go to a movie with me at the weekend, Carla?"

"Err... I'm sorry, Josh, I have a lot of homework to do."

"Oh, that's okay."

I passed him the blanket and got out of the car. Starting to open the front door of my house, I remembered that I forgot to thank Josh for the lift. I turned and waved to him. With a disappointed look on his face, he gave me a quick wave and watched me go inside.

After that day, whenever we bumped into each other, I always smiled at him. One day while walking to the parking lot, I heard a commotion coming from the back of the school. Others began running in that direction and I followed.

Two jocks were beating Josh up. In the past I had dated one of them, who was now pummelling him. Shoving my way through the crowd who were cheering the jocks on, I screamed at them to stop.

The guy I dated, Chris, his face distorted by anger, glared at me, "Have you gone soft on him, Carla?"

I screamed at him, "Leave him alone. He hasn't done anything to you! This isn't a fair fight and you know it."

Chris spat, "Well, stay away from him, Carla and I might be fairer." Chris punched Josh in the mouth before letting him drop bloodied down to the ground.

"You make me sick, Chris! You're nothing but a dumb bully, and I will be friends with whoever I like." I rushed to Josh and tried to help him up.

Chris laughed. "Don't know what I ever saw in you anyway, Carla. You're a slut and he's welcome to you." Storming off, he pushed a kid out of the way who was in his path.

Staring into my blue eyes, Josh muttered, "Thanks, Carla." In the same moment, he suddenly seemed shocked, mouthed something I could not understand, before having a seizure. At the hospital, the doctors had no idea what was wrong with him.

I visited Josh on a daily basis; his poor mother often weeping on my shoulder. Four days later, Josh regained consciousness. There was a marked difference in his personality. He seemed more confident and his mood more upbeat almost happy. I laid Josh's upbeat mood on news the police had arrested Chris and charged him with grievous bodily harm.

Strangely, when Josh returned to school, I got the distinct impression he tried to distance himself from me. Whenever, our paths did cross, I would smile and say hi, but he only nodded. In June of the year, Josh graduated.

A few months later, I saw him heading to True Value Hardware on Main Street.

I crossed the street and caught up with him. "Hi, Josh."

"Carla, hi, how are you?"

"I'm good. You?"

He smiled, "I've started college and have high hopes for the future."

I smiled back at him. "That's great. We should catch up."

"I guess. It's your birthday soon isn't it?"

"Yeah my birthday is next month; want to come to my party?"

He shrugged. "I am not too keen on parties."

I reissued the invitation. "Sure you don't want to come?" He opened the door to the hardware store, said, "See you later," and walked out of the store.

Confused by his behaviour, I stood there staring at the door.

The night before my birthday, I lay in bed watching hands on the clock creep forward. I'd officially be eighteen at 2 a.m. As the clock ticked two o'clock, I gasped as memories transported themselves into my head. The world swirled into darkness.

Three days later, I awoke in the hospital. Momma sat in a chair by my bed holding my hand. Tears running down her cheeks, she cried out and hugged me. Daddy rushed into my room, followed by Josh. It all fell into place. Josh had known he was my soul mate after Chris assaulted him and he'd realised he truly loved me. He had patiently waited on the sidelines for me to turn eighteen.

I could hardly contain my happiness as we looked lovingly at each other, tears in both our eyes. After the doctor assured momma and daddy about the state of my health, they decided to have coffee in the hospital cafeteria.

The moment they left, Josh closed the door and took me in his arms. My heart turned to butter when his mouth covered mine. We laughed, kissed, then laughed some more. Adam told me how hard it was to keep his distance.

Gabriel popped up, his face beaming. "It wasn't challenging this time for you two to find each other. I wished all of your lifetimes were like this one."

Adam chuckled and gave Gabe a hug. "You and me both."

"Hey, guys," I told them. "Some love over here wouldn't go amiss."

They grinned and walked to my bedside. I tried to hug both of them at the same time, but Gabriel's height and large size made that impossible. My attempt left all of us laughing.

After the doctor released me from the hospital, Adam spent all his free time with me. Prom night arrived before I knew it. Even though it would shock my friends, having Josh to them, but Adam to me as my escort, it filled me with unspeakable happiness.

Chris, out on bail, vented his anger when I turned down his offer to be my date. He demanded to know why I'd let a nerd of epic proportions like Josh, take me to the dance. I informed Chris that Josh was more of a man than he would ever be. Chris stormed away, but not before he gave me a rage filled look.

On Prom night, my date arrived at my house, I proudly walked down the stairs, my long hair fashioned into black ringlets and pulled to the side.

"You look amazing," Adam grinned and pinned a purple, orchid corsage on to my dress. The flower matched my lilac coloured dress so perfectly. We kissed and laughing we walked to the car. Gabriel, who insisted on tagging along with us to the dance, chose to sit in the back. He said that he'd soon leave us to enjoy life together.

I turned and smiled at him from the front passenger seat. "You've never stayed with me this long before. Gabriel. I'll miss you."

"I shall miss the both of you. It's my pleasure to support you until the original soul mates reconnect."

Eyes damp with tears, I told him. "Even though at times I act like a right bitch, I'm truly grateful for your presence."

Gabriel laughed and rubbed his head. "Yeah, you can be difficult like when you conked me with that frog statue."

The three of us laughed, filling the car with promises of a happy future.

Still grinning, Adam glanced at me, his hazel eyes full of love. I smiled back. He turned his focus back to the road. His eyes widened. Another car suddenly slammed forcefully into ours. The force hurled Adam through the windshield. Drifting in and out of consciousness, I realised mangled trapped steel ensnared the lower half of my body.

Blood seeping from my forehead, I whispered, "Gabriel?"

Unable to focus my eyes, I heard Gabe say, "I'm here Eve."

Fighting unconsciousness, I asked, "Is Adam—"

"I am sorry, Eve, he is dead."

Tears mixed with blood blurring what little vision I had. "It's not fair, Gabriel. Is God mad we found each other so easily?"

"Don't be silly, Eve, this has nothing to do with God, but I do agree this is very unfair."

"The other driver...?"

"The other car also has a fatality, Chris, your ex-boyfriend. Evidently, he was waiting at the intersection and deliberately crashed his car into ours."

Encroaching darkness grew. I whispered "See you in the next life, Gabe."

His voice choked with emotion, he softly replied, "I'll be waiting."

The tragic memory swirled away from me.

Tears streaming down my face, I realised that I still stood in a fitting room at The House of Dior in Paris. I suddenly felt certain Lucifer had fuelled Chris' anger. Determined to defeat Lucifer in this lifetime, I swiped at my eyes with the back of my hand.

I walked out of the dressing room looking like an over-emotional freak.

My personal saleslady, who looked like she enjoyed a manicure and facial daily, held out a box of tissues. Obviously, a lot of girls became blubbering wrecks when trying on a Dior dress for the very first time. Sniffling, I decided although it had brought back painful memories, I would choose the lilac dress. The saleslady complimented me on making an excellent choice. While I changed back into my street clothes, she packed the dress in a lovely box.

Smiling and clutching the box, I walked toward Malcolm who was enjoying a nice frothy cappuccino, while listening to relaxing music. He sat aside and stood on seeing me. "I'm guessing something caught your fancy," he said pulling out his wallet.

"You really didn't have to do this."

Eyes sparkling, he grinned. "I know, but the happiness on your face at the moment is priceless."

~~ *Chapter Twelve* ~~

In my hotel room, I spread the dress on the bed, wondering if Malcolm would approve of my choice. I changed into the dress and went over to the closet. Where were my white pumps? I thought to myself, as I was sure I'd packed them. I dumped the rest of the contents of my suitcase onto the bed, no sign of them. My navy ones would have to do. I put them on but saw they just didn't go with my dress. Pissed, I pulled them off and threw the cursed, wrong coloured shoes across the room. They narrowly missed poor Gabriel who had suddenly appeared.

He picked the shoes up and laughed. "Whatever it was, I didn't do it."

"I am sorry, Gabriel. I just cannot believe I forgot to pack my white heels. The navy ones really don't suit my dress. I truly don't know now what to do!"

He grinned. "Unlike most girls, you have a guardian angel to save the day."

I suddenly realised what he meant and laughed. "Pun intended, will you be an angel and fly to my house and get them for me, please?"

With a big grin, he bowed and said, "My pleasure, my

lady." Gabe disappeared and within minutes, he was back.

"Sorry I took so long," he said passing the white heels to me. "Bonnie was in your room guarding them. Her teeth marks on my hand testify she really likes those shoes."

"Gabe, you're a life saver." I stood on the bed, gave my big guardian angel a hug, and kissed him on the cheek.

He nodded and winked before disappearing.

I checked the white high heels for chew marks. Bonnie was notorious for devouring shoes. They looked mark free so I slipped them on. I checked my outfit in a cheval mirror. The shoes looked perfect with my dress.

Someone knocked at my door. When I opened it, Malcolm eyes lit up. "Wow," he said giving me a quick kiss. 'You look more beautiful than usual."

I beamed at him. "Glad you approve."

"Are you ready?"

"Yeah, just need to grab a few things and I'm all set."

I collected my mobile, compact mirror and lipstick, and put them in my cream coloured clutch bag.

As we walked down the corridor, Malcolm couldn't take his eyes off me. Inside the lift, he reached inside his blue Armani suit and retrieved a card. "Jasmine, I'd like you to have this key card to my penthouse in London." He pressed the card into my hand. "You may come and go as you please. Even if I am out of town you're welcome to stay there if you like." He grinned.

"Thank you; I don't know what to say." I said before putting the key in my bag.

"You needn't say anything. You're always welcome," he replied kissing me passionately until the lift door slid open. An older couple waiting for the lift looked at us and shook their heads in disgust.

Waiting in the lobby for the chauffeur to bring the car

round, I turned to Malcolm. "Where are we going?"

He grinned. "Can't tell you, or I'd have to kill you."

Sitting next to Malcolm in the limo, I watched the cityscape of Paris streaming by, even more beautiful at night. When the car stopped near the Eiffel tower, I glanced over at Malcolm, who wore a grin.

He helped me from the car and gestured toward a walkway. "This way to the lift, my lady."

The private lift took us up to one of the world's most famous restaurants, Le Jules Verne, on the tower's second floor. A waiter welcomed us and escorted us to a table by a window. I was completely gob smacked at the breathtaking view of Paris at the night. I gasped when inspecting the menu. "Wow, it's certainly not cheap here is it?"

Malcolm winked at me. "Nothing, but only the best for you."

A waiter took our order and while we were waiting for it to be delivered, Malcolm asked me to excuse him and walked towards the Men's Room.

I gazed out the window by our table. A storm was rolling across the city and lightning splintered the sky, illuminating the beautiful skyline of Paris. The brilliant flash of light backlit the window and I saw a grotesque face reflected in the glass. "Lucifer!" I muttered.

Horrified, I jumped to my feet and stumbled away from the window, bumping into a waiter who glared at me. Hands sweaty, heart pounding, I scanned the restaurant for anyone who might be Lucifer in disguise.

I needed help and fast. "Gabriel, please," I whispered. "I need you." No response.

I noticed Malcolm walking toward me.

"Jasmine, are you okay," he asked. "You look like you've seen a ghost."

Feet superglued to the floor, I mumbled, "Err… I'm fine… lightning near the window startled me."

Malcolm looked slightly amused. "No need to worry, Jasmine, you're perfectly safe. The Eiffel Tower has grounded lightning rods that dissipate any charge." He gently escorted me back to our table and pulled out my chair.

A wine steward, after receiving Malcolm's approval of the chosen vintage, filled our glasses. Needing something to steady my nerves, I immediately drained my glass.

Malcolm, watching me, raised one eyebrow. "Sure you're okay?"

"Actually I need to use the restroom," I replied, making a beeline for the Ladies Room. Cloistered inside a cubicle, I leaned against the wall and took a deep breath. I jumped when someone knocked on the door. Relief flooded me to find Gabriel standing outside the cubicle door.

Worried Lucifer might be lurking somewhere, I checked every stall in the bathroom. Finding we were alone, I looked up at Gabe. "Lucifer is here! I saw his reflection in the window. Can you get rid of him please? This evening is an important step to make Malcolm remember our past and I don't need Lucifer ruining it."

Tone deadly serious, Gabe said, "It's not quite that easy when Lucifer is in his true form. So if you notice a mini-tornado whirling through the restaurant. I strongly suggest you and Malcolm get out of the restaurant on the double. I may have to whip up a storm to force Lucifer back down to hell."

Sarcasm dripping from my voice, I said, "Terrific… just terrific."

Gabe rubbed my shoulder. "Don't worry; I'll do my best to keep him from spoiling your evening. I think Malcolm is close to falling in love with you and I won't let Lucifer jeopardize that. I'm going to find the troublemaker and boot him back into the pit."

Gabe kissed my cheek and popped out of sight.

Feeling less anxious, I checked my hair and makeup in the mirror. On the way back to the table, the waiter I previously bumped into intercepted me. "Madam, I have a message for you from my lord and master, Lucifer. He would like to speak with you. He's waiting for you at the top of the tower."

I was about to tell him to go to hell until I noticed Malcolm was nowhere to be seen. I glared at one of Lucifer's many followers, and demanded, "Where's Malcolm?"

A grin spread across the Satanist's face. "Mister Dice is having a little chat with his highness."

Panic stricken, I pushed past him, raced out of the restaurant and down the corridor to the Tower's main elevator. Inside, I frantically pressed the up button repeatedly. By the time the lift made it to the top, my heart was pounding so hard, it felt as if my chest would explode. On the observation deck, I anxiously looked for signs of Gabriel. None.

Suddenly, an icy aura enveloped the deck. I shouted, "I'm here; show yourself, you coward!" Horrified by my sudden braveness, I clamped a hand over my mouth. Whatever possessed me to challenge Satan so openly?

He instantly appeared wearing a malicious grin. So did Gabriel, at the far end of the walkway with hatred for Lucifer written on his face.

Gabriel, his eyes locked on Lucifer, told me, "Its okay, Malcolm isn't with him, just another lie to suit his twisted purposes. Malcolm has stepped outside the dining room to take a phone call."

I held my breath as Gabriel began striding towards us. Lucifer started to walk towards Gabriel. In an instant, Lucifer turned and pushed me over the railing. I let out a piecing scream as I grabbed the bottom of a metal baluster. Lucifer peeked over the balcony and laughed at me, then disappeared.

Dangling from the metal spindle, I screamed, "Gabe!"

Gabriel reached over the railing and shouted, "Take my hand."

Despite being terrified, I let go with one hand and stretched it towards his. But I could feel his fingers slipping through mine. Panic stricken, I released my other hand from the rain-slicked baluster and tried to grab onto his wrist. But that slid down also, screaming I started to plunge fast towards the ground.

Gabriel leaped over the railing, swooped down and caught me up in his arms. A collective gasp rose up from people gathered on the sidewalk below. I saw the shock on their faces turn to bewilderment when Gabriel cloaked me in invisibility.

Sobbing hysterically, I clung to Gabriel as he flew to a grassy area near to the Tower. When Gabe lowered me to the ground, my legs wobbled. He led me over to a nearby bench.

Trembling, I sank down on the bench. "So Lucifer's plan is to kill me?"

Gabriel sat beside me and took my hand. "No, he knew I'd save you. He pushed you over the railing to distract me from kicking his arse."

Looking at the Eiffel Tower made me nauseous and faint. Feeling, blackness cloak my vision I sunk down on the bench. Gabriel yanked me back up.

"My nerves are so rattled I can't face going back inside there. In fact, I may never be able to step foot inside that awful place again, but I need to get a message to Malcolm."

"Don't worry, I will handle it," Gabe replied, unexpectedly morphing into a man of normal height, minus wings and dressed in a three piece suit. He grinned and said, "Wait here."

After what seemed like ages, I saw a Malcolm, concern written on his face, looking for me.

I shouted, "I'm over here, Malcolm."

He rushed to my side and sat on the bench. "Jasmine, some guy informed me you were unwell. What's the matter?"

"I felt dizzy and thought some fresh air might help, but it hasn't. I'm sorry, but it appears I've spoiled the lovely evening you planned."

Malcolm placed an arm around my shoulder. "Don't give it another thought. I'll call the car this minute. If you feel up to eating later, I'll have a meal sent up to your hotel room."

Inside the car, I looked out the window; the reflection staring back matched the sadness I felt in my heart. My run in with Lucifer had ruined a perfect opportunity for me to secure Malcolm's love.

At the hotel, Malcolm escorted me to my room and offered to stay until I felt better. Dejected, I refused his kind offer and bid him evening.

Gabriel appeared in the corner of my room. "I am sorry Lucifer put a damper on tonight. If only I'd found him before he lured you up to the observation deck."

Weary, I sighed. "Its okay, Gabriel, it wasn't your fault, but may I ask a small favour if you will?"

"Of course; what do you need?"

"I'm convinced Lucifer intends to destroy me, whether it is mentally or physically. I'd feel better if my guardian angel watched over me, just in case he decides to come back soon."

"No worries, I'll not leave your side until morning," Gabe told me, reclining across the foot of the king size bed.

I donned a nightgown, crawled under the covers and closed my eyes. Every time I started to fall asleep, plunging off the Eiffel Tower would flash through my mind and I'd cry out. Each time, Gabriel rubbed my shoulder and reassured me everything was all right. I finally managed to drift into restless sleep.

My dreams transported me back to Roman times when I was a slave named Aula.

My master, Tiberius Culleo, was a rich and well-respected Roman merchant of fine fabrics and wines. Like my mother and her mother, I accepted along with my sister Jana our birthright was one of slavery. People often described me as exotic looking because unlike my kinsmen, I had light brown hair and blue grey eyes. In hope of securing lucrative goods to sell, my master Tiberius brought most of his slaves, including me to Egypt. Severe punishment rained down on any slave who angered or disappointed Tiberius.

While in Egypt, I turned eighteen and fell into a death like coma. I woke up in a dark purification chamber. Clearly, assuming I'd died, I had been bathed and wrapped in a burial shroud in preparation for embalming. In Egypt, even slaves got some respect after death. Had I still been in Rome, I would have already been thrown into a mass dirt grave, without even so much as a cloth covering me. So it would seem, coming here to Egypt, may have actually saved my life.

Having awakened now with complete knowledge, and lying on a cold marble slab. Gratefulness flooded me after Gabriel helped me to remove my burial shroud. He then helped me to sit up and offered me some water, which I gulped down.

Sadness filled Gabriel's eyes. "You've suffered mightily in this life. Many a time I wanted to reveal myself, but unaware of your true nature, it would have only frightened you. Plus, as you know I am not normally permitted too."

"You're not to blame, Gabriel." Tears rolling down my face, I told him, "I'm the one who disobeyed God and ate that cursed apple. Your presence is my only enduring blessing."

Gabe waggled his head. "At the moment, I feel that I've failed you miserably."

"We can argue that point later; right now, I need to get out of this creepy death chamber."

With Gabe's help, I stood and finding my legs steady, I walked across the chamber door and banged on the locked door, no response.

"Here, let me," Gabe said pounding his big fist against the door.

I heard gasps and screams, echo from the other side.

I pressed my ear against the door and made out the chatter of women. After several minutes, a nervous eyed slave slowly opened the door. I nearly bowled the woman over in my haste to escape the burial chamber. Although in truth, I was exchanging one hell for another.

Desperate to save my little sister from Tiberius evil clutches, I quickly sought her whereabouts. It seemed I had got to Jana just in the nick of time, as Tiberius had her naked over his bed about to rape her. A fury burned in my blue eyes setting them ablaze. But Tiberius appeared overjoyed to discover his favourite slave was alive. Throwing my sister from the bed, he grabbed me and ripped off my burial robe. On seeing my sister cowering on the stone floor, and along with the knowledge that I now knew who I was, I screamed as I slapped him across the face. He hit me back, hard and I slumped to the ground. One of Tiberius' advisors quickly appeared on hearing the commotion. He gasped on seeing me alive.

Tiberius wickedly laughed, "Look who has returned from the dead. Hell must have decided she needed more punishment."

The whispers from his advisor convinced him otherwise. He decided I must have faked my death in an attempt to escape. Tiberius dragged me to the public square, threw me on the ground and beat me in front of his slaves and other spectators. Tiberius raised his whip again; it looked from the corner of my bloodied eye, like Gabriel was struggling hard with his conscience to not intervene. But for once, I had a second guardian angel. As Tiberius brought his whip down, a Roman centurion grabbed his arm.

"Enough, Tiberius," the solider barked. "What is her crime?"

"She faked her own death in an attempt to escape. She is lucky I don't tie her to my chariot and drag her through the streets. She's a lazy slave," he yelled, kicking me in the ribcage. I cried out in agony.

The centurion shoved Tiberius away from where I lay. "How much do you want for this worthless creature? My mother requires a new kitchen slave?"

Tiberius laughed. "I'll never sell this one; she tends to all my personal needs."

I looked up at the centurion through blood stained hair dangling in front of my eyes. He had pitch black, shoulder length hair, and his eyes were the colour of honey tea. I realised salvation wearing Roman armour stood above me. The endless candle of hope in my heart lit up once again.

The centurion studied me for a moment through narrowed eyes. Tone gritty, he told Tiberius, "If injured too badly she could not fulfil your needs."

Cackling, "You're quite right, Manius, she has much to make up for in my bed tonight."

Bitter bile filled my throat when Tiberius' laughter ricocheted through the air as he cast the whip aside. Tiberius suggested Manius accompany him home and sample some his fine wine. They strode away leaving me sprawled on the ground. My friend Lucia, also a slave, helped me back to my quarters where she and my sister, tended to the wounds Tiberius' lash had carved into my skin.

With tears in her eyes, Jana asked, "How are you alive my sister? I prayed that someone would save me."

I hugged her tight to me, "I was never dead, I banged my head and got knocked out."

Pulling gently away from me, she wiped her tears on the back of her hands, "I should go, I have many chores to attend to."

I nodded and kissed her cheek.

When she and Lucia left, Gabriel appeared to me. Placing his hand on my head, he asked, "How are you feeling?"

I winced in pain, "Not great."

"I've often noticed Manius staring at you and assumed he was curious about your exotic and beautiful appearance. His reaction to you being whipped made me believe it was something more."

"Strange," I told Gabe, "because I can't remember seeing him before today."

"Under Tiberius' watchful eye, I doubt you dared notice any man."

In spite of the pain, I managed to half smile. "True in the past, but today changed everything, because I've found my soul mate again."

Gabriel kissed my forehead and disappeared. Exhausted, I fell into fitful slumber.

A noise roused me. I saw Manius enter the slave quarters. With the beat of my heart dancing like fireflies, I pushed my aching bruised body from my bed and stood.

His voice a harsh whisper; he told me, "We don't have

much time. I'm going to help you escape."

"Why? I'm a mere slave."

"I can no longer bare, to watch Tiberius...." His voice broke, and he pulled me to him kissing me passionately. Releasing me, he stared into my eyes. "Because... I am in love with you."

There it was; the look of soulful reconnection on Manius' face! His eyes rolled back in his head as he began to shake, before he slumped to the floor.

"Help me," I pleaded to Gabriel who stood in a shadowy corner of the room.

He rushed across the room. "I'll take you both to a safe place 'til he comes around."

I shook my head, "I can't leave yet, I must find my sister. Can I bring her with us?"

Gabriel looked sad, "I can't do that, Eve. How would you explain me and your true identity to her? If she was much younger, I could get away with it."

"Gabriel, please! I can't leave her here. God knows what Tiberius will do to her, especially if I have escaped."

Looking into his citrus coloured eyes, I waited anxiously for his reply.

Much to my relief he nodded, "I guess I can make an exception in this case." He smiled.

I kissed Adam's forehead, and whispered, "We'll be together soon, my love."

Gabriel picked up Adam and ran toward the back entrance of the slave house.

They'd barely gotten out of sight when Tiberius burst in and searched the entire room. Anger carving his features, he strode toward me. "Where's Manius?"

I took a couple of steps backward." Why would I know where the centurion is?"

The words barely left my mouth before Tiberius struck me. "You worthless little, harlot! I overheard everything. Where did Manius go?"

I swiped at blood trickling from the corner of my mouth. "I don't know."

Tiberius grabbed my hair and pulled me outside. Spectators didn't bat an eyelid as he looped a leather thong round my neck, and dragged me kicking and screaming to his chariot. At the Pyramid Khufu, the largest one of the three pyramids in Giza, he ordered two Egyptian slaves to carry me to the top. Tiberius followed behind us up the steps. At the top, Tiberius sized my arm and dismissed the slaves. Struggling to break free, I promised Tiberius I'd do anything he desired. Blubbering and looking completely terrified, I knelt at his feet praying for mercy and fearing the outcome. Although having died many times, it wasn't my favourite experience, especially with the knowledge I would begin another life. There was also the painful fact, that I had only just found Adam and got him to remember us again.

Bending down and putting his face close to mine, he hissed, "This is your fault, not mine! Why couldn't you give me the one thing I wanted? Your lover will meet his just punishment also." Face devoid of any emotion, he jerked me upright and pushed me screaming off the pyramid.

Gabriel heartbrokenly found my broken body and sadly broke the news to my soul mate when he woke. In a fit of rage, he attacked Tiberius and beat him to death. Adam's own fellow soldiers then killed him.

Someone knocked on the door to my suite. Screaming Adam's name, I bolted awake and realised I was back in the Paris hotel room.

~~ *Chapter Thirteen* ~~

Gabriel told me it was Malcolm, he apparently heard me cry out another man's name and beat a hasty retreat. I bounded from bed, threw on my robe and rushed to Malcolm's room. I knocked on the door and waited, no response. I knocked again and still nothing. Gabriel faded through the door and confirmed Malcolm wasn't in his room.

I muttered, "Crap," and returned to my suite.

I plopped down on the bed and mulled over what to tell Malcolm. I couldn't tell him the truth, not yet anyway. I prayed a foolish dream hadn't shredded the bond forming between Malcolm and me. After fiddling with my hands for five minutes, I decided to see if someone at the front desk knew where Malcolm might be. I dressed and with Gabriel trailing me, I headed for the lift.

As the elevator sank downward, Gabe asked, "Decided what you're going to say to him yet?"

"No. Got any suggestions?"

"Say you were having a nightmare about an ex-lover who beat you or something."

"Not positive that'd work. Besides, I don't want Malcolm to think I'll accept abuse from any man."

"Why did you cry out Adam's name anyway?"

"I Dreamt I was Aula, the Roman slave girl."

"Oh, I didn't like that life one little bit," Gabriel said, shaking his head.

I frowned at Gabe and spat, "You? I can assure you that it looked and felt worse from my point of view."

Gabe, looking sheepish, mumbled, "Yeah, bet it did."

In the lobby, I walked to the reception desk and asked the young, blonde woman behind the counter if she'd seen Mr Malcolm Dice. At the very exact moment, I caught a glimpse of Malcolm exiting the main door with a dark haired pretty woman. The man accompanying Malcolm and the woman directed a strange smile at me. A queasy feeling hit my stomach. The man's eyes possessed a distinctive reddish hue, like hellish hot embers.

I muttered, "Oh no, you don't." I raced out the door and onto the sidewalk. Down the street, I saw the man say something to Malcolm and laugh. He opened the car door and the woman and Malcolm got inside.

I ran after the car but it sped away. "Dam it!"

"Easier to follow them if I fly you," Gabriel told me.

"Too many people around for me to suddenly vanish; follow them and I'll hail a cab."

He nodded and flew in the direction the car had gone.

I waved down a cab, scooted inside and told the cabbie to drive in the same direction. A few minutes later, Gabriel appeared beside me. To prevent the cabbie from thinking I was a nutcase, I took my mobile from my handbag and pretended to talk to a friend. "Well?"

Gabe said, "They went to La Palette on 43 rue de Seine 6e."

I gave the cabbie the address. The moment we arrived at La Palette, I shoved money at the driver and jumped out.

The interior of the Art Deco style bar emitted a bohemian atmosphere. Taking everything in, Gabriel elbowed me and said Malcolm and the woman were sitting at a table on one of the leafy covered terraces. I followed after Gabriel as he waded through the crowd. All at once, I noticed the man with a reddish gleam in his eyes that I'd seen earlier with Malcolm and the woman, standing near the bar and glaring at me. I stopped in my tracks.

Gabe whispered in my ear, "Don't worry, you go and find Malcolm; I'll take care of red eyes"

The man sprinted towards the front entrance with Gabriel right behind him.

On the terrace, I saw Malcolm and woman at a table, laughing and drinking. Anger at Malcolm burned deep inside me, but I mostly blamed Lucifer. I started walking towards Malcolm then stopped. I still didn't have a clue how to explain why I cried out another man's name. I reversed direction and ordered a stiff drink at the bar. Trying to shore up my nerve, I swigged it down, ordered another and then two more. I caught the bartender's attention and held up my empty glass, but he shook his head.

All of a sudden, I noticed some of the waiters were moving tables and chairs to the sidelines. People started dancing in the middle of the floor. Thinking what the hell, I started dancing. When Gabe showed up cloaked in invisibility, I laughed as he began to dance with me. Gabe and I were really getting down with the music when I noticed Malcolm striding towards us.

"What the hell are you doing here, Jasmine," he demanded, "following me?"

"I'm dancing," I replied giggling, "and yes, I followed you here."

"You've been drinking."

I snapped, "So what?" Staggering towards the bar, I added, "And I intend to drink a whole lot more."

Malcolm grabbed my arm.

I tried to jerk away. "Hey, whatdaya think you're doing."

"You need some fresh air." He pulled me through the crowd and outside.

"You have no right to..." I felt it coming and clamped a hand over my mouth but it didn't help. I vomited all over Malcolm's shoes. He stared at the disgusting mess decorating his black real leather shoes. I burst into tears.

Malcolm wrapped an arm around me. "Let's get you back to the hotel."

I glanced at the bar and caught a glimpse of Gabriel doing what looked like a single man conga dance. The sight sent me into a fit of giggling.

Malcolm shook his head. "Jasmine, do me a favour; promise never to get drunk again."

For some inexplicable reason, a movie star asking me for a favour, seemed exceedingly funny. I dissolved into uncontrollable laughter. Malcolm scooped me up into his arms and carried me to his limo.

In my room at the hotel, Malcolm called room service and ordered a pot of black coffee. He ignored my protests and forced me to try a cup of the hot beverage. The second the inky liquid hit my stomach, I rushed to the bathroom, gripped the toilet bowl and upchucked. Too much liquor on an empty stomach exacerbated an already sorry situation. I could almost hear my mother droning on and on about the dangers of drinking. When I emptied out, Malcolm helped me to the bed, removed my shoes and covered me up with a blanket.

I woke up smelling of stale liquor and vomit. Holding my pounding head with both hands, I crawled out of bed and staggered to the bathroom. In the shower, I leaned against the wall and let hot water flow over me until I felt almost human. Still a bit unsteady on my feet I dried off; pulled on jog pants and a pink plaid t shirt, which I'd, decided to bring at the last minute. I ran a brush through my tangled hair, and tied it up in a ponytail. One more glance at my ghostly-pale complexion in the mirror, made me splash a bit of colour on my cheeks and eyelids. Though looking rougher than normal and a bit dizzy, I made my way downstairs. Malcolm had insisted we have breakfast before taking the plane home.

I found him sitting at table, reading a British morning newspaper. I breathed an inward sigh of relief when he stood smiling and pulled out my chair. Maybe I hadn't tossed our relationship in the bin after all. The thought was short lived though, as Malcolm passed me the newspaper and told me to look at page four. Much to my total horror, there were two photos of Malcolm and me from last night. The headline above them read, Heartbroken from split with Lily Olson, Malcolm Dice captured boozing it up with mystery woman in Paris. The first photo snapped when I barfed on Malcolm; the second one, showed him carrying me to the car.

I muttered, "Oh dear god."

Malcolm chuckled. "You gotta love the paparazzi."

I stared at him open mouthed. "Nice to see you find it amusing." I threw the paper down on the table. "I'll never hear the end of this."

"Trust me, you'll survive."

I heaved a disgusted sigh and took a sip of orange juice.

Malcolm said, "Can I ask you a question?"

"Yeah, of course."

He locked unblinking eyes on mine. "Who's Adam, is he someone important in your life?"

Oh my aching head; how could I possibly answer that one.

"Err... an ex-boyfriend. I had a nightmare about him getting hurt last night. Though he isn't currently in my life, truth is that I do care quite a lot about him."

"Any chance he may put in an appearance in the future?"

I didn't want to tell him an outright lie. Mulling over the way things were going between Malcolm and me provided a halfway honest answer. "Highly unlikely."

He gave me one of his dazzling movie star smiles and went back to drinking his coffee.

Studying his handsome face, I wondered what would have happened if I hadn't tracked him down last night. Would he have taken the woman to bed? Too fearful to broach the subject, I focused on my juice.

The car arrived and took us to the airport. On the plane, thoughts about my parent's reaction to the photos consumed me. Maybe they hadn't seen the photos. But the string of bad luck I was having lately made that extremely doubtful. Tension framed the little conversation between Malcolm and me on the flight home. When the plane entered British airspace, he pulled an envelope from his jacket and handed it to me.

I opened it. It contained an invitation to an after party to celebrate Malcolm's latest movie, Rough Diamonds, opening in London the following month.

"Thank you," I smiled, "sounds like quite the affair."

"I would have invited you to the premiere itself, but the list of invited was written up a few weeks ago. Back then, I also said that I'd escort the leading lady, Sharon Barnwaith."

Smiling, "That's fine; I completely understand and don't like my photo taken anyway."

Sitting down across from me, and smiling he leant slightly forward, "Are you free next week?"

"I'll have to check my calendar but I think it's clear. I'm

starting University the following week."

"Would you like to see my penthouse in London?"

I nodded, "yeah sounds, great."

"Actually, what say we stop off there before I take you home? You missed a fantastic meal at the Le Jules Verne and while I'm not a Cordon Bleu chef, I know my way around a kitchen."

Thinking a stopover would give me more time to prepare a cover story for Mum and Dad, I said, "Sure."

Malcolm grinned. "Then London it is."

His eyes suddenly clouded. "Oh, that reminds me of something strange that happened at Le Jules Verne."

"Oh really?"

"I swear the guy who told me that you'd been taken ill was the ice cream man from the park last week."

I smiled. "It's said we all have a double."

"Like I've told you before, I have a gift for faces and I'm nearly a hundred percent certain it was the same guy. It's strange he keeps popping up." He frowned. "Really frustrates the hell out of me, because I know him from somewhere before we ever met."

"I'm sure it's only random coincidences."

He shrugged his shoulders. "Guess so."

~~ *Chapter Fourteen* ~~

A limo waited at the airport when our plane landed. When we arrived at Malcolm's Kensington residence, the doorman welcomed him back. We took the lift up to the fifteenth floor. Malcolm swiped his key card and the automatic door swung open. The inside of his penthouse flabbergasted me. Serene turquoise tiles covered the foyer and a hallway that led into an expansive living room. A large bronze statue of Buddha, sat at the bottom of a wrought iron staircase I assumed led up to bedrooms. Vibrant paintings lined the whitewashed walls. In the living room a gothic style chandler hung high up in the centre of a domed ceiling and an oriental coffee table sat in front of a poppy coloured sofa facing a massive TV. A large, gorgeous, oil coloured painting of a peacock, hung above a log filled open fireplace.

Malcolm walked over to a mirrored bar in a corner and offered me a drink.

I shook my head. "I don't believe I'll want any alcohol for quite a while."

He chuckled and poured himself one.

Taking in my surrounding, I saw a framed photo of Malcolm and his brother James on the fireplace mantle. They looked so happy. The memory of witnessing rescue workers pulling James from a mangled car flashed through my mind. Closing my eyes, I tried to think of something, anything else.

Malcolm touched my shoulder. "Jasmine, are you okay?"

Startled, I flinched at his touch. "I'm still a little hung over that's all."

"I have just the cure; come with me," he said, pulling me along behind him to the kitchen.

The kitchen countertops were marble and an American style stove, plus a combo fridge and freezer stood between cupboards finished in onyx black lacquer. I stared at the lavishness. "Now this is a kitchen!"

Malcolm informed me a personal chef usually whipped up meals but it was his day off.

Perched on a stylish stool by a kitchen island with a butcher block top, I watched in fascination as Malcolm began chopping up onions with the expertise of a Sous chef. "So what are we having?"

He grinned. "I make a very mean, spaghetti and meatballs."

Smiling, "Oh really? My all time favourite."

His mobile phone rang. Quickly wiping his hands on a kitchen towel, he pulled it from his pocket and looked at the screen. "Sorry, I need to take this." He walked toward the living room. I heard him say, "Come on, Mum, please don't be like that." After a few minutes, looking upset, he walked back into the kitchen. "Jasmine, I'm afraid dinner will have to wait for another time. My Mum is in a bad way and I need to visit her."

I got off the stool and took his hand. "I understand; is there anything I can do?"

"No, but thanks anyway." He kissed my cheek then grabbed some car keys hanging on a key rack next to the microwave. "My chauffeur will take you home. I'll drive my personal car over to Mum's." Heading for the front entrance, he called his chauffeur and instructed the car be brought around.

Inside the lift, he pulled me to him and kissed me passionately. Desire threaded me and I returned his kiss in full. His arms tightened and the kiss deepened. Suddenly, the most bizarre picture of Malcolm poor Mum crying flashed through my mind. I pulled away.

He looked at me with puzzlement in his eyes. "Sorry, am I coming on too strong again?"

"You can't afford to be distracted. Your Mum needs you."

He nodded.

The lift door slid open and Malcolm escorted me to the limo waiting by the curb outside. He kissed me lightly and opened the door for me. I slid into the backseat and waved to him as it set off.

Checking my phone, I read a message from an old friend. In the midst of replying, I heard the chauffeur laugh. I looked up and saw him studying me in the review mirror.

"It wasn't really Malcolm's Mum on the phone," he told me with a slight chuckle. "But I do a great impression of her voice though, even if I do say so myself."

My fingers immediately froze on the keypad and I had trouble breathing. Staring at Lucifer's reddish eyes reflected in the mirror, I wanted to yell for Gabriel and have him rescue me. At the same time I needed to know exactly what Lucifer's endgame was.

"What is your problem?" I demanded. "You got us thrown out of Eden and caused God to punish us for all eternity. Seriously, why make things more difficult?"

"Isn't it obvious? You humans make me sick. You are all weak, inconsequential cretins. Yet the Creator thinks his children of earth are superior to greater beings like me. Seeing how he doted on the two of you when you were first created, made me mad with jealously."

"Okay, so you have a personal vendetta against me and my soul mate. What will this possibly achieve in the end?"

Lucifer turned his head towards me. Eyes wide and glaring, he cackled, the sound reverberating inside the car. "Well, stick with me darling and all shall be revealed in due time."

I nodded towards the extremely pissed off guardian angel now standing in the roadway. "I'm quite sure that he doesn't agree with your plan."

Lucifer jerked his attention back to the road ahead. Gabriel put out his hands and the car hood hit them. The limo ground to an abrupt stop.

Lucifer spat, "Oh, bollocks! It's bloody wonder boy here to save the day yet again. Doesn't he ever take a day off?"

He cursed God, Gabriel and me... especially me, before going poof.

Gabriel opened the car door. "Eve, are you okay?"

"I guess so, just shaken up a bit. This is becoming far too common for my liking."

"Agreed," Gabriel replied looking concerned.

"Okay, now what?" I asked Gabe. "We can't very well leave the car here. I can drive it home, but I need to see it's returned to Malcolm's penthouse. He may need it soon and how will I explain the chauffeur disappearing."

He grinned, shrunk down to human size, and his wings vanished. "Not to worry, I shall be your chauffeur for today Madam."

With Gabriel behind the wheel safely steering the limo homeward, I leaned my head against the car seat, closed my eyes and sank into sleep born of exhaustion.

Vivid memories of a past life invaded my dreams again. The year, 1971 and I was a deaf girl named Louise who lived in Australia. Having never heard sound and embarrassed by clumsy attempts to speak, I preferred to communicate by sign language. Plagued by health issues from birth, I had Wegener's Granulomatosis, a rare immune disorder where inflammation in my blood vessels restricted blood flow to my lungs, kidneys, and other organs. For seventeen years, I managed to cope with chronic ear infections, conjunctivitis, shortness of breath and joint pain. Shortly before my eighteenth birthday, a consultation with yet another specialist resulted in a prognosis that didn't bode well for my future; kidney failure.

When I woke up from the traditional coma and first saw Gabriel, I told him in rude sign language to leave me the hell alone. I didn't see any point in finding my soul mate after my recent diagnosis. I gave up and accepted my fate, but Gabriel didn't. Insisting being deaf heightened my other senses, so he encouraged me to put the honed senses to good use and search for clues to my original partner's whereabouts. I refused.

For two years, my health continued to decline as I underwent dialysis. One day while keeping my urology appointment, I'd rolled my wheelchair into the waiting room at St James' hospital in Melbourne. All at once, a guy brushed past me, sending my chair banging against a nearby wall. Without a word of apology he continued on his way. I signed, "Jerk" at him, though by then he was too far away to notice, leaving me boiling in anger. Suddenly, my heart started to race and I begin having trouble breathing. I clutched my chest and tried to suck in much needed oxygen. A nurse rushed to my side and pushed me to the emergency room. Not one nurse or doctor knew sign language, so I submitted to numerous needle pricks and having the leads of cardiac monitor attached to my body.

Defeated, I lay on a gurney waiting for tests to determine if I'd had a heart attack. Gabriel materialised and signed what happened. I signed back the preceding events that led to me landing in the E.R.

Gabriel's eyebrow rose up.

"What?" I signed as the doctor abruptly walked back into the exam room.

"It's nothing." He replied. But I eyed him suspiciously and he looked away.

The doctor told me in writing on the little pad that I always had with me, that the tests confirmed I'd suffered a panic attack. He wrote a nurse would give me a mild sedative.

When the doctor and nurse left, I looked at Gabriel and signed, "I wish this miserable life would end now."

Gabriel's brow furrowed. "I plan to track down the bloke who caused you to end up in the E.R."

Still steamed at the idiot who nearly bowled me over, it really made me mad how some people often had such disregard for anyone with disabilities. I signed a brief physical description then added, "He wore a black t shirt with 'I Love New York Hot Dogs' on the front."

Gabe nodded. "The shirt will make it easier to find him if he's still in the building. When I do, I'm going to bump him into a wall, hard."

"No; just find out his name and where he can be found. I intend to give the inconsiderate jerk a piece of my own mind."

Anger carving his features, Gabriel strode off.

Shortly after Gabe left, ambulance attendants rushed five accident victims into the E.R. Facing a sudden bed shortage, a frazzled nurse checked my blood pressure and helped me into a wheelchair. She pushed my chair to the waiting area and shoved a magazine at me and wrote on my pad that it may be some time before the doctor can fill out your discharge papers.

Disgusted by having to wait, I flipped open the two year old Vogue magazine. Midway reading a story about Emma Fairwood I sensed someone. I found Gabriel reading the article over my shoulder.

"She was in grade school when it happened," he said.

I frowned at him and checking no one was around, signed. "What are you talking about?"

"When Emma's sister Haley was diagnosed with leukaemia. For more than a year she fought to live, but the child knew her days were numbered."

I threw the magazine on the table beside my chair and signed, "Don't beat around the bush, I know my days are limited."

"You must trust anything is possible," Gabriel signed back.

I heaved a sigh. I realised Gabe was trying to comfort me but no amount of kind words could stop impending kidney failure. "Did you find the thoughtless idiot?"

"Thoughtless maybe, but he's certainly not an idiot."

Glaring at Gabriel, I said, "What does that mean?"

"He's an American doctor who works in this hospital. His name is John Umber and he specializes in lung cancer."

I signed, "Well he's a very rude doctor..." Noticing the nurse walking towards me, I stopped and pretended to be fiddling with my hair. I'd land in the Psych Unit if she thought I was holding a signing conversation with an invisible companion. She stuck a treatment instruction sheet in front of me and I scrawled my name across the bottom. I snatched my copy out of her hands and rolled my chair to the Urology Department.

My urologist reviewed my chart and ordered more tests,

which I despised but endured. Three hours later, I was given a date for a follow up visit. The mess of a day left my eyes filled with tears as I gripped the wheels of my chair and rolled it towards the front entrance.

Gabriel manifested. "So do you want to meet the doctor who banged you into a wall?"

"Thought I did, but my heart really isn't in it now."

"Wouldn't hurt to take a peek at him and say your piece to him. You know how you like to defend your rights. Might get your mind off other things?"

I shrugged. When no one was looking, Gabriel wheeled me to the Pulmonary Medicine Department of the hospital. He stopped at a door with Doctor John Umber written on it in large gold letters.

Confused, I looked up at Gabriel and signed, "Now what?"

"That's up to you."

I glared at Gabe. He raised his eyebrows expectedly. Shaking my head in disbelief, I knocked on the door. A tall man with messy red hair, a scruffy beard and wearing a doctor's white coat opened the door.

Reading his lips, I made out him saying, "Hello, can I help you?"

The t shirt promoting hotdogs under his white lab coat confirmed it was the right guy. My eyes meet his, my heartbeat began to race, and I had trouble catching a full breath. I signed, "I'm lost; could you direct me to where they do blood tests?"

His brow furrowed. "Sorry, but I don't know sign language."

I smiled and put a thumbs up, guessing he would know it meant okay.

He smiled back, then said, "I'll find someone who can help you. Please, wait here," and strode toward the main lobby.

I scowled up at Gabriel signing. "Did you know?"

Wearing a smug grin, he said, "I suspected as much."

I put all of my anger into signing, "Would've been nice if you'd given me a heads up!"

His grin widened. "And spoil the surprise?"

"Sometimes you're a complete arse!"

I saw a dark haired nurse walking my way. In front of my chair, she signed that her son was deaf and asked how she could help me. Uncertain how to explain, I glanced at Gabriel, hoping he could offer some inspiration. Invisible to the nurse, Gabe showed me a paper he had obviously stolen from Dr Umber's office. The document outlined the doctor's research on the link between smoking and cancer.

I applied a half lie. "An article I recently read, stated there isn't definite proof smoking causes cancer and other health problems. Since I was here for a check up, I wondered if Dr Umber might be the right person to ask if it was true."

She glanced at Doctor Umber striding down the hallway toward us. "Here he comes now; suppose we ask him?"

When the nurse relayed my interest, the doctor became quite enthusiastic and asked if she had time to act as his interpreter. She said her work shift officially ended five minutes ago and she'd be happy to sign for him.

He gestured for us to follow him and the nurse pushed my wheelchair into his office. The doctor spread an array of graphs and documents on his desk. He told me they proved tobacco companies had conspired to keep the truth from the public. Recent studies conducted by tobacco companies' own scientists confirmed a chemical added, amplified the dangerous effects of nicotine.

Most of the time I had no idea what the charts he showed me meant, but I found his passion fascinating. The doctor's long and complicated explanation seemed to bore Gabriel and he began fiddling about with a model of a human chest sitting on the desktop. The nurse noticed organ parts in the model apparently moving on their own. Her eyes widened. I glared at Gabe. He smiled and tried to move the plastic lungs back to their proper place. The model broke into separate parts and scattered across the floor, startling both the poor nurse and Dr Umber. The nurse stared open mouthed as the doctor picked up the pieces and reassembled them.

Gabriel grinned at me and mouthed, "Oops sorry."

The nurse, still staring at self animated lungs who threw themselves across the room, signed her kids would be out of school soon and she needed to get home. I thanked her for helping me converse with the doctor. Dr Umber shook my hand and for a moment, I saw something akin to some recognition in his light green eyes.

Heart full of hope, I gave him a big smile and signed, "I admire your dedication and I know your work will be taken seriously someday."

He thanked me for the interest in his work and bid me goodbye.

Tears of disappointment blurred my eyes as the nurse wheeled me to the front entrance of the hospital. I assured her a friend would pick me up and she left.

"What's wrong?" Gabriel asked.

I swiped at my tears. "My soul mate in this life has a greater purpose and I shouldn't try to make him remember."

"Why?" Gabe asked. "Your health could be reasonably good for years. Surely, even a day together as true soul mates would be worth it?"

"You don't understand, Gabriel. If he falls in love with me, he'll focus on my health issues and lose interest in the important work he is doing. His research could save millions of lives."

"Sometimes," Gabriel said, kissing me forehead, "I wonder who the real angel is, you or me?"

A year later, lying in a hospital bed waiting for a kidney transplant, I was reading the newspaper when a headline caught my eye. Dr John Umber Found Dead In His House Under Suspicious Circumstances. During their investigation, authorities discovered evidence a tobacco conglomerate, attempting to hide that their products contained amped up nicotine, had bribed government officials and threatened workers with physical harm. The list of those involved in the cover up seemed endless. The murder of my soul mate had confirmed his research. The newspaper slowly slipped from my hand onto to the floor. Filled with hope my next life would prove kinder, I lost the will to carry on and surrendered to death.

~~ *Chapter Fifteen* ~~

Gabe roused me from my dream of the past by gently shaking my shoulder.

Head still ringing with memories, I pried my eyes open and found myself still in the back of Malcolm's limo.

"You're home," Gabe told me. "I should return Malcolm's car to his penthouse, but I can wait around until you explain things to your Mum and Dad."

"No, that's okay; just give me a minute to prepare myself for the full on lecture I'm sure to receive."

Gabe chuckled. "I wouldn't worry. They can't be worse than your dragon of a mother in Victorian times. What a hissy fit she threw when you chose a coalminer over the son of a wealthy Parliament member."

Trying not to laugh at the memory that bounced into my head, I quipped, "You're right. That woman knew how to use her oversized lungs. Luckily, my Mum is this life is much more placid. Still, she's not a total pushover. She has a tendency to ramble on, but still manages to get her point across extremely well."

I smiled at the irony. Here I was, the original mother of the human race and worrying about my Mum giving me a lecture. I told Gabe to return Malcolm's car. I then paused on the door steep and mentally assembled a list of excuses, before inserting my key in the lock. Opening the front door, I apprehensively walked inside.

I called, "Mum... Dad?" Silence answered. A note propped up against a vase of flowers on a living room table, caught my attention. I set my suitcase down, crossed the room and picked it up.

Jasmine honey, we tried calling your phone numerous times but got no answer. We are at the vet; a car hit Bonnie and I am afraid it doesn't look good. Please call your Dad's mobile the moment you get this. Love you, Mum.

"Oh my gosh, no!" I dug around in my handbag for my phone only to find the battery dead. I raced to the landline and discovered I couldn't remember Dad's mobile number. Realizing I had Dad's mobile number stored on my iPhone, I tried to find the charger and couldn't. Panicking, I grabbed my car keys from off the key tree and scurried outside.

On the drive to the veterinarian clinic we used, unrestrained tears ran down my face. At the clinic, I braked hard in the car park; I jumped out of the car and ran to the door; locked. I rang the doorbell. It seemed forever before a veterinary nurse opened it. Rushing inside, I asked if a dog named Bonnie was there. The nurse mumbled something and avoided my gaze.

I shouted, "Mum... Dad?"

Mum, her eyes red from crying, appeared from one of the exam rooms. The look on her face confirmed the worse. I rushed into her open arms and we clung to each other.

I finally managed, "Is she?"

"Yes, honey," Mum sobbed, "she's gone."

"Where's Dad?"

"He's still in with her," she whispered. "I think he would

like a few moments alone with her."

"What happened?"

Mum led me to a bench in the waiting room. Sitting by me, she clutched my hand. "It was the strangest thing. I was walking Bonnie at the park. As I went to put some waste in a bin, she followed me. A little boy on the other side of the roadway called Bonnie. Oddly, instead of shying away as she normally does, she wagged her tail and started to go, I managed to grab hold of her collar but she was so forceful that I lost control of it. Once free, she ran straight towards the boy and into the path of an oncoming car.

"Who was the boy and where were his parents?"

She wiped her eyes on an already soaked tissue. "It all happened so fast. I only got a fleeting glimpse of the boy before the car hit her. Strangely there wasn't any sign of him afterwards, and no one seemed to know his identity. I should have never let her off the lease... if only..." She broke down again.

I held Mum while she cried, but in my head, I was silently screaming at the monster from hell who murdered our beloved Bonnie. A thought suddenly flashed. Why didn't Gabriel know about Lucifer's plan? Gabe could normally sense the evil one's presence if Lucifer wasn't in his original form. My anger and pain was boiling, I planned to find out why Gabe had failed both my family and me.

Dad finally emerged from the room where Bonnie was. Mum and I hugged him. Voice raspy with emotion, he told us, "I need to make arrangements for Bonnie. There's a nice pet cemetery not far from here and I'm going to make her coffin myself."

Back at home, none of us felt the need to talk. No amount of words could bring Bonnie back. I kissed Mum and Dad goodnight and grabbed hold of my handbag off the sofa. I climbed the staircase wrapped in misery. As I opened my bedroom door, my cell phone rang. I pulled it from my purse and hit talk. "Hello."

"Hi, gorgeous," Malcolm said, "You got back okay, then?"

"Yeah; but the situation at home could be better."

"Oh dear, are your parents giving you grief about the photos?"

"No; I forgot all about the photos. To be honest though I wish that was why." I started to weep.

"Jasmine baby, what's wrong?"

"It's our dog, Bonnie," I sobbed, "She got hit by a car and died."

"You're joking?"

I mumbled, "Afraid not."

"Wow, that sucks; I'm so sorry. Is there anything I can do?"

"Not really, but thanks anyway." Sitting on the bed, I switched the phone to my other ear, as I grabbed a tissue from the box on my nightstand to dry my eyes. Sniffling, I asked Malcolm, "How's your Mum?"

"I think she's having a nervous breakdown. When I arrived, she and Dad were calmly having tea. I asked her how she was feeling and she said reasonably well under the circumstances. When Dad left the room, I questioned her about the phone call. She looked at me as if I was daft and denied calling me, but I insisted she had. She began to tear up so I dropped the subject."

"I'm sure grief and stress is making her forgetful," I told him.

Noticing a pair of red eyes glaring at me from behind my bedroom curtains, I stammered, "Err... sorry, Malcolm, but I have to go."

"Okay; goodnight and once again I'm sorry about your

dog."

My hand trembling I whispered, "I'll call you tomorrow."

The call disconnected, but clutching my phone as if it could somehow protect me, I stared transfixed at the lilac coloured drapes.

The curtains parted and the demon kid walked toward me. His lips curled into a grin. "Did you have a pleasant evening?"

Avoiding looking directly into his eyes, I stood and took a couple of steps towards the door. "Lovely, thanks for killing my dog."

His cackle echoed through the air. "You're most welcome. You have always shown impeccable manners, I expected you to thank me for getting rid of that dirty animal."

"Why? Bonnie posed no threat to you."

"I was a tad pissed. You see, I hoped to chat with you on the ride back home, but goldilocks decided to put in an appearance. I don't like being interrupted and decided to get your full attention in another way."

A malevolent grin spread across the demon boy's countenance. "The next time we can't have a private chitchat, your Dad or Mum might have an accident!"

Despite knowing it wouldn't help the situation, I launched myself at the little demon. Suddenly Gabriel crashed through the ceiling, his gigantic feet landed on the devil's head. Similar to a nail hit by a hammer, mini Lucifer went straight down through my bedroom floor. Gabriel standing in all his glory wore a very satisfied grin.

I hurled myself at Gabe and wrapped both arms around his waist. "Thank god you came!"

He chuckled. "Now that was fun."

Noticing I was weeping uncontrollably, he whispered, "I'm here now, please don't cry. Everything will be okay."

I wailed, "He killed Bonnie. What if my Mum and Dad are next?"

Holding me tightly, Gabe said, "Lucifer's bark is often far worse than his bite. You see, energy makes up everything and believe it or not, every evil committed by Lucifer drains some of his stored power. That's why he usually avoids the hands on approach and tries to influence the choices people make."

I swiped at the tears stinging my eyes and looked up at Gabe, "What about you? Do you ever run out of power?"

"Sometimes; but not often, because I'm like an appliance plugged directly into God's spiritual power socket. Lucifer isn't connected to God anymore, so he draws power from the evil mankind creates." He kissed the top of my head. "Don't worry, I won't allow Lucifer to harm you or your family. I'll ask other angels to keep an eye on your parents."

Reassured but weary, I didn't bother changing into night clothes, just threw back the covers and curled up on the bed.

Gabriel pulled the blanket up over me. "Goodnight, I hope you sleep well."

"Thanks, you too."

A weird thought though struck me. "Do you ever sleep, Gabe?"

"Not exactly; when I have time off, I do rest, but that rarely happens. When I'm not helping you, I try to assist other souls."

I smiled. "Goodnight, Gabriel."

Watching him pop from view, I realised Gabe really was my best friend. Grateful to have such a loyal guardian, I closed my eyes and surrendered to exhaustion.

The house felt strangely empty the next morning. Bonnie wagging her tail and holding one of Dad's shoes proudly in her mouth usually greeted me. There was no sign of Mum and Dad. Alone with my thoughts, I sat at the kitchen table.

After a few minutes, Mum came in the back door. Still wearing her garden gloves, she picked up a teapot and started making tea.

"Where's Dad?" I asked. "He is normally up way before I am?"

"He wanted to get an early start on a coffin for Bonnie, so he's in the work shed."

"Oh," I replied looking down at the floor.

Mum turned to me. "Your father and I saw some interesting photos in the newspaper yesterday."

"About that, Mum, it wasn't as bad as it actually looked."

"Meaning what exactly?"

"It was a matter of bad timing, that's all. I had a few more drinks than I should have. Malcolm was taking me back to the hotel when paparazzi snapped those photos. Nothing happened, mum, I slept it off in my hotel room. Alone."

"You know, Jasmine, even as a child you were always sensible, and I've always thought you a level headed adult, but lately you're like someone I really don't know. I'm very disappointed in you." She gave me a scornful look only a mother can give.

"Mum, I'm still me, but at some point everyone tries to discover who they really are."

"Well, I believe the change in you somehow stems from your coma. For example, you never played the piano and now you play like you'd had lessons ever since a very young child." She shook her head. "Where is my Jasmine? I don't know you?"

Resting both elbows on the table, I put my face in my hands. "Mum, please, I do not know what to say; apart from I'm still your little girl. Perhaps being in a coma woke something dormant inside me."

Dad entered the tension filled kitchen. "What's going on in here?"

I sighed. "Mum thinks body snatchers have taken over my body or something, because I'm a little different these days."

Dad looked weirdly at Mum. "I thought that you were going to wait for a better time to discuss this with her?"

Oh great! I thought. He's cottoned on to the fact I'm different also.

Mum glared at dad. "I bloody well can't just sit back and watch Jasmine mess up her life. That no good womanizer has obviously led her astray. Nothing good will come from her associating with Malcolm Dice and his Hollywood lifestyle."

Dad looked to me. "I'm worried about her too, but I think you're going a bit too far. I know my daughter, fame and money does not influence her."

Mum didn't back down. "You may think so, but I believe she's going off the rails. She acts like getting drunk out of her head and having unflattering photos of her splashed all over the newspapers is only bad timing. How do we know Malcolm isn't plying her with drugs also?" She folded her arms and hissed at dad, "Have you thought about that? She's not the daughter I raised, bringing such shame on our family."

I leapt out the chair and shouted, "Hello! In case you guys haven't noticed, I'm right here... and I don't need to listen to this bullshit from you, Mum."

"Watch your mouth, young lady," she ordered.

"Or you'll do what, Mum? Ground me?" I screamed, heading for the stairs.

In my room, I covered my head with a pillow, but it didn't block out the argument going on downstairs. Poor Dad was now on the receiving end of Mum's fury.

I heard her yell, "I tell you something is going on here!

Jasmine goes into a coma for some unknown reason and wakes with a talent for playing the piano and then turns into the promiscuous girlfriend of a globetrotting movie star."

Dad said, "How do you know she's promiscuous?"

Mum yelled, "Because I remember my Jasmine and the girl upstairs isn't my baby."

I'd expected something along these lines but Mum was on the verge of hysteria. I mumbled to myself, "What the bloody hell has gotten into her?"

"Maybe Lucifer?" a voice answered.

I peeked from under the pillow and saw Gabriel standing at the foot of my bed. "No, I think it's more likely the menopause. I have been through it enough times myself and Mum is the right age after all."

Gabe waggled his head. "Getting into people's head and doing a bit of rearranging fits Lucifer's M.O."

Thinking about Malcolm's poor brother James, and the tragedy that happened, panic rushed through me. "What can I do Gabriel?"

"I'll try to find an angel named Serenity who's notorious for her healing and restorative powers. She'll help calm your mother's worries," he told me, before vanishing like a popped soap bubble.

"I love it when you do the bubble thing," I said, but received no reply.

Things seemed quiet downstairs... too quiet. After a few moments of arguing with myself, I decided to check on them.

When I walked into the kitchen, Mum was making scrambled eggs. She glanced up and smiled at me. Dad, his brow furrowed sat at the table.

I eased into a chair next to him and whispered, "How are things with her?"

"Bloody weird is all I can say," he replied, looking up at

Mum. "She was about to launch into another crazed rant, when suddenly her eyes glazed over and she started humming a tune. Then she smiled and asked me if I wanted an omelette or scrambled eggs."

Must be the work of the Serenity angel I thought, looking around the kitchen for any other sign.

"What are you doing?" Dad asked.

"Oh nothing; thought I saw a moth."

I spied a white feather on the floor by the stove. Assuming it confirmed Serenity's presence, I walked to where Mum stood. Watching her whisk eggs that filled the skillet, I inquired, "Mum, you okay?"

"I'm good," she answered, looking at me with a bright smile on her face. "You want some eggs too?"

"No thanks, I don't feel very hungry."

"Sweetheart, I know you're upset about Bonnie, but you should eat. An empty stomach will only make you feel worse."

"Don't worry, Mum, I'll grab something later. I thought you were working today."

Dishing up Dad's breakfast on one of her plates normally reserved only for special occasions, she said, "I told them I'm not feeling good today."

I frowned and looked at dad. He shrugged his shoulders.

"Okay," I told Mum. "I am going to pop out for a bit. I need some things from the market. Can I get you anything?"

"I don't think so, dear," she replied putting the dirty pan into the sink.

I walked to where Dad sat and rubbed his shoulder. "See what I mean?" he told me, quietly. "Bizarre, or what?"

"Yeah, probably a delayed reaction from witnessing what happened to Bonnie."

"You might be right," he replied, sounding glad of some

possible explanation.

Upstairs, I put on a pair of jeans and a t shirt. In the midst of tying the laces on my running shoes, I glanced up and saw Gabriel. "I grinned at him. "Serenity has fast mojo."

"I told you she's good. She confided Lucifer had definitely manipulated your mother's fears. Serenity will do her best to block those thoughts and keep your mother calm."

"Great, please thank her for me."

He grinned. "Already did."

I checked the life of my phone battery then grabbed my keys and purse. Downstairs, I tiptoed across the living room and peeked around the kitchen door. Mum stood by the stove enjoying a mug of tea while dad ate his breakfast. Relieved things seemed somewhat normal; I left by the front door.

As I unlocked my car door, my phone rang. I punched the talk button and listened in stunned disbelief, to the malevolent voice on the other end. Shocked, the phone slipped from my fingers and tumbled underneath the car. Why couldn't Lucifer leave me alone for more than five minutes? Lucifer had told me not to have faith in anything or anyone. He said that no one, not even Gabriel could block him for long. With Lucifer's evil laughter still ringing in my ear, I bent down and looked underneath the car. My phone had skittered to the other side. All at once, a hand reached beneath the other side and grabbed it. Heart thumping with rising dread, I stood and come face to face with Malcolm.

He grinned. "Here's your phone, butterfingers."

I took it and surprisingly discovered the protective case I bought had prevented any damage. "Thanks," I told him. "I'm so clumsy sometimes."

Studying me, Malcolm said, "You look pale; sure you're okay?"

"I'm fine, just gutted about Bonnie."

"I can empathize. James and I had a dog when we were young. A flash flood rolled through where we lived, and the current swept our dog into the floodwater. James tried to save the animal and couldn't. My Dad managed to rescue James before the water took him too."

"Bonnie was like a member of my family." Unable to contain my anger, I spat, "That bastard!"

Malcolm looked confused. "Who, the car's driver?"

"Err... yeah. Though, it's really unfair of me to be angry at the driver, as it wasn't his fault, because he didn't have time to stop his car. And he kindly drove Mum and Bonnie to the vet."

He pulled me into his arms. "It's the pain talking." Raising my chin until our eyes met, he kissed me gently, and said, "Where are you off to?"

"I need to pick up a few things, but mostly, I wanted to clear my head."

"Would you like some company?"

Hypnotized by his sexy eyes, I whispered, "I'd love company."

He gestured to his vehicle parked by the curb. "Shall we take my car?"

"Fine by me."

As Malcolm steered the blue Mercedes down the street, I rested my head against the Corinthian leather seatback. Lucifer's warning crawled like dark cockroaches through my mind. Should I be leaving? What if Lucifer messed with Mum's mind again? I wished Gabe would appear, so I could double check on mum.

"Where did you want to go first?" Malcolm asked.

"There's a supermarket near the centre of town. I need a few toiletries and some painkillers for my headache."

He laughed. "Still hung over, eh? You, lightweight!"

"No, my Mum had a bitch fit about the newspaper photos and everything."

"I see; I suppose I'm forbidden to take you out again."

"Don't worry, Mum will be fine, just needs some faith healing or something."

He cast a puzzled look at me. When we arrived at the market, Malcolm opened my car door, I quickly jumped out. Malcolm closed the door and sat back in the driver seat.

"Oh, you are not coming in?"

"Nah, I don't have my awesome disguise." He smiled.

"Okay, well I won't be long." I then headed off towards the automatic doors.

Inside I collected the items I needed, paid and walked back towards Malcolm's car. From the corner of my eye, I saw a toddler break free from his mum and run in front of a delivery van, cruising through the parking lot. The driver stomped the brakes and the squeal of tires filled the air, but the van kept skidding straight toward the toddler. A white blur streaked in front of the van. Suddenly, the little boy stood on the other side of the parking lot, crying but unharmed. Gabriel stood next to him. The tot's mother rushed to his side, hugging and kissing him.

"Geez, that was a close call," Malcolm said.

"You can say that again."

In the car, Malcolm asked, "Where to now?"

After thinking about it, I decided it was for the best that I went home, as I was still worried about Mum. "I hope you don't mind, but I think I should go back home, I am concerned about Mum with everything that has happened with the dog."

"No problem, I completely understand."

When the car came to a stop at my house, Malcolm looked at me. "How about catching a movie this weekend?"

"Yeah, sounds great!"

He got out of the car and opened my door. "Call you later then." He gave me a quick kiss and whistling, walked back to his side.

I returned Malcolm's goodbye wave and went inside the house.

Dad was coming down the stairs.

I asked, "Where's Mum?"

"She's having a lie down. Everything has affected her more than I realised. I wanted to work on the coffin for Bonnie, but didn't want to leave her alone."

"Go do that, Dad and don't worry, I'll check on mum."

He kissed my cheek. "Thanks, sweetheart."

~~ *Chapter Sixteen* ~~

Upstairs, I quietly opened the door to my parent's bedroom. Mum was sound asleep, so I eased the door closed and walked to my room.

I sat on my bed and kicked off my shoes.

Gabriel appeared. "Your Mum will be more tired than normal. Nothing to worry about, it's just Serenity working her magic."

"Good to know. Gabriel, you did an admirable thing saving that toddler today."

"Think nothing of it. I try to help however I can, especially when children are involved."

A half forgotten event moved to the forefront of my mind. "It was you, wasn't it?"

He frowned. "What do you mean?"

"When I was five, I got lost in town. You were the man who found me sobbing behind a bin and reassured me that you knew where my Mum and Dad were. You took my hand and led me to them."

"Yeah, that was me. I guess you were too young in some previous lives to remember when I helped you,"

"Which lives?"

"Do you recall the Titanic sinking?"

"I must have been only three at the time, so most of it is hazy. I remember the panic when the ship started to sink, and my hand slipping from my mother's when we fell into the water." I paused and looked at Gabriel. "Wait, something rings a bell. You saved me... must have, because I couldn't have survived the freezing water."

Gabe nodded solemnly. "Guilty as charged. When you went under, I flew down, grabbed hold of your dress and pulled you to the surface. After warming you underneath my wings, I quickly placed you into one of the lifeboats when nobody was looking. I will never forget the desperation in your chocolate brown eyes when you begin crying for your mother. I dived back in the water but unfortunately, I couldn't save her. I flew to the nearest ship in the area, the Carpathian, but it was too late when it finally arrived on scene to save many."

He sighed. "A catastrophe like the Titanic is a reminder, even angels have limited power. Heart heavy with sadness, I said, "I survived such a tragic event only to die of the Spanish flu six years later."

"Some you win, others you lose."

"Were there other times you intervened?"

"You were even younger another time, so I doubt you'd remember anything."

Curiosity piqued, I asked, "What happened?"

"When the Vikings invaded York and plundered your village. Your parents weren't home when the raiders attacked, but they killed your older brother and grandma before setting your house afire. I saw you trapped in the burning building and flew through the flames, then carried you to safety. You stopped crying the moment I wrapped my wings around you. When I saw your parents running toward their smouldering home, I set you on the path in front of them."

Puzzled, I raked through my past lives. I gasped as horrible memories flooded my mind "But the Vikings took me captive. Considering what happened you should have let me perish."

Gabe, fiddling with a flight feather on his wing, stared at the floor. "After what took place, I thought the same, but I couldn't stand by and watch you burn alive. And I shouldn't have let you see me before you turned eighteen, but I am a sucker for little kids. "

Stressed from dealing with Mum and overcome by memories, I told Gabe, "I think I'll try to rest while Mum is asleep."

"Good idea. Call if you need me," he said as he then vanished.

I stretched out on my bed and stared up at the ceiling.

Visions of another time begin flowing through my mind.

When my father learned the Vikings killed my brother and grandmother, he joined a group of men who ambushed the Norsemen as they returned to their ships. The Norseman hacked my father and his companions to death. The savage brutes, bloodied from battle, captured every woman in sight, including my mother who wouldn't let go of my hand. A bearded Viking dragged both my mother and me to a longboat.

In Denmark, a warrior made my mother his slave. Trying to keep me alive, she quietly consented to his demands. The English Crown retaliated by killing every Dane within their kingdom. When the news reached Denmark, crazed Viking warriors dragged English slaves from their huts and slaughtered them. Sobbing, I clung to my mother's headless body. I would have died also if not for Etta, the wife of a high ranking Norseman. She snatched me up and carried me to her house. Her own babies had died right after birth. She told her husband Arnvidr, that she intended to raise me as her own, insisting I would know only Norse language and tradition.

Snow topped mountains and lush forests surrounded our village. There was a farmer's market and a crystal clear lake nearby. With food, meat and water plentiful, our village thrived.

My adopted parents named me, Brynhild and I became a Norse child in every way, but one with an emotional scar festering in my soul. Others deemed I had a wild spark in my eyes. With black hair and dark brown eyes, I stood in sharp contrast to other children in our village. Most of them had light coloured hair and eyes. Many thought me fierce because when taunted, I threw myself at my tormentor and beat them until dragged off. My father nicknamed me, blakkr úlfr, which meant, Black Wolf. Obvious pride in my fighting spirit confirmed he wished me a boy. Much to my mother's dismay, my father instructed me in all forms of combat and taught me to hunt. He told me to respect the land and all wildlife. Whenever we killed an animal for food, he stressed the importance giving thanks to the Gods for blessing our hunt. Slowly, I realised my warrior father had a gentle side to his nature and we developed a close relationship.

As the eldest son of a powerful chieftain, my father was friends with King Sweyn Forkbeard. When Forkbeard died, the throne passed to his son, Canute. My father commanded Canute's armies and often had first choice of looted treasures. On one occasion, my father gave me a silver necklace with a large ruby pendant.

Etta my mother, tried hard to get me interested in sewing and cooking. I did make myself a lovely tunic out of cow hide and fashioned it with opal beads. But due to yet another scuffle with a village boy, I soon ruined it. My father suggested I only wore armour, as it may last longer. My mother gave him a scornful look.

Between the age of twelve and fourteen, most girls married. Having deemed men in my village unworthy, I refused all suitors. One persisted and I knocked him over the head with a jug, which made my father laugh hard and long.

One wintry day, a strange malaise overcame me and I sank into unconsciousness. I awoke screaming and fought anyone who tried to touch me. In the following days, my mother and father kept a close eye on me, but I spoke to no one. Part of my soul was missing. Gradually, things returned to normal.

One day while I hunted alone, Gabriel manifested standing on a felled oak tree. He did not speak, just stared at me. Anger filled me. I notched an arrow and drew back my bowstring.

"Shoot me if it makes you feel better," he said.

I sent my arrow. Fast and straight it went, the wind screaming through the red feathers on its shaft. Faster and faster, it sped toward my target, the oak next to my guardian angel. A loud thud resounded as my arrow sank into the tree. Tears streaking my cheeks, I lowered my bow and let it fall from my hands. I sank to my knees and sobbed.

Gabriel touched my shoulder. "I'm sorry."

"I know who you are and it's not your fault."

"Is there anything I can do to help?"

I jerked out of his reach. "Yes, leave me to my misery."

"Whatever you wish," he said, vanishing.

I lay on snow covered ground and sobbed until I had no tears left.

At supper that evening, my mother seemed preoccupied as she ladled venison stew into three wooden bowls. Aware of father glancing at me from time to time, I slowly spooned the meaty mixture into my mouth.

King Canute plans to conquer England," he said to my mother. "I'm to lead the first wave of raids."

Hearing the name England irritated the scar on my soul. Leaping upright from the wooden stool, I cried, "Let me come with you, father! I can fight as well, if not better than most of the men in the village."

He laughed. "Brynhild, war isn't for women. Your mother is getting older and she needs your help."

Longing to see my homeland, I grew angry. "But father—"

"I will hear no more or I will marry you off to old Eric!"

Chastised by the thought of submitting to old Eric, I sat down and stared at my bowl of stew. The idea of battle excited me, but something else vexed my mind.

That night, I came up with a plan but I'd need Gabriel's help. I called his name softly. He appeared instantly. I whispered my plan to him.

He looked at me as if I had lost my mind. "Denmark is a big country. He could be here?"

I shook my head. "I feel certain Adam isn't here because instinct is drawing me to England."

He nodded. "When you're prepared, I'll return."

Lying in bed under a warm bank of animal hides, I listened to a wolf howling in the distance. The eerie sound sent a chill of foreboding through me. I hoped I was making the right decision.

The days crawled by until the appointed time arrived. I watched as mother packed loaves of bread and other supplies for father's trip. She started humming a familiar song. Unexpected sadness washed over me and I hugged her.

She gave me a quick squeeze. "My child, is something troubling you?"

"Nothing at all; that song is the one you sung to me when I was little and I needed to feel your arms around me for a moment."

She smiled and patted my cheek. "I'm grateful the Gods blessed me with you. You didn't come from my loins but you're my daughter in every way. I couldn't love you more."

Taking her hand, I kissed the worn fingers that had shown me so much love. "And I couldn't ask for a better or kinder mother."

Tears filled my mother's eyes.

Father walked in to our longhouse and mother swiped at her eyes.

He pulled us both to him and held us tightly in his strong arms. Looking down at me, he said, "I trust you will take care of your mother?"

I nodded, but bitter bile boiled up in my mouth.

Two weeks after my father left for England, I summoned Gabriel.

"Are you sure about this?" he asked.

"I cannot rest until I know for sure."

"But you're a Viking at heart. Have you considered what may happen if your soul mate is loyal to the English throne?"

"My heart may be Viking but England is my homeland."

"I judge your plan a foolish one, but nevertheless, I shall do as you ask."

I donned the armour of a warrior, grabbed my sword and shield then plonked an iron helmet over my plaited hair. Gabriel lifted me into his arms and took flight.

When we arrived over the English coast, a throng of Viking longboats were rowing ashore.

A horde of armed Norsemen flooded ashore. Gabriel landed nearby. Cloaked in invisibility underneath Gabriel's wings, we moved closer to the Norse raiding party. As they marched past, I pushed Gabriel's wings aside and fell in behind them. I glanced back at Gabriel. He smiled and waved, but worry etched his face.

Nervousness hit full force when I noticed father led my column of warriors. He turned, glanced my way and stepped to the side. Certain he'd recognized me, I ducked my head and staring at the ground, marched past him. I breathed a sigh of relief when he rejoined warriors leading the charge.

Without a hint of warning, blade and axe wielding villagers from the town ahead burst from the bushes. I looked at the throng of Englishmen rushing toward me but couldn't sense the presence of my beloved. I suddenly realised how foolish my plan truly was. Once again, I'd allowed my heart to lead my head.

I didn't want to kill, but I needed to defend myself. Man after man rushed me. I tried to inflict non-life threatening injuries, but sadly knew I'd still be responsible for many deaths. Most would perish from wound infections. The body count on both sides mounted, and the ground became slick with blood. I looked for my father. He was battling two English soldiers. He mowed down one and whirled to face the other. Sunlight glinted off a blade. My heart lurched as I saw an English sword pierce his neck. I ran to his aid and screaming in rage, swung my blade and sliced off the head of the English foe. I dropped to my knees and cradled father's head. He tried to speak but only blood trickled from his mouth. Tears staining my cheeks, I raised him into a semi-upright position.

He gurgled, "Brynhild, I..." then his eyes closed forever.

Agonizing pain sank into my back. I looked up and saw an Englishman pulling his sword from my body. I felt blood soaking my back and I couldn't breathe. A strange buzzing filled my ears and everything became a slow motion blur. I begin to fall sideways, but someone caught me. Trying to maintain focus, I peered through the fog of blood loss and saw the face of my original mate. In disbelief for two reasons, I tried to take this all in, as it was him all along. I had not seen him in three years since he was manly away in Norway. I could not believe it as I tried to keep breathing and my eyes focused. Looking down at me, his light green eyes gave the impression of being sympathetic. As I stared into the eyes of my beloved, Lord Canute, I murmured, "Why?"

Lord Canute clutched me closer to him and pulled my helmet off. "Brynhild!"

I struggled to explain our true connection, but blood filling my mouth stole my voice as my life ebbed away.

~~ *Chapter Seventeen* ~~

The throbbing of my head jarred me back to present day reality. I grabbed my handbag from off the floor and found the painkillers I'd bought earlier at the store. Needing a glass of water, I headed downstairs. Mid-staircase, a chilling premonition shuddered through me. I retraced my steps and walked quickly to Mum and Dad's bedroom.

I turned the knob, quietly opened the door and whispered. "Mum, are you all right?" An empty bed with the covers tossed aside greeted me. Repeatedly calling her name, I looked in every room upstairs. I tamped down rising panic, legged it downstairs and checked the living room and kitchen; no sign of her.

I rushed out to Dad's work shed and swung open the door. I shouted over the noise of his sander, "Dad, where's Mum?"

He turned off the sander and removed his safety glasses. "What did you say, Jasmine?"

"I can't find Mum."

"Isn't she in the house?"

I shook my head.

We rushed to the house and re-checked each room, then looked up and down the street, but no sign of her. Racing back inside, Dad checked to see if Mum had taken her keys and purse. Both lay on a table by the sofa.

Dad grabbed his keys from the small table in the hallway. "Jasmine, I am going to take my car, she can't have gone far. You stay here, if you see or hear anything let me know?" He left before I could answer.

Time slowed to a crawl as I paced the living room floor. Unable to restrain my fears, I rushed to the window and looked for any sign of Mum or Dad's car. I saw our neighbour Thomas exit his front garden and run towards our house. I jerked the door open before he could ring the bell.

Struggling to catch his breath, he wheezed, "Quick, Jasmine, your Mum needs her first aid kit."

Shocked Mum was at the neighbour's, I mumbled, "What?"

"Tom was cleaning out the gutter and fell off the ladder. I warned him the ladder was too rickety, but he never listens to me."

"Oh god; is it bad?"

His eyes filled with tears. "She thinks he has a broken nose and a cracked rib."

I took Mum's medical bag from the coat stand and locked the door behind me.

Next door, Tom lay on a black leather sofa in obvious pain while Mum tried to stem the blood gushing from his nose.

"Quick, Jasmine, I need my bag."

Nosebleeds gave me the heebie jeebies, so I shoved the bag at her and backed away.

Mum took a sterile pouch from her medical bag. She peeled off the paper covering, removed two nasal sponges resembling mini-tampons and wedged them up Tom's nostrils. Maintaining pressure on Tom's gauze filled nose with one hand, she looked up at me. "Where's your father?"

"He went looking for you. It worried us when you disappeared and left your phone and purse at home."

She looked surprised. "What silly worriers you guys are. Where did you think I'd be?"

"Well, certainly not here. Why didn't you tell us where you were going?"

"For Pete's sake Jasmine, should I really have worried about telling you or your father, instead of rushing over here to help Tom?"

I shrugged my shoulders, "I guess not."

I flinched when Gabriel popped up beside me. He stared at Tom lying on the sofa with gauze up his nose. Gabe grinned. "Not one of Tom's best looks. He reminds me of a stuffed chicken."

Fighting an urge to kick Gabe in the shins, I gestured for him to leave. Noticing Mum frowning at me, I pretended to be swatting at a bug. Gabe finally got the hint and vanished.

Mum frowned at me, shook her head and sighed. "You're of no use here, Jasmine; go home and get hold of your father. Tell him we need to transport Tom to hospital and get his ribs X-rayed."

I raced home, grabbed the phone and called Dad. I warned him not to ask Mum why she didn't tell us before going next door, unless he wanted his head bitten off. The moment I hung up, Gabriel reappeared.

I glowered at him. "Mum already thinks I'm a sandwich short of a picnic. It doesn't help when she sees me shooing away invisible moths."

The grin he wore grew. "Sorry, couldn't help myself."

Worried about Tom, I spat, "Best leave before I fling another statue at your head."

Although looking a bit sheepish, he muttered, "But he did resemble a half-stuffed... "

I reached for Mum's most prized statue. Gabe popped like a balloon and disappeared.

Hours passed before Mum and Dad returned home. Mum reported Tom had a broken nose and two cracked ribs, but would recover in time. Relieved, I went up to my bedroom.

I logged onto MSN messenger and happily discovered Malcolm online too. We chatted about trivial things for a while, then tried to arrange a time for our movie date. Malcolm suggested Saturday, but I explained Mum insisted I stay home on the weekend. A distant cousin, Lucy, who we hadn't seen in years was coming over from Ireland. Lucy and her new husband were to stay with Aunt Grace for a few days. Malcolm graciously accepted my regret, but said he really missed me. I smiled to myself and replied I missed him also.

I looked forward to seeing Lucy, but when Saturday came thoughts of Malcolm filled my head. I wondered what he might be doing. Was he with another woman?

The bell ringing almost made me jump out of my skin. Mum rushed to the door. Chatty laughter drifted from the hallway then Mum escorted Lucy and her husband into the living room. Diminutive and plump with bright red hair, Lucy almost seemed an unsuitable match for the rugged Irishman beside her. Tall, muscular, with dark hair and piercing green eyes, Lucy's husband would make any woman's heart stutter.

With a big smile, Lucy rushed to hug me. "Jasmine; wow look at you! You've certainly grown since last I saw you."

I giggled, "Yeah that does have a tendency to happen."

Releasing me, she glanced around. "Didn't you have a dog when last I visited?" Laughter bubbled from my cousin. "I remember once, she became over-excited and nearly knocked me flying. Is she in the backyard?"

Awkward silence hovered and grew until it filled the room.

Poor dad seemed unable to find his voice. "Err...uh..."

Mum said what Dad could not. "A car knocked Bonnie down a few days ago and the vet couldn't save her."

Lucy blushed. "Oh dear, I'm so sorry."

"Its okay, Lucy, you didn't know," Dad muttered.

Attempting to lighten the mood, I said, "So this is your husband Mark?"

Lucy nodded happily and putting her arm around Mark, she introduced him to everyone. Dad and Mark shook hands.

I found Mark's thick Irish accent intriguing and commented how I'd longed to return to the Emerald Isle soon.

Dad frowned. "Jasmine, what are you talking about? We've never been to Ireland."

Mum raised her eyebrows. Jasmine, please don't tell me Malcolm Dice took you there and you failed to tell us."

"No... uh... what I meant, Mum, is that we have ancestors from there and it'd be great to see Ireland and trace our roots."

Mum was about to post a follow up remark when Lucy butted in. "You guys wouldn't believe what interesting family history I've discovered."

Everyone seemed interested, so Mum suggested we chat about it over dinner. Glad Mum's attention was off me, I agreed enthusiastically.

During dinner, we toasted the newlyweds and extended wishes for their happiness. While we enjoyed homemade lasagne, Lucy shared what she had found out regarding our genetic link to Ireland.

"As you know, Grandfather George was adopted, so it proved difficult but I tracked down some old family records," she told us, excitement dancing in her eyes. Well, it turns out that our great-great-grandmother was no other than Rachel Haynes!"

Shocked, I spewed the red wine I was drinking all over dad who sat opposite from me. Everyone stopped eating and stared at me, and then at poor dad who had wine trickling down his face. Mum, her eyes wide with horror, glared at me. Face heating, I bolted from my chair, apologised to Dad and ran from the room.

In my room, I closed the door and whispered Gabriel's name and he immediately appeared. Bewildered, I stared at him. "This is seriously messed up. Lucy just implied I'm my own great-great-grandmother. That can't be true, can it?"

Gabriel grinned.

Annoyed, I slapped his arm, hard. "This isn't funny, Gabriel, it's damn bloody freaky! I'm a blood relative to myself. Don't you find that somewhat disturbing?"

He laughed. "Not really. You've had many lives, so I don't find it surprising at all."

"You knew about this?"

He rolled his eyes.

"Wow; what was I thinking? Of course you bloody well knew! What don't you know?"

"I don't know what lottery numbers will win tonight. Otherwise I'd help a woman who recently lost her husband and can't afford food for her three kids."

I snorted. "Yeah, right, God doesn't approve of gambling and that includes playing the lotto."

He winked. "Obviously, and that's why I don't know the numbers."

I suddenly realised Gabe had drawn me off the original subject. "Don't try to distract me. My family is discussing a woman I know extremely well because I was once her! Not sure I can accept being my own ancestor."

"Eve, you need to look at the whole picture. As you and Adam were the mother and father of the human race, so everyone is your relative, including Rachel Haynes. Your family could have easily been having a conversation about Cleopatra and then you would be in the exact the same situation. Rachel Haynes, was just not as long ago as her."

I opened my mouth to speak but Gabriel abruptly vanished. In the same instant, my bedroom door swung open. Mum, wearing a frown, walked towards me. "Jasmine, are you alright?"

"Of course, Mum. Finding out Rachel Haynes is a relative surprised me, that is all. Strangely, she's the assignment I'm currently working on for my history course."

With guests waiting downstairs, Mum swallowed my lie. "I'd like to serve the brownie dessert I made before the hot chocolate sauce cools, so please come back down."

"I will, Mum, just need to check my makeup first."

Mum glared at me. "Really, Jasmine, I'd think you'd be more considerate. Your cousin Lucy doesn't visit us often."

"I will not be long, Mum... I promise."

After she had left, I checked my makeup in the mirror. Studying my reflection in the mirror, I thought about what Gabriel told me. Staring at my curly red hair, I knew fate had smacked me again, as when Rachel Haynes, I was a redhead then too. Clearly, that gene had passed down through many generations.

As Rachel, I was born in 1897 in Belfast, an era when men who ruled Ireland viewed women as insignificant. My father was a burly man, but he was actually a gentle giant. Unlike other rough edged Irishmen, my father had a passion for the piano and taught me to play. After the tragic death of my mother, my father and I became even closer. He often took me to the Giants Causeway, on the northeast coast and told to me to envisage the stones made by cooled lava as big piano keys. He instructed I should imagine the musical sound of each key and jump from one rock to another. I spent hours dancing over the rocks while magical music played in my head, increasing my soul's connection to music.

Although born with natural talent, it increased tenfold after I recovered from turning eighteen. My father decided I should turn professional and I agreed, but a professional female pianist was quite unheard of. To succeed, I knew a mighty struggle lay ahead, but father was a determined man who refused to accept no for an answer. How he convinced another pianist, Samuel Bracket, to hear me play I'll never know, but it was something I would be eternally grateful for.

When we arrived at the Empire Music concert hall, I begin trembling from a sudden attack of nerves. Father went to look for the maestro, leaving me alone in great hall. Feeling like a lump of coal in a silk purse, I stared at the intricately carved ceiling and ornate walls. A grand piano sat centre stage. Fascinated by the magnificent instrument, I skirted the orchestra pit and climbed stairs leading up to the stage. Light cast by a chandelier made the piano gleam like rich oil. A red velvet covered bench in front of the treasure beckoned. I gingerly sat on it and ran my finger over ivory keys polished to silk like perfection. Without hesitation, I surrendered to the magical moment and begin to play.

Lost in the harmonic cadence of the great classics, I don't know how much time passed before I played the last crescendo in Beethoven's Sonata in F minor. The last chord barely sounded when I sensed someone's presence. A man stood just off stage with full attention fixed on me. Wondering how long he'd been there, I bolted upright and turned to leave.

"No! Stay where you are," The man ordered.

Terrified and chastising myself for touching such a priceless piano, I froze in place.

With his cool blue eyes locked on mine, he slowly walked toward me. Every step he took made me more apprehensive. I'd broken every rule of socially accepted behaviour. My heart began to pound and taking a full breath became impossible.

In front of me, the man asked, "Who do we have here?"

Unable to meet his gaze, I stared at the floor. "I... I'm... uh...Rachel..."

"Does Rachel have a last name?" Amusement framed his words.

I managed to find enough breath to say, "Haynes... Rachel Haynes."

"So you're the ingénue who wanted to audition for me."

Oh lord, he was the pianist Dad persuaded to hear me play. I'd thrown away my one and only chance. With no other choice left, I gathered all my courage and met his gaze. A sudden feeling of goose bumps shivered over me. The maestro was my Adam; at least his soul was!

It seemed like a lifetime had passed before he spoke again. "I've never heard such pure perfection. You play right from your soul."

"Thank you." I placed a hand on my chest. My music wells up from deep within my heart."

"It shows, because each note captures the listener's very being. Can I persuade you to play another piece?"

I smiled and said, "My pleasure," And settled on the bench.

"Mind if I sit beside you?"

I said, "Not at all," but my fingers poised over the keyboard trembled as he did.

He smiled and took my hands. "Forget I'm here, just play from your heart."

I blushed and reluctantly removed my hands from his.

Gabriel appeared on stage and winked at me. Beaming

with pure happiness, I played a true heart song for my soul mate. Unlike in other lives, my one and only true love soon became his original self. Under his guidance, I became the first professional female pianist in Ireland, renowned for playing enchanting music.

Mum yelling Jasmine at the very top of her lungs jerked me from the past.

I ran downstairs and apologising for taking so long, sat back down at the table. Comforted by the luscious, hip fattening dessert Mum served, I did not find Lucy prattling on about Rachel Haynes and other dead relatives so shocking.

Dad insisted we played a few hands of cards. Lucy's husband, Mark proved an expert at Texas Hold'em. Strangely, despite countless lives, I still couldn't muster a convincing poker face and lost nearly every hand. The game finally broke up in the wee hours. After hugging both Lucy and Mark as they left, I bid Mum and Dad goodnight.

I undressed and tossed my clothes at the chair in a corner of my bedroom. Most landed on the floor. Too tired to care, I donned PJs and plopped down on my bed. I hardly closed my eyes when music echoed. Who the hell could be ringing my mobile at this ungodly hour? I sighed and fished the phone from my bag. I saw Malcolm's number flashing to my new ring tone. Hearing his sexy voice chased away any exhaustion I felt. I lay in bed and chatted with him, laughing when he said a group of teenagers mobbed him outside a shopping mall. The squealing mob chased him into one of shops, where he hid in a cleaner's cupboard until one of his personal assistants arrived and rescued him.

"That's the last time I go clothes shopping on my own. Think I put far too much faith in my disguise."

"To be honest, it really isn't the greatest one."

"Maybe I should buy a priest costume to match your nun

outfit?" He chuckled. "Now there's a saucy thought, plenty of fun could be had there."

I giggled. "Not so sure the Vatican would approve and I certainly don't want more photos of me splashed all over the tabloids."

"Don't worry, I can be very discreet. I'd keep those pictures only for my own enjoyment."

I laughed at his brashness.

After a brief silence, he said, "Is Tuesday night, say around 7:30 okay with you? There are two movies playing I haven't seen. One is Dark Wishes, which is something to do with the devil. I've read good reviews on the other one, Space Dream; it's a science fiction film. Either one is fine with me. So why don't you choose?"

In no mood to be reminded about the devil or anything along those lines, I said, "I have heard good things about the sci-fi one also."

"Okay, Space Dreams it is then."

He reminded me all about the after party and jokingly suggested I wear the bin liner. I informed him that I had something more intriguing in mind.

He made several outrageous guesses about my possible attire. I answered each speculation with teasing laughter. I ended the conversation by saying, as always he'd just have to wait and see.

~~ *Chapter Eighteen* ~~

On Tuesday, I decided on a black Chinese style dress with embroidered red and gold dragons. The mandarin collar flowed to an asymmetrical front held closed by floral frog buttons. A slit in the ankle length skirt permitted a brief glimpse of my leg when I moved. I slipped my feet into black heels with a satin bow on painted toes.

Tying my hair up in a low ponytail I judged my image in the mirror, I decided black was definitely my colour. A car horn beeped and I rushed to the window. Malcolm's car sat by the curb and he was striding toward the house. Hoping to abort an awkward situation, I grabbed my handbag and ran down the stairs.

Too late, Malcolm stood in the foyer with a bouquet of flowers in his hand. His hair was slightly dishevelled and he was sporting an impressive goatee since I'd last seen him.

Dad greeted Malcolm warmly and shook his hand. Much to my surprise, after kissing me on the cheek, Malcolm gave Mum the flowers. Mum, quite unimpressed, muttered polite but very cool appreciation and immediately laid the bouquet aside.

I told Mum and Dad, "See ya later," and Malcolm escorted

me to his car. He opened the passenger door, and careful not to wrinkle my dress, I slid onto the seat.

Once in the driver's seat, Malcolm turned to me. "I don't think I'll be able to concentrate on the movie now."

Oh no, Mum's reaction to his gift had spoiled everything. Dreading the answer, I forced, "Why?"

"Because, you're so gorgeous." He smiled.

I laughed. Admiring his marooncoloured silk shirt and black chinos, "You don't look so bad yourself."

He grinned, leaned over the handbrake and kissed me passionately on the lips. Instantly, a hot flash of desire threaded my body, but much too soon, he broke the connection.

He smiled, kissed me lightly, then started the car and floored the accelerator.

When we arrived at the cinema in London, we didn't go in the main entrance like everyone else. Instead, a male theatre employee guided us to a side door that led to a private screening room. The only attendees inside the dimly lit room, we had our choice of seats. Malcolm said the midsection offered the best viewing point. We had barely settled into our seats when the usher asked us what refreshments we'd like.

Malcolm told him, "Two cokes and a large tub of popcorn... no, wait." Turning to me, he said, "Sorry, Jasmine, how rude of me. Would you like something else?"

I smiled. "No; that's great and salted, please."

Malcolm relayed my request and the usher hurried to the door. The lights blinking signalled the movie was about to start. Malcolm put an arm around my shoulder and I leaned against him. Seconds later, darkness cloaked the room. Tilting my chin up, Malcolm covered my lips with his. The kiss deepened and I eagerly surrendered my mouth to his. His tongue sliding inside my mouth sent electric shards of wanton need coursing through me.

The theatre employee clearing his throat broke the spell. The tray in his hand contained our refreshments. Malcolm passed me a coke. As he reached for his drink, the usher lost control of the tray, spilling coke on Malcolm and sending popcorn flying.

Malcolm shouted, "What the hell," and jumped to his feet.

Shock and fear painted on his face, the man jerked a handkerchief from his pocket and dabbed at coke trickling down Malcolm's shirt. "I'm... I'm so very sorry, Sir." I can't apologise enough."

Malcolm snatched the handkerchief from the usher and tired to prevent drink from staining his slacks. Too late, dark rivulets covered his trouser legs. Glaring at the usher, Malcolm snarled, "You bumbling idiot!

The usher said, "I apologise, Sir," and brushed a popcorn kernel off Malcolm's shoulder. "Please send me the bill for your shirt."

Malcolm threw the cola stained handkerchief at the usher. "This shirt cost more than you make in a year!"

Malcolm looked ready to punch the guy, so I tried to defuse the situation. "It was an accident."

Malcolm's attention remained on the target of his anger. "I'm going to make damn sure your arse is fired. Hell, I might even press charges. Get out of my sight!"

The poor guy ran toward the door, tripping and nearly falling in his haste to escape.

Once again, I tried to calm Malcolm.

"No! I won't forget it, Jasmine. I'm sure the idiot deliberately dumped the drink on me. He's probably a crazed fanatic."

I suggested he visited the men's room before the stains set. Saying he intended to speak to the manager first, he stormed off.

I breathed a sigh of relief, sat down in my seat and stared up at the screen. I'd missed the opening of the film and couldn't understand the plot. Suddenly, I sensed someone's presence. I turned and said, "Malcolm, what did the manager..." Shock stole my voice.

A few rows down a pair of faceless red eyes were staring menacingly at me. Lucifer!

I jumped to my feet. "You gotta be kidding me."

Every light on the ceiling begin snapping off and on; then I felt a whoosh of cool air pass by me. I frantically tried to discern Lucifer's whereabouts. I saw the velvet curtains by the movie screen move and I heard a loud garbled cry. The lights abruptly returned to normal. In almost the same instant, I realised Gabriel now sat in the seat next to mine, sucking down my drink.

He grinned. "Sending Lucifer back to hell always makes me thirsty." He gathered a handful of scattered popcorn, and stuffed it in his mouth.

I glared at him.

Crunching popcorn, he mumbled, "Nothing's better than a spot of popcorn while watching a movie."

"You're unbelievably, but I'm glad you turned up." I brushed a stray hair strand off my face. "I'm guessing Lucifer is responsible for Malcolm being doused in coke and ice."

"Yep; but gotta admit it was amusing though; reminded me of the time when you christened me with a milkshake."

"You bloody well deserved it." I laughed. "You looked quite funny with it running down your face."

He chuckled. "I reeked of strawberry for days."

At the sound of the door opening, I glanced over my shoulder and realised Malcolm had returned. He looked unimpressed, wearing now borrowed trousers and an over large t shirt emblazoned with the cinema's logo. He did not look like a suave movie star, in fact he looked a bit clownish. I clamped a hand over my mouth, but a giggle still escaped.

Even Malcolm smiled. "The manager is going to have my clothes dry cleaned. They're going to restart the movie and bring us new refreshments. The manger also threw in a year's worth of tickets for two."

I sank into my seat. "What about the guy who spilled the drink?"

He said, "That's a complete mystery," and sat next to me."

"What do you mean by that?"

"Well, when I complained, the manager said the employee assigned to the private auditorium was late for his shift and had only just arrived. I insisted someone served us, so he asked me to describe the usher. Surprisingly, he informed me no one matching my description works here or ever has."

I glanced at Gabe and frowned. He smiled sheepishly and shrugged his shoulders.

"That is strange," I told Malcolm. "Most likely he was a fan who posed as an employee to ask for your autograph and lost his nerve?"

"Could be; I've ran across more than one wacko." Pulling me closer, he kissed me. His arms around me tightened and the kiss deepened. It took all my willpower to pull away. When he released me, I noticed something quite unexpected.

"Is that a tattoo?" I asked, pointing to a faint image beneath a sleeve of his shirt.

"Yeah; a few years ago I saw an illustration of a weird design displayed in a tattoo shop window. Curious, I went inside and asked what it meant. I'd never dreamt of ever having a tattoo until I saw this image," he told me, pulling up the sleeve of the t-shirt. "The tattooist claimed its Aztec and means united."

I gasped.

He frowned, "What's the matter, Jasmine, don't you like tattoos?"

"Uh... its... err... I just thought an actor wouldn't be permitted to have tattoos."

He grinned and pulled the sleeve down. "Oh, I see. The makeup artist covers it up when I'm working."

I managed to smile thinly and stood. "If you'll excuse me, I need to visit the ladies room."

"Okay; but hurry back. They should be restarting the film soon."

In the loo, I leaned against the wall and tried to regain control over my racing mind, to no avail. After seeing his tattoo my thoughts flashed back to the beginning of the eighteenth century.

Once again, I was a member of a native tribe. Called the Tapirape, we lived deep in the Brazilian rain forest. My name then was Latuie.

We resided in mud huts with leaf thatched roofs and honoured the old ways by worshiping the moon and the sun; content in the knowledge the stars contained the souls of our ancestors who protected us. Life was often hard, but isolated, unaware of other civilizations, we were happy. We helped each other and parents taught their children to respect nature and the jungle that provided us with food, shelter, clothing and medicine.

My father, Pacon, designed ritualistic symbols and applied them to the bodies of members of our tribe. Only men performed such special tasks, but both of my brothers died young. Desperate to keep the trade in our family, father taught me the art. He demonstrated how to extract dye from green Jenipapo fruit and mix it with sap from the sacred Copal tree and other pigments. I learned to sharpen an animal bone into an instrument used to cut patterns into the skin before applying the dye. By the age of thirteen, meticulous detailed tattoos covered my small frame. One was particular striking; a black anaconda snake that coiled up my arm and rested its head on my shoulder. A year later, my father died and I felt it a great honour when the tribe elders permitted me to tattoo them.

On the eve of my fifteenth birthday, the village elders paired me with Toyon, a slightly older man. Once united in a bonding ceremony, it was customary for husband and wife to have their partner's name tattooed on their arm. Toyan and I submitted to the custom, marking us as one until death. I loved my warrior husband and bore him two children, a boy and a girl.

One day, I was tattooing Toyon's father, Axon, when fireworks suddenly exploded in my brain. My bone instrument cut deep into his skin and I begin convulsing.

I awoke three days later in a blind rage. I threatened to kill anyone who came near me until tied down on my woven leaf bed. Shunned, my only visitor was an elderly woman who cared for my needs. Each day I begged my caretaker to fetch my husband but she refused.

A week later, Toyon and our children entered the hut. I held out my arms and my precious children rushed into them. Toyon pulled me into his arms, but my husband's reassurances didn't calm my troubled mind. Tears welled in my eyes watching the children playing with their pet Marmoset on the floor by my bed.

My eyes widened in horror when my father in law entered the room. Instead of a bird tattoo, a deep red gash marked Axon's thigh. I reluctantly met Axon's dark eyes. My husband's father shockingly was my original soul mate! After several tries, I managed to mumble, "I'll tattoo over the mark and stain it with brilliant colours."

"No you must still rest. My cut needs to heal until the next full moon."

After both men left to go hunting, I left the children with my mother and sought solace in the jungle. I expected Gabriel to manifest, but he did not.

Most men in our tribe took more than one wife and Axon had two. I often caught Axon studying me with a man's interest in his eyes, but I was married to his son. The tribe would shun us if we formed a relationship. I stared at the black snake tattooed on my arm. I think with my mind in turmoil, I imagined that the snake grew, deforming, with its mouth widened and baring two large fangs. Grabbing up a sharp stone, screaming I beat the evil image and then tried to scrape it off my arm.

A man's strong hand forcefully ripped the stone from my grasp. Crying, I beat Gabe's chest with my fists until all strength drained from me and I collapsed on the ground.

Gabriel shouted, "Breathe; you're hyperventilating, Eve, breathe."

My lungs refused the order, as the tree canopy above me, began spinning like a wobbly top. He picked me up and carried me to a nearby stream, where he splashed water on my face. When I calmed down, I realised that I'd at least managed to scrape the deceptive serpent's face off my arm.

Gabriel washed my battered arm and applied sap from the Croton lechleri tree to stop the bleeding and prevent infection. "I take it Axon is your original mate."

"Yes, my punishment continues." Tears threatened to over flow my eyes. "God wants to ensure I suffer as much as possible."

"No, Eve! It's pure coincidence."

I looked at him madly, till a sudden noise echoed and branches near us moved. Gabriel pushed me against a tree and assumed a protective stance in front of me. The foliage parted, revealing the object of my despair.

Axon had a large fish impaled on his hunting spear. "Latuie, what are you doing this far from the village?"

Gabe nudged me and I reluctantly started walking towards Axon.

Toyon emerged from foliage behind Axon. He rushed to my side and examined my battered limb "What is this?"

Unable to find my voice, my focus shifted from my husband to Axon who appeared more confused than I felt.

Toyan tugged me in the direction of our village. He ordered me to remain in our hut and ran to fetch my mother. Mother inspected the image father had painstakingly carved into my arm when I had become a woman. Our tribe believed the snake consumed evil and father told me the tattoo would always protect me.

"Why have you done this thing to yourself?" mother demanded.

Unable to explain, I threw myself on the bed and sobbed uncontrollably. Mother ordered Toyan to summon the shaman. The medicine man thought demons had seized possession of my soul during the seizure I'd suffered. He thought me attempting to remove the sacred image confirmed his judgement. The shaman told my mother to see I didn't leave my hut while he consulted with the elders.

Gabriel soon appeared. "The shaman has spread the rumour you were possessed while you were comatose. The elders will hold a meeting at the sacred circle in the jungle tonight to decide your fate. If the shaman gets his way, it won't be a pleasant one."

I whispered, "Toyan won't let them harm me."

"Don't be so certain, the Tapirapes are a superstitious lot," Gabe insisted.

I started to answer but mother frowned at me. "Who do you speak to, Latuie?"

"No one, mother, I speak to no one."

Gabe left to monitor the shaman's activity.

Assuming I'd been speaking to demons, mother kept a watchful eye on me through the day. When dusk fell, I pretended to be asleep.

Time stretched endlessly until I heard mother begin to snore. Now was my chance!

I inched past mother and peeked through the reed curtain covering the doorway. No guards stationed outside the hut. Careful not to cause the reeds to rattle, I drew the curtain aside and slipped outside. At the sound of approaching voices, I hid behind wicker baskets that held my tattoo utensils.

Two warriors walked within inches of my hiding place and stopped. After a quick glance around, they continued to the communal area. Amazed they hadn't seen me, I removed the stone I used to extract dye from the Jenipapa fruit from one of the baskets. Using all my strength, I threw the instrument into shrubbery near to where they stood talking. Startled, they both ran to investigate the noise. I seized the opportunity and ran into the jungle.

Minutes later, I stood hidden behind a tree near the meeting circle. The village elders and others seated around a bonfire, listening to the shaman. Suddenly, someone grabbed my arm. Relief flooded over me when I realised it was Gabriel.

We eavesdropped on the elder's conversation. The shaman told the elders that I was no longer myself. I was one of the walking dead, a Mantowa, which was the most feared demonic spirits. Questioned by the shaman, Toyon admitted I wasn't myself and that strangeness hid in my eyes. Tears began streaming down my face as I watched my husband's betrayal. After a brief debate, the elders decided my fate;

death.

Gabriel pulled me to him. "It's alright; I will take you somewhere safe."

I whispered, "I won't leave my children behind."

"But the world is far different than the life your children enjoy here."

"Please, Gabriel, the tribe may think they're cursed also and kill them."

Gabriel agreed and prepared to lift me into his arms. Suddenly, Axon leaped from a cluster of Awarra palms, wrapped an arm around my waist and clamped his hand over my mouth. Terrified, I tried to break free.

Axon's voice in my ear was a harsh whisper. "Shh... be quiet or they'll hear you."

I nodded and he released me. Looking into his eyes, I knew he was trustworthy. Clasping my hand, he pulled me deeper into the jungle. We ran until my lungs felt like they'd explode and I sank to my knees.

"Come," Axon pleaded, "it's not safe here."

I shook my head and gasped, "Can't go on."

After I caught my breath, he helped me climb a tree with a thick leafy canopy. Once safely settled in the crouch of two large branches, I asked, "Why are you helping me?"

"The spirits of our ancestors spoke to me from the stars. They said you were innocent and I must protect you whatever the cost."

I studied Axon. Did the soul of my original mate hidden inside Axon fuel his desire to protect me, or had he actually received a heavenly message? Betrayed by both the tribe and my husband, I longed for a comforting touch. I wanted to feel Axon's lips on mine, but uncertain of his reaction, I dared not express my love for him. Cool night air threaded the forest and I started to shiver. Axon scooted across the branch and put his arms around me. The warmth of his body against mine melted my restraint. Caressing his bare chest, I looked into his dark eye. His lips lightly brushed mine, and finding no resistance, he kissed me. I slid my arms around his neck and returned the kiss in full. He pressed me against the tree trunk and spread my legs. When he entered me, a feeling of completeness coursed through me. Gripping the tree branches, I eagerly met each of his thrusts until pleasure pulsated through the centre of my body. Axon's seed flowed into me. Lust satisfied, his eyes met mine and I saw full recognition flood his face. His eyes glazed over and losing his grip on the tree, he plummeted to the ground.

I screamed, scrambled down the tree, and ran to where he lay.

Heart filled with fear, I tried to confirm if he was alive or dead. A sudden blow to the back of my head blurred my vision and I slumped on top of Axon. Another blow to my head made the world descend into darkness.

Someone tapping my shoulder freed me from the past.

I jumped, and found myself back in the theatre bathroom with a woman asking if I was okay. I nodded.

The woman peered at me through narrowed eyes. "Are you sure?"

"Thank you, but no need for concern," I told her. "I felt a bit dizzy, but I'm fine now."

Wondering how long I'd been in the ladies room, I jerked the door open and hurried back to the screening room.

"Sorry, I took so long," I told Malcolm.

He smiled. "No problem, I'm used to waiting for women in the bathroom."

I rolled my eyes. Seconds after I took up my seat, the manager personally served us refreshments, and apologised again before leaving. The lights blinked off. The screen lit

209

up and a trump of music heralded the film's opening scene. Malcolm handed me a drink, then draped an arm around me. Leaning my head against his shoulder, I took a handful of popcorn from the container in his lap. Bad dialogue and a flawed plot made the movie downright awful. Malcolm and I soon lost interest.

Malcolm kissed me and trailed his mouth down to my neck, causing tingles of pleasure to slide down my spine. Placing a breathy kiss in the curve of my neck, his hand caressed my thigh. "What say we forget about the film and go back to my place?"

Wanton lust urged me to accept. But the ring tone in my bag threw cold water on desire. Silently chastising myself for not turning it off, I felt beneath my seat and retrieved my bag from the floor. I fished around inside it and found my mobile. "Hello."

Dad's voice sounded in my ear. "Jasmine, your Mum is in the hospital." A ragged sob sounded. "She tried to kill herself."

I nearly dropped the phone, suddenly feeling faint. "I'll be right there!"

"Please do hurry, sweetheart."

"I will, Dad." I hung up and threw the phone back in my bag.

In a panic I told Malcolm, "I'm sorry, but I need to go." I stood and rushed toward the door.

Malcolm caught up with me. "Jasmine, what's wrong?"

"My Mum is in the hospital."

"Oh no what happened?"

"I'm not really sure...uh...I think she fell."

Saying, "Let's go" and taking my trembling hand, he led me to the car.

~~ *Chapter Nineteen* ~~

Traffic in London at night was always horrendous and the hospital was at least two hour's away. Time slowed to a crawl and counting off the minutes, I nibbled on my fingernails. Where was Gabriel when I needed him? I knew Lucifer was behind Mum's attempted suicide. Lucifer would stop at nothing to prevent me and Malcolm from making a proper connection. Perhaps I should forget about Malcolm and allow him to enjoy a normal life.

The car sped up and Malcolm glanced at me. "We're clear of traffic now and I'll have you there in no time."

Our eyes locked for a second. In that instant, a rush of timeless love for him filled my heart and I felt ashamed. Whatever possessed me to consider abandoning my quest?

Resigned to the trip home, I closed my eyes and imagined how things might turn out. Would a fairytale romance happen in this life or would fate tear Malcolm and me apart? The more I thought, the deeper I sank into a confusing maze of darkness.

My mind drifted back to a time when hedge mazes dotted the landscapes of grand estates and elaborate ball gowns were all the rage.

In 1866, I was twenty year old, Adele Joie, Bessette. I lived in the chic, medieval town of Albi in France.

As a young girl, I spent many days enjoying the manicured gardens on my family's estate. I marvelled at the rainbow of flowers and roses and delighted in watching our male Indian Blue Peacocks perform their mating dance in the spring.

When lavender burst into bloom, surrounded by sweet perfume, I'd settle on my favourite bench on a hill. Watching a sea of purple blossoms ripple in the breeze evoked peace in my soul.

But over the last two years, no amount of roses, flowery perfume or peacocks soothed my troubled mind. An arranged marriage filled me with melancholy. I cared for my husband, I truly did. Isaac was a good man and I could find no fault in him. My parents had declared my betrothal to Isaac shortly after my birth. Only a week after Isaac and I were married, I fainted and awoke days later with full knowledge of my past lives. Gabriel offered words of wisdom, but most fell on deaf ears.

One morning after breakfast, Isaac left to go shooting fowl with my papa. I was strolling through the garden when the sound of someone crying distracted me from my own despair.

The sound of a voice asking, "Why oh why," drifted out a hedge maze.

I followed the sound through the turns and twists and found Isabella, our scullery maid on a bench by a fountain in the centre of the maze. Upon seeing me, she scrambled to her feet and ran into a maze hallway. The toe of her shoe caught on roots sticking out of the ground and she fell.

I offered my hand. "Are you okay?"

Her watery blue eyes uncertain, she cautiously placed her hand in mine. "Yes, Madame."

I helped her stand and inspected her ankle. Finding it sound, I led her back to the fountain's bench and sat beside her. "Pray tell; please release the burden you carry."

She shook her head.

I squeezed her hand, "It often helps to share a problem."

A tear slid down her cheek. "Nothing can help me now, Madame.

"Nonsense, there's always solution to every problem."

She sobbed, "You're too kind, Madame. But I've disgraced my family."

A slightly rounded belly revealed she carried the source of her misery inside.

"Ah, I understand, but if you'll permit me, I'm willing to help you."

"Madame would be the last person to understand what I've done."

"You're with child, yes?"

She nodded.

"Who is the father?"

Trembling, she stammered, "But...I...can't..." and jerking her hand from mine, she jumped to her feet.

I stood too. "Please name the father. I know far more than you suspect."

Tears streaming down her face, she knelt at my feet. "I tried so hard to resist but I love him dearly."

Annoyed, I ordered, "The name, girl!"

Sobbing hysterically, she kissed my feet and cried, "Tis Isaac, your husband, Madame."

Dumbstruck, I stared down at the blubbering girl. Unable to look at her one moment longer, I turned to walk away. Grabbing the hem of my dress, she sobbed, "Mercy, my lady; I beg you, please have mercy on this wicked girl!"

What a fool I'd been; caught up in my own problems, I

never dreamed my husband might crawl in bed with one of our servants.

I jerked my skirt free. "Rise, girl!"

Despite being clearly terrified, she did as I asked.

"Even though I care for Isaac, ours was an arranged marriage, and I do not love him the way a wife should. What's done is done. I shall speak to him and sort this thing out."

She fell to her knees and gazed up at me. "You're an angel from heaven, Madame; I cannot believe you to be no other."

I turned my back on the pitiful creature and skirt swaying, hurried to the maze's entrance.

In the suite of rooms I shared with Isaac, I paced the floor, thinking how best to broach the subject of his pregnant paramor. I stared at the bed where I'd surrendered my virginity to Isaac on our wedding night. Despite knowing now he wasn't my soul mate, the thought of Isaac pleasuring another cracked my composure. Sagging to the floor, I sobbed uncontrollably.

Gabriel appeared. "Is there anything I can do to help?"

I shook my head, "Not unless you have a magic wand and can make all of this go away."

"Wish I did."

"It's okay; other lives have been far worse." I swiped at my eyes.

Gabriel gently rubbed my shoulder. "I'm here if you need me."

I mumbled. "Thanks," and he vanished.

The rays of a setting sun filled my bedroom with watercolour hues. When I finally regained my composure, drying my eyes, I summoned my personal maid, Elise. She then helped me dress for dinner. I chose to wear a blue satin gown with a low neckline edged with beautiful white lace.

The door to the adjoining bedroom opened and Isaac entered my room. He'd changed out of his hunting clothes into dinner attire. I walked to my dressing table and picked up a perfume bottle. Dabbing fragrance behind my ear, I studied Isaac in the mirror. He looked handsome in a maroon waistcoat, a ruffled white shirt and tailored black trousers. Rich sunlight highlighted his brown hair and turned his eyes electric blue.

He slid his arms around my waist and kissed my neck. "Did you have a good day, my darling?"

I steeled myself and faced him. "I spent the afternoon in the garden where I chatted with a kitchen maid." I searched his eyes for some hint of guilt and found none. "And you; did you and papa enjoy your hunt?"

"A fine day of birding has left me quiet ravenous." Offering an arm, he smiled. "Shall we go down to dinner?"

He escorted me down the curved, mahogany staircase and into the sitting room where mama and papa waited. Isaac and papa discussed their day and Mama attempted to engage me in conversation. In no mood to discuss triviality, I answered her only when absolutely necessary. Relief flooded me when the butler announced dinner.

White candles in candelabras cast a golden aura over an oak table set with delicate china, etched crystal goblets and gold plated cutlery. Always the perfect gentleman, Isaac pulled out a chair for me. I thanked him and sank into the cushioned seat. Picking up the monogrammed napkin by my service, I laid it across my lap. The butler filled our wine glasses with Merlot, and then served the first course.

Not interested in food, I turned my attention to papa. "Isaac tells me you bagged several birds?"

Papa spooned onion soup into his mouth before saying, "That we did."

Isaac chuckled. "Fifteen pheasants between us."

The butler removed my untouched soup and served the second course. Papa and Isaac concentrated on devouring Coq au vin swimming in wine sauce, but mama kept glancing over at me. I forced down a few bites of meat and nibbled on a bread roll.

Mama inquired, "Are you well, Adele?"

"My appetite seems to have fled this evening."

Concern wrinkled her forehead. "Shall I send for a doctor?"

"Heavens no, mama; I have a simple headache."

"Are you sure nothing else troubles you?" The expectant look in her eyes revealed what lay underneath the inquiry. Both mama and papa were eager for me to produce a grandchild.

"Quite sure, mama," I replied, slowly standing. "But if you'll excuse me, I'll retire." Isaac stood. "I'll escort you upstairs."

I shook my head, "Nonsense, I'll be fine; finish your meal."

Closeted in my bedroom, I threw myself across the bed and released my tears. Once again, fate had turned my life upside down. I couldn't resolve the predicament between Isaac and myself by lying about and wailing. I dried my eyes and pulled the bell cord.

Elise arrived and helped me undress and put on my nightclothes. "Would Madame like me to brush her hair?"

"No thank you, Elise; I will attend to my hair."

"If you wish, Madame." She turned down the bed covers. "Does Madame require anything else?"

I waved her away. On the stool in front of my dressing table, I picked up a hairbrush with an ivory handle, part of a vanity set Isaac had purchased for me on our honeymoon trip to Spain. Running the brush through my long brown hair, I wondered if I should ignore Isaac's trysts with his mistress, most women did.

A knock sounded on the door and I answered, "Come in."

Isaac entered. "How's the headache?"

"It is much better, thank you."

"Splendid." Isaac removed his waistcoat and vest.

I laid the brush aside, gathered my thoughts, took a deep breath and stood. "Isaac, may I have a word with you?"

He tossed the vest and jacket on a chair and unbuttoned his trousers. "Of course my dear."

"I know about your discretion with the maid."

Colour drained fast from his face and he fastened up the waistband of his pants. He stared at me for the longest time. Aware he was testing the truthfulness of my declaration; I maintained my composure and stared back.

His facade crumpled and sitting in the chair, he stared at the floor. "I first met Isabella before we were married. In need of womanly comfort, I took her into my bed. Pressed to fulfill the contract arranged by our parents, I ended the affair. When your parents invited me to Chateau De Bessette, I discovered your mother had employed Isabella as a kitchen maid... and... we..."

"I don't need the sordid details! I understand ours was an arranged marriage, Isaac, but I've tried to be the wife you needed."

He rushed to my side and clasping my hands, kissed them. "My dear, Adele, no flaw of yours led to my infidelity. You have been a perfect wife. It's my failing not yours."

His pleading eyes tore at my resolve to protect my family's name, but revealing the truth might destroy any chance of finding my original soul mate. I applied a half lie. "I do care deeply for you, Isaac, but my heart too belonged to another before we were wed and like you, I felt compelled to honour my parent's wishes."

He released my hands and stepping back, stared at me in disbelief. "Who is this man?"

"His name doesn't matter because our time together has passed."

"Does he feel the same?"

I averted my eyes. "I no longer know his whereabouts."

"This is fine mess… and Isabella…"

I said what he could not. "Is pregnant with your child."

"What should I do?"

Unexpected anger filled me. "You have done quite enough! I will not sacrifice the honour of my family to your lust for a scullery maid. We shall keep up the charade in public, but I will no longer indulge you in bed."

"But…"

"Good night, Isaac."

He collected his clothing and opened the door to the adjoining bedroom. Pausing, he looked back at me. "Adele?"

"Please, Isaac, leave me be!"

I adopted false happiness around others, but the knowledge Isaac continued to visit his paramor tortured my mind. I feared papa and mama might discover Isaac's indiscretion. As time passed, Isabella's condition became obvious and rumours were adrift. Facing social and financial ruin, Isaac urged Isabella to be patient and lay hints a villager had taken advantage of her. I breathed a sigh of relief when papa accepted the story.

One warm summer evening, feeling trapped in a house filled with deceit, I sought peace in the garden. A loud commotion sounded. Gathering up my dress skirt, I hurried toward the sounds. Isaac stood near a lake with a dripping wet, unconscious Isabella lying in his arms. My first thought almost shattered my mind. Had Isaac drowned his inconvenience? Then I noticed Isaac's clothing was also wet. He laid Isabella on the ground and tried to breathe life into her, but it was too late. Isabella and her unborn child were dead. Clutching Isabella to his chest, a great scream of anguish tore from Isaac.

Everyone in the house came running. Papa urged Isaac to let the servants tend to Isabella, but he refused to release her. He slowly stood and lifted Isabella into his arms. He stared at me for the longest moment and then carried his dead lover to the house.

Papa thought it a tragic accident, but Isaac insisted Isabella, unable to swim, avoided the lake. When pressed to contact the local gendarme, papa declared that having shamed her family Isabella must have killed herself. Isaac flew into a rage and alleged Isabella was murdered. Papa scoffed the idea. Isaac argued that papa had uncovered their plan to run away together and orchestrated Isabella's demise. Papa shouted at Isaac, saying his charge was absurd and how dare he make such an accusation.

Isaac broke down. When I tried to comfort him, papa grabbed my arm and restrained me. Face hard with anger, papa told Isaac he was no longer welcome at Chateau De Bessette.

Defeated, Isaac quietly arranged for Isabella's burial and packed his belongings. He left immediately after the graveside service for Isabella.

With the truth out, I become a social outcast. Falling into despair, I remained in my bedroom for two weeks. One morning mama insisted I come down for breakfast. Minutes after I took my seat at the table, the butler gave papa an envelope. Papa read the enclosed message then passed the note to me. I scanned the page and gasped. A villager had found Isaac hanged from a rafter in a barn. Uncontrolled sobs shook my body.

Papa spat, "Stop that wailing, Adele; it's a blessing! Isaac did the only honourable thing. His death removes the stain on our family and frees you to marry someone more suitable one day."

I screamed at him, "How can you be so cold hearted? Two people are dead and all you're concerned about is our good name." I ran up to my room; a room I once shared with Isaac.

Days passed and Gabe tried to keep my spirits up, but nothing broke my melancholy. I gave up all hope of ever finding true happiness again. Summer faded and fall turned into winter. One night snow began to fall, draping a blanket of white over the garden. Unable to sleep, I watched the sunrise; its light made the snow glitter like billions of diamonds. I put on a fur-trimmed cloak and pulled its hood over my hair. Careful not to wake the household, I slipped out of the house.

In the garden, I inspected the delicate beauty of a frosted spider web and admired the perfection of a snow dusted pinecone. The pristine beauty of the landscape reminded me of the Garden of Eden, and my connection to God. In the first garden, an amazing peace radiated from it and there was no pain, suffering or sadness, only utter joy. Shimmering, sapphire coloured water, flowed from magnificent waterfalls, surrounded by beautiful flowers of every conceivable colour. Nothing ever withered or died and unicorns and magical beasts roamed the land without fear. How I longed to feel that serenity again. Sometimes, I wondered if the garden ever truly existed, or if in fact it was just a figment of my tortured mind. I shut my eyes and tried to envisage the garden, but could only summon a faded image. Frustrated, I sighed. I could remember most lives in vivid detail. So why couldn't I visualise my original home; it was probably part of my punishment for allowing Lucifer in the guise of a snake to lead me astray. My sin forever tainted all of humankind, proving we didn't deserve God's unending blessings.

Once again, the reality of my sin washed over me, filling my eyes with bitter tears. The harsh cold seeped through my cloak. Shivering, I turned towards the house. Near the maze, I stopped and watched a small robin flitter from bush to bush, then perch on a snow covered branch. Listening to it trilling a sweet tune, I smiled and dried my eyes with the edge of my cloak.

Near the house, I saw a horse drawn carriage ramble down the road and stop near the front entrance. A tall man and two male companions stepped from the carriage. My heartbeat sped up and drawing a breath became difficult, telling me the soul of my original mate lay inside one of the strangers. I hastened my steps. Eyes fixed on the men I slipped on a patch of ice and crying out in pain, I fell, landing face down in the snow.

I pushed myself into a sitting position and gingerly touched my ankle. I heard the sound of boots crunching snow and saw the tall man in the carriage running to my aid. Much to my surprise, I realised he was Harry Wentworth, Duke of Oxford.

Concern filled his green eyes as he bent over me. The Englishman spoke in perfect French when he inquired, "Are you okay, Madame?"

"My ankle failed me."

The Duke glanced at my swollen ankle. "I see." Before I could lodge a protest, he lifted me up into his muscular arms and trailed by his two companions, he trudged to the house. I looked into his handsome face; it was perfect, like it had been carved from out of marbled stone. His disheveled, dark brown hair rested slightly above his shoulders. Wrapping my arms tighter around his neck; I near enough kissed his neck from taking in his wondrous scent.

The butler opened the door. He brushed past the butler, strode to the sitting room and placed me on a red-velvet settee.

The butler summoned mama and papa. They rushed downstairs. While the Duke explained what happened, mama removed my shoe and placed my foot on a cushion. At the sight of my ankle, she sent the downstairs maid for a vinegar compress. Papa thanked the Duke and his companions and then offered a brandy to warm them. The men readily accepted. The Duke smiled at me and bowed slightly before following his companions into papa's private salon.

I looked up at mama. "What has brought the Duke of Oxford here?"

"I haven't the faintest idea." She laid the compress across my ankle. "I don't pry into your papa's business."

She ordered a maid to fetch the physician.

More curious about the Duke than worried about my injury, I said, "Wonder where his wife is... maybe he isn't married?"

"Adele, you're still in mourning!

"But mama, if he isn't..."

"The Duke's private affairs are none of our business, and..." Her eyes clouded thoughtfully then cleared. "It would be an excellent match, but it's only been six months since Isaac died. What would people say?"

"Everyone knows Isaac broke his marriage vows. Surely you can't expect me to continue to mourn a man who betrayed me. "

She studied me for a moment then declared, "I will hear no more on this matter."

"Mama..."

"Adele, enough!"

Crossing both arms, I sulked into a pout.

She sighed. "But I shall invite the Duke to dine with us. Now, we must get you to bed."

I smiled sweetly. "Thank you, mama. Maybe the Duke will tell us about his experiences on behalf of the English throne."

She laughed then said, "Perhaps," and summoned the butler to carry me upstairs.

Mama followed us to my bedroom and fussed so much over me that I finally sent her away.

Gabriel appeared. I smiled at him.

He chuckled. "It's so nice to find you in a better mood. Is it because of the English Duke?"

I felt my cheeks heating. "Tell me, Gabe, do you know if the Duke is married or engaged?"

Gabe grinned. "He isn't."

My heart leaped with joy.

Gabe glanced at the door and went poof. The door opened and mama bustled into my bedroom followed by the doctor. He examined my ankle and determined it wasn't broken, just badly sprained. He bandaged it and gave me crutches.

Aided by my maid, Elise, I bathed and began dressing for dinner. She brushed my hair and highlighted my coiffure with pearl tipped hairpins. Clinging to a bedpost, I sucked in my breath and held it while she laced up my corset. I donned my most extravagant, gold brocade ball gown and Elise fastened the clasp of my favourite diamond necklace. A jewelled hand mirror confirmed I looked my very best. Elise summoned a footman who helped me manage the staircase. At the bottom, I insisted on making a proper entrance and took up my crutches. As I executed a turn into the sitting room, one crutch slipped on the marble floor and I lost my balance. Strong arms wrapping around my waist prevented a hard landing. I gazed up at the Duke. "Thank you."

He smiled. "My pleasure; I was coming down the stairs and saw you slip."

"I am most grateful for your assistance." I smiled back. He retrieved my fallen crutch and escorted me to the sitting room. It came as no surprise mama had invited several of her friends. At dinner, the table held a veritable feast. Halfway through dessert, the sound of sleet and snow hitting the windowpane sounded.

Mama looked at papa. "We mustn't send our guests back out in this weather."

Papa nodded. "Yes indeed; travel would be dangerous tonight. I insist the Duke, his companions and your friends spend the night at Chateau De Bessette."

"Most gracious of you, Sir," the Duke replied. "My men and I accept your kind offer."

While the gentlemen enjoyed an after dinner cigar in papa's salon, the ladies settled in the sitting room. When the men joined us, the butler served drinks. Clustered around roaring flames in the fireplace, we chatted the evening away.

When I announced my decision to retire, the Duke insisted on helping me manage the stairs. At my bedroom door, he said, "Goodnight, my lady, pleasant dreams and I hope your ankle is much improved by morning."

"You are most kind, my grace."

"Do call me Harry, please."

Face heating, I smiled.

He took my hand and placed a light kiss on it, then strode down the hallway.

In bed, I lay wrapped in happiness. My one true love and I were under the same roof. An unsettling thought made me bolt upright. What if he left and I never saw him again? I swung my legs out of bed and grabbed my crutches. Making sure no one was in the hallway; I hobbled to his room and lightly rapped on the door. Tortuous moments passed before it opened.

Upon seeing me, he grinned and drew me into the room and shut the door. He caressed my face and whispered, "Adele," then his mouth covered mine, setting my soul singing. Clinging to him, I met his passion with my own. He scooped up and carrying me across the room, eased me down on the bed. Lying beside me, he reclaimed my lips. Adrift on a reckless sea, I heeded passion's call and parted my lips. With a soft moan, he crushed me against him and invaded my mouth with his tongue.

He traced kisses to the sensitive spot on my neck, where my pulse throbbed wildly. Unbuttoning my gown, he kissed my nipples. Wanton desire threaded me and arching my back, I rubbed my pelvis against him.

He slowly slid my nightgown up and eagerly entered me. All control gone, I surrendered to the sensual waves washing over me. Digging my fingers into his back, I cried out in ecstasy as my body shuddered out of control. Encapsulated in the moment, I clasped him to me, savouring ebbing gratification. Passion faded into utter contentment and I snuggled against him.

Early next morning unable to quickly find my nightgown, I grabbed a sheet from our love nest. Wrapping it around my naked body, I absconded to my own room. Although not without Elise my maid noticing. Smiling to her, I tapped my finger on my lip. She smiled back, before quickly opening my door and closing it behind me. Back inside my bedroom I stood and stared out the large bay window into a garden. The snow looked to be almost five feet high now and still falling. I smiled to myself, knowing it was likely the Duke and his men would be stranded here for at least a few more days. At breakfast my thoughts were soon happily confirmed. Father was adamant that the Duke and his men remained here as our honoured guests until the weather improved. The Duke smiled at me, thanking father again for his generous hospitality.

For the next two days we spent every moment we possible could together.

Mama's eye brow rose on numerous occasions, when she noticed our obvious flirting.

Each night secretly I crept into his bed and into the loving arms of my true love.

One night he whispered in my ear, "You have captured my heart and I shall never be able to retrieve it. Having taken you, I'm left with little choice but to ask your papa for your hand."

I laughed. "I believe a gentleman should ask the lady first."

He propped on an elbow and captured my eyes with his. "Will the lady agree to become my wife?"

I laughed and threw my arms around him. "The lady most certainly does!"

We make love again and languished in bed until first light cracked the sky. Like an errant child, I hurriedly put on my discarded nightgown. After making sure the household still slept, Harry carried me back to my room and kissed me soundly before leaving.

After breakfast, Harry asked to have a private word with papa. In the sitting room, I ignored mama and her guest's tedious chatter, and kept glancing at the closed door to papa's salon. Several times, I heard raised voices. When my disastrous marriage to Isaac ended, papa had made it clear he viewed me as tainted goods and hardly spoke to me. What if he didn't permit Harry and me to marry? On the verge of invading papa's private chamber, I heard laughter. The door opened and both men walked into the sitting room. Papa, wearing a proud grin, announced my betrothal to the Duke of Oxford. Harry took my hand and we accepted congratulations from the assembled.

Over the next weeks, the household was abuzz with preparations for the wedding preparations. Mama reminded me I was marrying a Duke and insisted on ordering a cream coloured wedding gown, a diamond encrusted tiara and veil from Paris. Harry's family arrived from England, accompanied by a few other people of nobility.

The morning of the wedding, red roses, gypsophila and ivy decorated the stairway railing and every room. Gabriel, cloaked in invisibility, wearing a big grin joined other guests assembled in the banquet hall. Wearing the Paris gown tailored to show off my figure and clutching a mixed bouquet of white and red roses, I followed my attendants down the staircase. At the bottom, I took papa's arm and he escorted me to the hall where Harry waited. By Harry's side, I smiled up at him and eyes full of love, he returned the smile. He then abruptly went limp and fell on the floor. A great gasp rose from the assembled and people rushed to his aid. Papa sent for the doctor and then ordered Harry to be carried upstairs.

After examining Harry, the practitioner shook his head. "It's puzzling since I find no reason for his condition."

Mama reminded him I had suffered the same sort of affliction two years previous.

The doctor nodded. Yes, strange, I will contact a colleague and ask his opinion. Until then keep him warm and try to get fluid down him."

Refusing nourishment or to rest, I remained by Harry's bed and spooned droplets of water into his mouth. One night while holding his hand I succumbed to exhaustion. A touch woke me and jerking upright in the bedside chair, I found Harry now my Adam, staring at me. I threw myself into his open arms and joint laughter sounded. After another wedding with a fewer guests and our parents present, we married and travelled by boat to England, where we lived contently in a castle overlooking a river.

Malcolm shaking my shoulder startled me out of the past.

I vaguely heard him say, "Jasmine, are you okay?" He repeated his inquiry several times before I comprehended that I now sat in a car cruising down a highway. I looked at him. Sounding concerned, he told me, "I called you six or seven times; you appeared to be in a trance."

I mumbled, "Sorry, I must have dozed off or something."

Staring out the car window, I thought about a psychiatrist who once told me whenever I regressed into a previous life, I emerged with a form of post traumatic stress. In that particular life, fed up with my erratic and strange behaviour after I woke from the coma, my parents had me committed to a mental asylum. Daily analysis sessions with my psychiatrist invoked hellish side effects. I constantly shifted from one life to another. It amazed my doctor that I could recall accurate details from many time periods. The process exacted its toll and I suffered a complete psychotic break. Considering everything, I viewed it a miracle that I wasn't a raving lunatic in every lifetime. One of the reasons I was still grateful to God, was for this smallest of mercies.

Malcolm steered the car into the hospital parking lot. "You don't look well; I think I'll come in with you."

"I'm okay, really. I'll call you later." I leaned over and gave him a quick kiss and opened the car door.

"Well, if you insist." Concern filled his eyes. "Call if you need me and I'll come straight away."

I sighed, "I am so sorry Malcolm, as it's my fault our dates end badly."

He twisted a grin. "I'll give you a chance to make up for that very soon." He waved and gunned the accelerator. Watching him drive away, I then rushed inside the hospital.

At the reception desk, I asked for my Mum's ward. The lady checked her computer then frowned at me and said they didn't have a patient by that name. I replied there must be a mistake and asked her to look again, but she came back with the same results. Confused, I walked to the main entrance and exited through the sliding doors. Standing on the sidewalk, I searched through my bag and found my mobile. I dialled my home number and mum answered.

"Mum, where are you?" I said my voice sounding shocked.

She laughed. "I'm home, silly; didn't I just answer the phone?"

"Are you okay?"

"Of course darling. Why would you think otherwise?"

"Err... no reason, just being silly me, I guess." A startling thought popped into my head. "What about Dad; where is he?"

"Your father is sitting right here watching a nature program on grizzly bears. Jasmine, is there something wrong?"

"I had a sudden feeling something bad might've happened, that's all."

"Well we're fine. How was the movie? Was it any good?"

"Yeah; I'll be home soon, I will tell you more about it then."

"Okay, see you soon then, bye."

I hung up; suddenly realising I was stranded, without a way to get home. Kicking my brain into gear, I whispered the name of my personal taxi service.

Gabriel materialised in a flash.

Annoyed another date with Malcolm ended in disaster; I

crossed my arms and stared at him. "Let me guess; Lucifer bloody faked my Dad on the phone, just as he did Malcolm's Mum?"

Gabe shook his head, "Nope, it really was your father."

"What! I spoke to Mum and she said dad is at home watching the telly."

"It's okay; Lucifer only influenced your Dad to subconsciously make the call. We found out because Serenity, keeping watch over your mother, sensed Lucifer's presence. She checked on your father and found him in the work shed unknowingly making a call. She broke the connection and guided your father back to the house."

I frowned." You sure Dad is okay?"

"Serenity pushing Lucifer out of your father's head gave him a slight headache, but other than that, he's fine."

Relieved, I asked if I could get a lift home. He nodded and gathered me into his arms.

At home, I found Dad had fallen asleep in his chair and Mum was engrossed in her favourite show. The only thing amiss was Bonnie's absence who had always greeted me.

Mum glanced at me and asked, "Sweetheart, could you put the kettle on, please?" and then she focused on the TV screen again.

"Sure, Mum. You want Tea?"

She nodded.

Dad stirred and smiled when he saw me.

"Do you want a cup of tea too, Dad?"

Still half asleep he mumbled, "That'd be great, love."

I walked into the kitchen, picked up the kettle and filled it with cold water from the tap. I turned to grab mugs from the cupboard and bumped right into Gabriel.

"You should take on a human form more often," I said, trying to scoot past him to get milk from the fridge. "Then you wouldn't take up half of the flipping kitchen."

"But I feel so naked without my wings."

A weird thought landed in my brain and I smacked a hand against my forehead.

Gabriel looked amused. "You're wondering what I'd looked like naked, aren't you?"

Guilt flooded my face with warmth, but I insisted, "Definitely not," and grabbed two fair trade tea bags, placing them in each mug.

He chuckled, "It's an extremely bad idea. Without my outer casing I'm far too bright for human eyes."

I drizzled a dab of milk into the mugs and poured boiling water into each. Waiting for the tea to brew, I looked up smiling at Gabe. "Now we've established that interesting fact about angels, will you let me pass before the tea gets cold?"

He chuckled and stepped aside.

I carried the mugs to the living room and found dad had fallen back asleep, so I set his cup on a small table next to his chair.

I passed a cup to Mum. She said, "Cheers, darling," and took a sip of tea. "Jasmine, sit down and tell me about your date."

"Not much to tell, Mum," I said perching on the arm rest of her chair. "The film was okay but nothing special."

"I didn't mean the film, silly, I meant the company."

"Oh; I found the company quite agreeable."

Studying my face, she said, "Sounds like your relationship with Malcolm could be serious?"

"I hope so, Mum, because I do feel a strong connection to him."

"Your Dad and I have discussed inviting Malcolm over for dinner. Although, I will have no choice but to have to invite your aunt Grace, also."

"Hmm...Malcolm and Aunt Grace. What an interesting combo."

I thought for a moment then laughed. "Yeah, sounds like an idea. I think you'll really like Malcolm when you get to know him."

Remembering I needed to call Malcolm, I told her, "I think I'll turn in." I kissed her cheek. "Goodnight, Mum."

"Okay, honey." She replied finishing off her drink. "I have an early shift tomorrow so it won't be long before I hit the sack too."

I walked over to Dad, who was still out for the count, kissed his forehead and whispered, "Night, Dad." I then hurried up to my room.

I dialled Malcolm's number, but no answer. I tried again. It rang and rang; still no luck Maybe he was already asleep. I started to undress, but instinct urged me to try him again. I let the phone ring him a dozen or more times again. Nothing. A premonition crawled down my spine and I made a decision.

~~ *Chapter Twenty* ~~

I thought about my relationship with Malcolm while driving to his place. Things hadn't gone as expected, but given more time, I believed he'd fall in love with me and remember our mutual past. He simply must! I couldn't endure this lifetime, if another woman captured his heart. Nevertheless, I knew Lucifer would use all his power to prevent us from reuniting. By the time I arrived at his condominium, butterflies were dancing a wild tango in my stomach.

The doorman recognised me, nodded and opened the door. I showed the security guard the key card Malcolm gave me in France. A broad smile spread across his coffee coloured face and he winked. "Have a good night, miss."

I smiled back, got into the lift and the doors slid close. The short ride up to Malcolm's penthouse seemed to take forever, causing me to tap the toe of my red stilettos against the floor impatiently. Worried Malcolm was growing tired of interrupted dates, I'd decided to throw caution aside and surrender to him. Except for the necklace he gave me in Paris, I wore nothing underneath my black trench coat.

The lift finally arrived at my destination. I hurried to Malcolm's door; my hands slightly shaking from nerves as

I swiped the card through the slot. Wanting to surprise him, I hoped he hadn't heard the lock click open. I walked inside and quietly closed the door. Aware at one in the morning, that Malcolm would most likely be asleep, I walked up the stairs. Unsure which room was the master bedroom; I headed to the nearest one. As I reached for the knob, someone on the other side opened the door. A buck naked, busty blonde woman walked out, leaving the door ajar.

She stopped giggling and looking quite surprised, said, "Oh, who are you? I thought it was to be only the three of us tonight."

Feeling as if my heart had stopped beating, I pushed past her and shoved the door open. I gasped. Malcolm was screwing another Barbie doll on a king size bed. The doorknob banging against the wall announced my presence. Malcolm glanced over this shoulder and frantically pushed the girl away. He bounded out of bed and began looking on the floor for his underwear.

Face red and struggling to put on his boxers, he cried, "Jasmine, I..."

Glaring at him, feeling as if my green eyes were burning a hole in his soul, I crossed the room and slapped him with all the strength of my anger. With the print of my hand blooming on his face, he stared at me in disbelief. I swiftly turned and rushed out of the bedroom, flying down the iron stairs and out the door.

He caught up with me at the lift. Grabbing my arm, he said, "I know this looks bad but..."

"Don't bloody touch me!" I jerked my arm free and entered the lift.

He used a hand to stop the door from closing. "Jasmine baby, please! It was just a bit of harmless fun, nothing more."

Quickly taking off a shoe, I used it to smack his hand.

He yelped and jerked his hand back. I punched the down button and the lift door slid closed, closing my quest to make Malcolm remember our shared past.

I nearly bowled the doorman over in my haste to escape the building. Running to the car lot, the sight of Malcolm having sex with that woman replayed over and over in my head. Feeling nauseous and dizzy, I tried to erase the horrendous image from my mind and failed. Ripping off the necklace he gave me, I cast it on the ground. Unreleased tears distorted my sight as I struggled to unlock my car.

Gabriel appeared. Taking the key ring from my hand, he unlocked the door.

I slid onto the driver's seat and slammed the door shut.

Gabe morphed into human form and got into the passenger side. "I know this is a big step backwards, but—"

"Don't you dare tell me everything will be fine!"

Chest hurting, bottom lip quivering, I snatched the keys from his hand and tried to start the car. Vision blurred by gathering moisture, I couldn't find the bloody ignition slot.

Gabe pulling me into his arms broke a dam of unreleased emotions and a tidal wave of sadness washed from my eyes. Clinging to him, I sobbed, "Malcolm never cared for me and I don't want him to... not anymore. How could he do this to me, especially when he didn't even know if my Mum was okay?"

I clamped a hand over my mouth trying to stem my grief and anger, but it continued to pour out. "I know the soul of my one true love lies inside Malcolm, but I can't penetrate his defences. Lucifer has done so much damage, making Malcolm numb to his real self."

Gabriel patted my shoulder. "I can only imagine your anguish, but don't give up on him yet. You need to have more confidence in yourself and faith in God."

I screeched, "How can you say that? God is the reason for my agony! He cares about me just as much as that black hearted rogue Malcolm."

Gabe lifted my chin and looked into my eyes. "You know full well that mankind is easily corrupted. For some reason Lucifer has ramped up his game in this lifetime but that doesn't mean he can't be defeated."

Anger contorted my face. "You're a fool but I'm not! I won't continue to pursue a man who's incapable of love and worships only himself."

Gabriel's eyes clouded with thought. After a moment, he nodded. "Like all humans, Malcolm has weakness in his soul, but I know a spark of love for you burns inside his heart. You always expect far too much too soon."

I shrugged my shoulders. "I've run out of options. The only comfort is that I didn't sleep with the conceited arse, because obviously that means nothing to him. I refuse to be another one of his many conquests listed in some little black book."

"Sadly, some people have difficulty distinguishing the difference between lust and love, but eventually they learn better."

I cursed under my breath. "Aren't you the self righteous one!"

He sighed. "The beautiful, headstrong woman I've known across many lifetimes would never give up so easily."

"Well that woman is weary and fed up with life. All I want is to go home and rest." Gabriel got out of the car and rounded the front. "Move over, I'll drive. In your state of mind you're likely to have a crash and kill yourself, or someone else."

I shifted into the passenger seat. On the journey home, I stared out the window, trying not to think about Malcolm, but a graphic image filled my mind.

Gabe switched on the car stereo. The sound of 'Nothing Compares to You' by the crossover group All Angels, filled the car. The song added to my sadness and fresh tears wet my cheeks. Gabriel frantically tried to find another tune, but the song strangely kept starting over. Frustrated, he thumped the stereo hard, breaking it.

At the house, I let myself in and careful not to wake my parents, crept up to my room. Sobbing, and crazy with anger at Malcolm, I grabbed the photo of us painted in Paris off the wall, and tore it from the frame. With my bare hands, I tried to rip it to shreds. Realizing it was too tough, I grabbed a pair of scissors from out a stationary pot on my windowsill. Cutting it up into pieces I stared at jagged strips of canvas littering the floor. Suddenly I regretted destroying such a beautiful painting. I dropped to my knees and attempted to reassemble the picture. Realising how foolish it was, I became even more upset.

Gabe appeared. "If knocking him about would help, I'd do it. However, as I said earlier, I see something deep within Malcolm's eyes and with a bit more work his true feelings for you will surface."

I snorted. "They just did."

"Jasmine! Please trust my judgement."

I glared up at him. "That hasn't got me very far in this life, or any other."

Gabe took my hand. "One more time, please."

Dedication to me shining in my guardian angel's eyes broke the back of my anger. Sniffling, I nodded. "I'll give it another try but after that I'm done. Do you hear me?"

"Loud and clear," he replied, hugging me to him.

After he left, I gathered up scraps of the painting and tossed them in the waste bin next to my nightstand. Noticing my mobile flashing, I picked it up and found numerous text messages from Malcolm. Hurt and shock still too raw and painful, I shoved the phone in a drawer. I undressed and went to bed, where I tossed and turned until finally falling asleep.

A rustling sound woke me less than an hour later. Rubbing my puffy eyes, I stared into murky darkness filling the room. Moonlight streaming through the window highlighted a metallic object on the nightstand. The necklace Malcolm had given me.

I whispered, "Gabriel?"

"I'm here."

I picked up the necklace, my hand shaking. "Thanks for retrieving it for me."

Sounding relieved I wasn't mad at him, he said, "You're most welcome."

A sound reverberated from the nightstand. I opened the drawer and removed my phone. It was yet another text, from Malcolm.

Please forgive me, Jasmine, I'm a terrible fool and plan to seek professional help. I certainly don't deserve it but please give me one more chance, please!

Even though I knew Lucifer was probably messing with Malcolm's head, I decided not to answer. I wanted Malcolm to respect me, to realise I wasn't some groupie who would come running whenever he jerked on my chain.

The next morning I couldn't resist checking my phone. With nothing new, I logged on to my laptop. Opening up my email account, I found a message from Malcolm in the inbox.

Jasmine, I'm a weak minded imbecile. Since you didn't answer any of my texts I've probably used up all of my nine lives with you, so I see little point in begging for your forgiveness, but I feel compelled to give it a go. I realise that saying I'm sorry won't suffice in this terrible situation.

You're unlike anyone I've ever met and I truly would like to redeem myself. Please give me one more chance. I promise you won't regret it. I hope to hear from you soon. Much love, Malcolm x

My heart urged me to believe him, but what if Lucifer wasn't behind the way Malcolm acted? What if three ways with women was just part of Malcolm's character and movie star lifestyle? Mulling over it, I decided to honour my pledge to Gabe. I'd try once again, but at the first sign Malcolm was toying with me, it was over. My heart couldn't take much more.

Another surprise visit might uncover the truth. The after party in London for Malcolm's film, Rough Diamonds, would provide the perfect opportunity.

~~ *Chapter Twenty One* ~~

Over the next week, Malcolm's betrayal played in my head like a repeating movie. I'd resisted answering his text. Instead I let him stew, hopefully in regret. After all, I had the needed pass to the after party in my purse, the invitation he gave me. Although I had contemplated ripping it to shreds on several occasions, but felt compelled to keep my word to Gabriel.

One evening Mum worked a late shift and Dad who had a bad cold, went to bed early. Bored and lonely, I strolled out into the back garden and sat down in a deck chair.

A crescent moon and twinkling diamonds filled the clear night sky. When I was small, Dad and I often sat outside on warm summer nights and star gazed. He taught me to recognise the different planets and constellations. A star cut a bright path across the dark blue canopy overhead. Dad told me to always wish upon a falling and never tell anyone my wish or else it wouldn't come true. Another streak flashed. Closing my eyes, I wished this would be my last lifetime. I couldn't go through this anymore. Trapped by my thoughts I gazed up at the sky.

A rustling sound broke the stillness. From the corner of my eye, I saw something dart towards Dad's work shed. I walked over there and saw yellow eyes peeking at me from behind a large terracotta flowerpot. I scooped up the kitty and petted the fluff ball. "Good thing Dad is asleep or you'd be sopping wet for prowling around in our garden." I cradled it in my arms and walked through the gate that connected our yard with the adjoining one. I saw Thomas standing at the kitchen sink near the window, doing the dishes. I knocked on the windowpane, giggling when he gasped jumping away from the sink.

Seeing me, he rushed to the back door, jerked it open and screeched, "Jasmine, you nearly scared me half to death! What are you doing out there?"

I showed him the kitten. "I believe this cotton ball belongs to you."

Tossing the dish sponge on the counter, he took the kitten and holding it up, stared into its eyes. "Marilyn, you naughty girl; what are you doing next door?" He kissed the cat and smiled at me. "Thanks, Jasmine, I hope Marilyn didn't do anything wicked in your Dad's prized flowers?" Puzzlement filled his eyes. "Come to think of it, I'm surprised she isn't wet. Where is your Dad?"

I rubbed the kitten gently behind the ears. "He has the flu or something so Marilyn got a free pass this time."

"Oh no; bless him. I'll give you a slice of carrot cake for him that I made to cheer up my poor Tom."

"Oh yeah, sorry, how is Tom?"

"Not too bad, his ribs still hurt but he is frantic about his nose."

I frowned "Oh; why's that?"

Thomas heaved a big sigh. "It doesn't look quite the same as before, and he's worried the difference will show in our wedding photos."

I stifled a giggle. "Bless him!"

"He wants to get a nose job but it's only two weeks left till our wedding. At one point the vain sod even wanted to postpone the ceremony." The strain of dealing with both Tom and wedding arrangements showed on his face. "Some men!"

I nodded. "Tell me about it; I'm nearly at the point of joining the church and becoming a nun."

"Get in here, girl." He took hold of my arm and dragged me inside the kitchen. "From the sound of it, we're long overdue for a good old chin wag."

I tried to protest but it was useless. Gabriel stood by the microwave stuffing a large chunk of carrot cake into his mouth.

Thomas said, "First, let me get your Dad some..." Looking at the butchered cake, he scratched his head. "That's strange, I could've sworn there was more a few moments ago."

I glared at Gabriel who grinned and wiped cake crumbs off his mouth.

Thomas shrugged his shoulders and removed a plastic container from a cabinet. "I hope one of the cats didn't get some. I left a plate of cooked meatballs out on the counter yesterday which was a big mistake." He placed the remaining cake inside the container and handed it to me.

"Thanks, Thomas; I'm sure Dad will love it."

He gestured to a black and white stool that matched the kitchen's retro style decor. "Please sit down cupcake."

I perched on the sixty's era stool and propped my elbows on the breakfast bar.

He filled the kettle with water and switched it on, then picked up two mugs off the draining board. "What's your poison, Jasmine, tea or coffee?"

"Coffee will be great. Thanks, Thomas."

He made our drinks and plonked a Twilight mug in front

of me. Sitting on the stool beside mine, he said, "Okay, first things first. Girlfriend, I've heard shocking things about you!"

Frowning and taking a sip, "From whom?"

"That nosey Irish broad at number six; you know, Mrs. Quinn. She claims you're going around with some guy in a chauffeured limo. But I know that busybody is economical with the truth; bless her white cotton socks. So tell me, Jasmine Brown, is there any truth to the rumour?"

Shocked I was the object of gossip; I twisted a lock of my hair and muttered, "Yes it's true."

Thomas' eyes widened. "What! But why in the heavens didn't you tell us?"

"Because it's complicated and I'm not sure of the outcome."

He grinned. "Matters of the heart are seldom ever simple."

Thinking you have no idea, I rolled my eyes.

"Girl, I can't believe you've been withholding such juicy information, especially from me! Now give; I want all the details."

A mantle of sadness settled over me. I stared into my cup. "To be honest, part of me wishes I'd never found him... I mean met him."

"I gather he's a womanising, cheating pig?"

My throat tightened up. I took another sip of my coffee, hoping it would help; it didn't. "Pretty much."

"My first boyfriend was a dickhead too. He cheated on me twice before I saw the light and dumped his arse. Get out Jas, before it's too late." Studying me, he shook his head. "Oh dear, you've already fallen for him."

I croaked, "I can't," The floodgates opened.

Thomas rushed to the counter and grabbed a box of tissues. He ripped out several and shoved them at me. "Oh, Jasmine darling, I'm so sorry the jerk hurt you."

I dabbed my eyes until I found some measure of composure. Not wanting to talk about Malcolm I changed the subject. "Where's Tom?"

"We had a little tiff and he's staying with his mum tonight."

I sniffed. "Oh no and here I am feeling sorry for myself."

He patted my hand and smiled. "Don't worry. We're just having a bit of time out." He half smiled. "Anyway, enlighten me, who's the heartbreaker?"

I sighed. "Malcolm Dice."

Thomas' mouth gaped open and he shook his head. "I don't think I heard right sweetie; what did you say?"

"Malcolm Dice."

His eyes narrowed. "Jasmine Brown! Are you kidding me? You don't mean the actual Malcolm Dice."

I nodded. "Yep, that's the one."

Thomas jumped to his feet and started to flap about like a crazed bird, chirping, "Oh my god, oh my god, oh my god!" Grabbing my hands, he implored, "How, what, where?"

"It's a long story. The main thing is I'm not sure of his true feelings. I believe they're hidden somewhere deep inside him." I frowned at Thomas. "Do you know what I mean?"

"I understand exactly. His screaming male hormones are drowning out what his heart is trying to tell him, right?"

I laughed. "Yeah, that's it in a nutshell."

Thomas started to say something but a ring tone drifted from my jeans. I stuck a hand in a pocket and removed my iPhone.

Thomas' eyes lit up like a blue neon light bulb and he started flapping again. "Is that him, is it, huh, is it?"

I glanced at the screen. "Sorry, it's only Mum."

Thomas' expectant face deflated.

I smiled and answered the phone. "Hey, Mum, what's

up?"

"Hi, sweetheart," she replied. "Saw your car outside when I got home and your handbag on the table, but no sign of you, so I was wondering where you were."

"I'm having coffee and a little chat with Thomas."

"Okay, are you coming home soon?"

"Yeah, be there in a minute."

I hung up and shoved the phone back in my pocket. I smiled at Thomas. "Sorry, I'd best be heading back home. I'll let you know how things with Malcolm go."

"You better, because I'm anxious to hear every sordid detail."

I kissed his cheek. "Thanks for listening to my pity party. Tell Tom not to worry; even with a broken nose he'll still be gorgeous in the wedding photos."

He escorted me to the door and patted my back. "Take care, Jasmine."

On the way home, I looked up at the starlit sky. Wishing on a hundred shooting stars that my punishment would end was useless. The odds were I'd win a multimillion pound lottery before that happened.

In the living room, I switched on the TV and flopped down in an armchair. I surfed through the channels and found nothing of interest. I finally settled on an old 'Friends' episode.

Mum walked down the stairs. "Hi, sweetheart. Your Dad is sound asleep." Looking at me slumped in the chair she said, "You okay?"

"Guess so."

"Come on, Jasmine, you can't fool me. What's troubling you?"

I sighed. "Nothing much, just wish my life was simpler. Being eighteen is tough. Sometimes I want to be a little girl again, innocent, with no worries."

She smiled and gave my shoulder a squeeze. "Happens to all of us, but there's nothing we can do about it." She pointed at the container on the coffee table. "What's that?"

"Thomas, sent Dad some homemade carrot cake to help him feel better."

"Well he's snoring away. What say we divide it into thirds and enjoy our share with a nice hot cuppa?"

"Had coffee next door, but I'll have a bite of cake." I smiled.

Gabriel popped up next to my chair.

Thinking about Gabe gobbling down carrot cake, I added, "No one can resist Thomas' cakes." Gabe grinned and winked at me.

Mum picked up the container and carried it to the kitchen.

Gabriel inquired, "How are you doing?"

I whispered, "Still having flashbacks of Malcolm banging that woman."

He nodded. "Remember your life back in the Ming Dynasty?"

"Yeah, why do you ask?"

He threw a glance towards the kitchen. "Tell you later. Your Mum is coming back."

Mum entered carrying a tray that held two dessert plates with carrot cake and her cup of tea. She placed it on the coffee table.

She handed me one plate. "Thought I heard you talking; were you on your phone?"

"Err... yeah." I lied. "I was talking with Susan."

"How is she doing? You guys planning a meet up?"

"She's coming over next week." I made a mental note to call Susan and arrange for her to visit. I would need her specialised talent to become a glamour queen anyway for the after party.

Mum sat down on the sofa and I joined her there. We ate cake and chatted about what the stars of 'Friends' were doing now. Saying it'd been a long day, she piled our empty plates on the tray and carried them to the kitchen. In a few minutes, she walked back into the living room and kissed me on the cheek. "Good night, honey, don't stay up too late."

I switched off the TV. "Think I'll turn in too."

In my room, I found Gabe reading 'Memnoch The Devil' by Anne Rice. Seeing me, he snapped the book closed and put it back on my bookshelf.

I sat on the bed and crossed my legs. "Why did you ask about the Ming Dynasty?"

"Not sure how you'll feel about this." He paused for a long moment. "The Chinese government has found the body of Jia Jiming."

I gasped and jumped to my feet. "Are you serious?"

"You know how museums intrigue me?" Wanting to smack him, I gave him one of my hurry up glares.

He got the message and spit it out, "I visited a Ming Dynasty exhibition at the British Museum. The dragon necklace you gave Jia is still around his neck."

Horrified, I croaked, "They have his body on display?"

"Afraid so; amazingly preserved in a glass case."

Anger conquered tears threatening my eyes. "That's awful; he deserves to be respected, not displayed as an object of curiosity."

Gabe placed a hand on my shoulder. "Shall I take you to see him?"

I nodded. Checking to see if the coast was clear, I found Mum and Dad both snoring in unison. The next minute Gabe and I were flying through the night. Damp air whistled past me, making me grateful Gabe insisted I wear a jacket.

When the museum came into view, I suddenly regretted my decision. Every instinct cried out, telling me to turn back, but my heart urged me forward.

~~ *Chapter Twenty Two* ~~

Gabe landed in an alley next to the museum. He told me to wait while he materialised inside the museum and found a way to turn off the surveillance cameras. After a few moments, the main door opened and Gabe motioned for me to join him. I ran to the door and cautiously stepped inside. The place was so huge you'd need a week to fully view all the exhibits. Gabe whispered, "Security guards are camped in the main control room. I couldn't turn off all of the alarms, so don't touch anything."

Apart from small lights in a couple of display cases, the museum was pitch black.

I nodded and squinting, peered into the darkness. A soft glow appeared around Gabriel.

I smiled. "Thanks for the light, angel torch."

"You're most welcome, Eve."

Gabriel lifted me into his arms. "Be faster if I take you to the Ming Dynasty section on the second floor."

He flew up marbled steps and lowered me to the floor.

The most renowned era in China, especially for its refined aesthetic and standards of perfection, the Ming dynasty exhibition swept me back through history. Exquisite works of arts painted on silk scrolls were on display. Delicate porcelain vases and plates decorated with hand painted landscapes, dragons, or birds filled many large display cases. Priceless Jewellery posed on black velvet pedestals were in smaller ones. Many magnificent statues, depicting the Ming emperor and other persons of nobility lined the walls. In the middle of the room, was a full size clay statue of a soldier on horseback guarding the many treasures.

A large clear box in a side room captured my attention. Trembling with rising trepidation, I slowly walked to the glass coffin. Even in death, Jia's face and black hair appeared well preserved and faded material covered some parts of his withered body. His body armour, helmet and engraved sword lay beside him. Vision blurred by tears, I turned to Gabriel. "Remove him immediately from the case, so we can give him a proper burial."

Gabe, sorrow carved on his face, shook his head. "I wish I could and do the same to all the other bodies in the museum. But as you know, I'm forbidden to interfere in these matters without prior permission."

I choked back rising sobs. "It's sacrilegious, to strip a great man of his dignity by having him gawked at as if he's just another historicall artefact."

Gabriel nodded and placed his hand on my shoulder trying to comfort me.

A jade pendant with a meticulously carved dragon hung around Jia's neck. Transfixed, I leaned over the case to get a closer look at the necklace. I felt my hand brush against the glass. A shrill sound sliced the air. Excited voices and the sound of running feet echoed.

Gabe cried, "The guards," and scooped me into his arms.

Cheeks wet with grief, I clung to my guardian angel as he flew me to safety.

At home, I found Mum and Dad still asleep. Concerned about my emotional state, Gabriel insisted on keeping me company.

Lying on my bed, I strolled through precious memories of Jia. A sudden thought made me gasp, "Oh no," and bolt upright.

Gabriel tensed. "What's wrong?"

"I forgot to read the plaque posted by Jia's glass coffin. I don't know where they found him or anything."

His voice soft, Gabe told me, "Archaeologist found his body three months ago, in a mountain cave in Beijing. Researchers believe an avalanche trapped Jia inside the cave and he froze to death. Deposits of arsenic in the cave walls helped to preserve his body. Some on the museum board wanted to remove the pendant and display it separately. The curator declared Jia wore the pendant in life and should continue to wear it in death. The board reluctantly agreed."

I grabbed a tissue from the box on my nightstand and dabbed at my eyes. "It's the least they could do for him."

Gabriel kissed my forehead and told me to rest.

Physically and emotional drained, I said a silent prayer memories didn't invade my sleep.

Even as I drifted into slumber, unwelcome images begin to form.

The Ming era was fraught with violence. As Kai-Ying Quan, I was locally renowned for wearing my black hair in a single braid that flowed all the way down my back, brushing the floor. Barely five feet tall, I possessed delicate beauty and a strong will; a combination many admirers found irresistible.

My family lived in a large clay and bamboo pagoda with four smaller houses surrounded by courtyards and beautiful gardens. All which were kept in meticulous condition by numerous servants. Colourful Koi filled several garden ponds. Sunlight on their shimmering scales made them appear like precious gems streaking through clear water. At night, delicately painted lanterns cast vivid colours across each courtyard.

Unlike peasant girls, I lived in the lap of indulgence. Only clothing woven from the finest silk covered my body and each garment bore an embroidered red dragon. The dragon medallion symbolized the Emperor viewed my family as special. Few ever gained such favour in his eyes. As a result my father Wei Quan, arranged a marriage for me when I was very young. My betrothed was Jia, the son of Wong Jiming, one of the Emperor's military advisors.

As children, Jia and I played together, often climbing a large Cherry tree in the centre of the main garden. I loved the springtime sweetness of the old tree's blossoms and even in present time, it was one of my favourite smells. Other times, Jia and I plunked pebbles in the ponds, terrorizing the carp. Sometimes Jia would wade into the water and pretend to be a black crowned heron, making me giggle until my belly hurt. To me Jia was almost like a sibling, I could never imagine in years to come we would be married.

Lack of respect and my rebellious nature displeased father to no end. Faced with another rebellion on my part, he'd curse under his breath and say I had disgraced our family, again.

A man of tradition, Wong Jiming expected Jia to follow the path he chose for him. Therefore, like most boys of noble birth, Jia left our providence to train under a master in the mountains before joining the emperor's army.

Unbeknownst to my family I fell in love with a servant named Kang Lee who took care of Koi fish in the garden ponds. Kang's dark smouldering eyes and seductive smile, made me swoon as if floating on air. One night after everyone was asleep I snuck out and met Kang. Taking my hand, he pulled me inside a Jasmine covered pagoda and kissed me. A servant saw us and summoned father. Vowing he'd return to me, Kang fled. I feared father's men would track him down and kill him. Anxious months followed but Kang evaded the searchers.

News Jia would soon return to seal our contract filled me with anger. I ran away but Father tracked me down within hours. I kicked, screamed and begged for release from marriage to a virtual stranger. Father would have none of it and ordered servants to drag me back to the house.

On the morning of our wedding, I saw Jia for the first time in years. He was taller and more muscular than I remembered. His dark hair now rested below his shoulders and an old battle scar kris crossed over his left cheek. Even though still handsome, his eyes did not make me go weak at the knees like Kang's did.

I cried throughout the ceremony and refused to submit to Jia on our wedding night. Although he was gentle and attentive, I still turned down his sexual overtures. Frustration in my husband's eyes increased with each passing day. My mother couldn't understand why I wasn't happy. She believed Kang had cast a magic spell on me. Having shamed him, father disowned me.

Torturous days turned to weeks without news from Kang Lee. I visited the holy temple daily and prayed he'd hurry back and rescue me.

Three months later, I heard rumours Kang had returned. Late one night, disguised as a peasant woman I went searching for him. A street vendor directed me to an abandoned hut on the outskirts of town. I hurried there and much to my delight found Kang standing by a lake.

Spying me, he cried out my name and I ran into his open arms.

I looked up into his eyes. "I thought you had abandoned me."

He caressed my face. "Not return for my lotus flower? You are the light in my soul. I might as well be dead if not with you."

His lips claimed mine and sinking down on the grass by moonlit water we sought shared pleasure.

Desire satiated, he cradled me in his arms. "I've found a magnificent house for us in the adjoining providence. We'll be happy there and have many beautiful children."

I smiled. "When can we leave? I can't bare being separated from you."

He kissed the palm of my hand. "Soon, my love, but we'll need money. It shames me to ask this, but your husband is wealthy and won't miss a few coins if you're careful."

The idea troubled me. If caught, my husband could drag me before the Emperor where I'd face execution, but I would do anything to be with Kang so I agreed to do as he requested.

"You should return home before you're missed," he told me.

I scrambled to my feet. "When will I see you again?"

"Meet me here tomorrow night and we'll plan our escape."

I dressed, gave Kang a quick kiss and hurried home.

The next night I gave my lover three Kai Yuan Bao coins I'd stolen. He kissed me and said we'd leave for our new home soon, but explained the trip would be costly. Happier than I'd ever been, I promised to get more money. After making love, we formulated our plan.

The appointed time arrived. Overjoyed, I packed essential clothing and a few cherished items. I retrieved the stolen money from its hiding place and clutching my belongings,

I slipped into the night. Seeing Kang waiting at the lake filled me with unspeakable joy. The sight of his companion stepping from the abandoned hut froze me in place. I stared at the young woman, her belly heavy with child.

Seizing Kang's arm, I implored, "My love, what's going on? Who is this woman?"

Laughter curled from Kang's lips and he grabbed the moneybag from my hand. "You stupid woman, I never cared for you! The only thing I loved was the money you could get for me. Now my wife and I can live in comfort."

I clung to him. "I don't believe you! You love me; I know you do. Please don't do this to me... to us. We belong together."

He answered my plea with the back of his hand. The blow sent me flying to the ground. Blood seeping from my mouth, I looked up at him. Cold indifference filled his eyes and he kicked me. Attempting to shut out the pain I closed my eyes, but another blow brought tears to them.

A strange whooshing sound filled the air. The scream of a woman echoed. Startled, I opened my eyes and saw Kang's head rolling across the grass. I watched in horror as Kang's body slumped to the ground. Jia stood by the headless body, his face angry clutching his bloody sword. Jia snatched the money purse from Kang's lifeless hand and thrust it at the pregnant woman. Terror written on her face, she took the bag and bowed low. Jia dismissed her and holding her swollen belly, she waddled fast down the road.

Jia walked to where I lay. "We shall never speak of this, but you will lie with me this night and bare my children like a good wife." I accepted his offered hand and he pulled me to my feet.

Unworthy of compassion and forgiveness, I nodded meekly and followed my husband home. I became the dutiful wife and a love for Jia blossomed in my heart. Like all men, Jia longed for a son and yet I did not conceive. I tried all manner of potions to increase the odds but a year passed without a single conception. Jia insisted it would happen in due time but I thought different. Clearly, a childless life was punishment for betraying my marriage. I deserved such a fate but Jia did not. Still, even without children, we were happy until an uprising led by a war chief, Li Zicheng, shook China.

The Emperor ordered his soldiers to defend Beijing against the coming attack. A revered warrior in the royal army, Jia answered the call to arms.

Pulling me close as he prepared to leave, Jia whispered in my ear. "Do not fear, little one, I shall return."

My eyes moist, I removed a small jade dragon necklace Jia had given me, and pressed the memento to his hand. "A good luck charm; I will mark the days until you put it around my neck again."

He nodded and kissed me. Enveloped in sadness I watched a white horse carry my husband into the distance.

The bodies of many fallen warriors were borne home, but no word of Jia. Some people suggested he must have deserted and fled. I knew he would never do such a cowardly thing. The realization he must be dead made me violently ill. Bouts of unrelenting nausea left me so weak that I became unconscious.

Three weeks after my eighteenth birthday, I awoke and noticed a strange fluttering in my abdomen. The village doctor confirmed what I suspected. I was pregnant. But that wasn't all I realised, I also painfully acknowledged my soul mate was its father!

Life without him proved hard. If not for the fact I carried our child, I think I would have taken my life. Tears streamed from my eyes as I held our son for the first time; a child who would never know his dad.

The loud alarm on my clock radio startled me and blearily I opened my eyes.

Free of the past, a shocking notion hit me. Jia certainly cared for me but he never suffered the coma of remembrance, not while we were together. What if Jia realised he truly loved me while in the cave, he would have become unconscious. That could be the reason he froze to death. But the idea love for me caused his death, was hard to bare. Only the knowledge that the soul of my original mate wasn't still in the mummified body, comforted my tortured mind.

Instead, his soul now resided in one Malcolm Dice.

I suddenly became aware Gabriel stood by my bed. "Have you been here all night?"

Concern etching his face, he nodded. "Perhaps I did the wrong thing taking you to see Jia, because you tossed and turned most of the night."

"I needed to pay my last respects, but it made me dream about my life with Jia. A reminder how flawed all humans are, especially me."

"What do you mean?"

"Look what I did back then. I foolishly betrayed my husband by having sex with Kang, a man who never loved me. Who am I to judge Malcolm so harshly?"

Gabe frowned. "For your own sake, remember self-centred people like Kang seldom live up to expectations."

A graphic picture of Malcolm in bed with two women flashed through my mind. "Don't worry; no man will ever take advantage of me again."

~~ *Chapter Twenty Three* ~~

Gabriel left, leaving me alone with my thoughts. I stared at the window, listening to raindrops crash against the glass. The tragic end to Jia's life made me understand why Adam never talked about his previous lives. They were too painful. He wanted to live in the present not dwell in the past. On the other hand, every detail of an endless time warp tortured my mind. Only fair since I got us exiled from the Garden of Eden.

Finally I dragged my sorry bones out of bed, shuffled downstairs and into the kitchen. After making myself a cup of black coffee, I looked in the cupboards for something to eat. Nothing stirred my fancy. Even though only 8.15 in the morning, I decided to make a batch of chocolate chip cookies. I turned on the oven to preheat and whipped up the mixture in a bowl. Unable to resist, I spooned some dough into my mouth before forming the cookies and placing them on a baking sheet. While they baked, I went to the living and turned on the TV. A news report about Malcolm's film, Rough Diamonds, flashed on the screen. An entertainment reporter managed to snag an interview with the man himself. Seeing him on the screen I tried to keep my emotions in check. I was going to switch the channel over, but felt constrained to watch and sat in an armchair. In the footage Malcolm talked about his role in the movie. His character was a righteous cop working with a partner on the take, which forced him to question his own ethics. How ironic! Malcolm's character possessed higher morals than he did. The ménage à trios at the hotel with two bimbos revealed Malcolm's true nature.

Suddenly a suffocating stench invaded my thoughts. Jumping to my feet, I legged it to the kitchen and jerked the oven door open. Smoke rich with rotten eggs, garlic, burnt cheese and bad fish rolled out. Fighting an urge to puke, I slammed the door shut. Too late, caustic smoke had filled the room. I used the tail of my pink bathrobe to cover my nose and mouth. The back door swung open. Gabriel!

Trying to breathe through thick terry cloth, I asked him, "What in heaven's name is that stench?"

"I sense Lucifer's presence. The odour of Hades clings to him sometimes."

The familiar jingle of Mum's charm bracelet announced she was on the way downstairs. I rushed to open every window but I was too late. Mum's scream echoed through the house.

She walked into the kitchen holding her nose. "Oh dear god, Jasmine, what has died?"

I whispered, "Gabriel, help. How do I explain this?"

He shrugged his shoulders and popped out of sight.

I gushed, "Don't panic, Mum. A failed attempt at making cheesy garlic bread created a bit of smoke."

"Garlic bread; sure you don't mean garbage bread? I've never smelled anything this bad in all my life."

I put on a fake smile and muttered, "Sorry, Mum."

She grabbed two cans of air freshener from a cupboard and went on a spraying frenzy.

Evidently awakened by her scream, Dad ambled down the staircase. Even with a bad head cold that adversely affected his sense of smell, he covered his mouth and nose. "Jasmine, we should sign you up for cooking classes. Your baking should be classified as a chemical weapon of nose destruction."

Having failed to disperse the odour, Mum pulled open the drawer containing a small stock of disposable masks she'd brought home during the swine flu epidemic. She gave Dad and me one and then donned a mask herself. I laughed to myself thinking what a funny sight we made wearing the face masks. My mood did an abrupt turn when mum put on oven mitts and walked to the oven. She opened the door and pulled out a tray filled with perfectly baked cookies.

Astonishment written on her face, she looked at me. "I thought you said it was garlic bread?"

"Err... I threw the garlic bread in the outside bin. I neglected to say I also made some cookies."

Dad toddled over, picked a cookie off the tray and took a small bite. I scrutinized his face and so did Mum. Instead of racing to the bin and spitting the cookie out, he smiled. "Forget the cooking lessons, these are yummy."

Mum shook her head and started transferring the cookies to a plate. "At least that awful smell has faded. Nevertheless, Jasmine, I don't want you to experiment in my kitchen, especially while your Dad and I are on holiday this weekend."

I smiled. "I promise not to cook anything while you're away."

Mum propped both hands on her hips and stared at me. "What a ridiculous statement. Do you plan to starve? I said no experimenting. Stick with things you know how to cook."

Dad chuckled. "That's my silly Jasmine."

I smiled at Dad and kissed him on the cheek. "Guess I've

done enough damage, best go upstairs and get dressed."

In my room, I heaved a sigh of relief and plopped down on the bed. Gabriel reappeared. "Lucifer seems to have gone but you can never be certain with him, so I rounded up a few angels to stand guard here."

"I don't feel right receiving such special treatment," I told him. "I'm sure other people need angels more than I do."

"Don't worry, there are many more angels than you realise. They far outnumber the living."

I smiled. "Oh... in that case, invite as many as you want; the more, the merrier."

Gabriel grinned and disappeared.

Nervous and jittery, I flinched at the slightest noise all day long, but nothing else unusual happened. Mum thought the odour had contaminated the drapes and sofa cushions, so she spent most the day cleaning them.

I attempted to clear my mind by listening to relaxing music. The strategy failed miserably. So I tried to organize things for Uni. I would start the MA History program at Cambridge in a few days. Not one of my old school chums planned to attend the university, so the idea made me quite nervous. With everything which had recently happened I could really do with a friendly face, so I was hoping that I wouldn't come across as a complete weirdo.

Even as I sorted through things I would need, thoughts of Malcolm rolled through my mind. Why hadn't he attempted to contact me? Gabriel was right. Self-centred people always failed to meet expectations.

I felt out of place on my first day at the Cambridge University. My classes were at King's College near the banks of the River Cam. I stared in amazement at the spectacular gothic architecture of the college built in the 1441. The emblematic chapel with its stained glass windows, wooden chancel screen and the world's largest fan vault was breathtaking. The mastery of design took my mind of fears of not being accepted my peers. As it turned out, I wasn't the only weird bird on campus. I ticked off days until Malcolm's after party, attending classes, but I couldn't focus on my studies.

My tutor Miss Bell, took me aside. "Jasmine, is everything okay? It appears you have lost interest in the course. You often seem miles away."

"I'm fine; just have a lot on my mind at the moment."

She placed a hand on my shoulder and looked into my eyes. "After seeing your previous grades, I predicted you'd be one of my star pupils. I'd hate for anything to interfere with you getting your Masters. Is there something I can help you with?"

I smiled and put false confidence in my voice. "Everything will be sorted by the end of the month and I'll be my old self again."

Miss Bell didn't look convinced. "I hope so."

I nodded. Clutching my work folder I hurried from the room. Lost in thought, I ran smack bang into my ex-boyfriend, Jack.

"Whoa," he said. "Where are you off to in such a hurry?"

Uncomfortable silence hung as I tried to find my voice. I'd forgotten he planned to attend Cambridge also. I finally managed, "Hi, Jack, how are you doing?"

"Not too bad."

Silence resumed. Avoiding eye contact, he ran his fingers through his brown hair. He did the same thing before asking me out for the first time. I never understood why a guy who could have his pick of girls was nervous around me. Cheeks heating, I leaped at the chance to date him. Things seemed simpler then, before the coma of rebirth turned my life on its ear.

The silence lengthened until he broke it. "Nice to see you again, Jasmine, take care."

"Yeah; you too, Jack." I lifted my hand to wave, but he turned and walked down the corridor. My heart sank. I never wanted to hurt Jack, but I didn't feel the same way about him after my coma. The list of people I'd hurt grew with each lifetime. If I ever make it to the afterlife, providing I went up and not down, I hoped to have a chance to apologise for the damage I'd done. Walking to my car, I said a prayer the pain I caused Jack and others wouldn't be for nothing.

At home, my phone spit out a ring tone. A text from Malcolm sent yesterday. Receiving delayed messages happened way too many times. Silently cursing my network, I read Malcolm's message.

Jasmine, I hope you are well. I thought it best to give it a few days before contacting you again. As you know, I'm not good at this kind of stuff. Although I know gifts don't impress you, I left something by your father's workshop. Now that you've had time to reconsider, I hope to hear from you, even if it's just to tell me to piss off. Love, Malcolm

Crying, "Bugger," I tossed the phone on my bed and raced downstairs. Low and behold, I found a package stuffed between the garden wall and the shed. I ripped off the yellow tissue paper and opened the package. I gasped. It held a jewellery box with a mother of pearl lid engraved with the image of a graceful Japanese cherry tree. I lifted the lid and a tiny Geisha figurine inside begin dancing to an enchanting tune. Smiling, I watched the perfectly detailed girl perform. I carried the beautiful gift up to my room and placed it on my nightstand.

Gabriel appeared. "Very nice. Let me guess; Malcolm?"

I nodded. "He's making it extremely hard for me not to

contact him before the premiere."

"Don't worry; outside of moping about, he's okay." He grinned. "A wise woman always makes a man woo her properly. It's all part of the fun."

I smiled and hugged him. "Hey wait a minute, how do you know what he's doing?"

He grinned. "I've kept tabs on him."

My mind at ease, I decided to stick to my original plan to attend the after party. I dismissed my personal assistant and headed to the bathroom for a bubble bath. Lying in a tub of warm water, I contemplated what life might be like if Malcolm realised he was my original soul mate. Would he carry on with his acting career? A celebrity, it would be impossible for him to fade into the background of society. I sighed, lathered up my bath sponge and scrubbed one arm. In the midst of washing the other one, I heard a strange noise coming from behind the door.

Frowning, I stepped out of the tub. Grabbing a bath towel, I wrapped it around my body and opened the door. A fierce gust of wind greeted me and sent me flying across the bathroom. My head hit the wash basin and everything went dark.

~~ Chapter Twenty Four ~~

When I regained consciousness, I heard a commotion downstairs. I rubbed the lump on my head. A stupid move which sent lightning bolts of pain through my noggin. I gripped the sink and hauled myself off the bathroom floor. The room spun like a wobbly carousel. The noisy din from below abruptly turned to eerie silence. Legs still unsteady, I ripped off the towel covering my naked body and put on my pink robe hanging on the door hook. Supported by the banister I carefully walked down the stairs.

I opened the living room door, but stopped dead in my tracks. It looked as if a mini cyclone had ripped through the room. Gabriel, his feathers rumpled, stood in the middle of the room. Dizzy, overwhelmed, the room began to tilt before my eyes. Half blinded by looming unconsciousness, I groped for the door frame. Gabriel grabbed me just as my knees gave way. He carried me across the room and placed me in the only upright chair left standing.

When the room stopped spinning, I stared up at Gabe.

He shrugged. "Sorry about the mess; took showering fists on Lucifer to make him leave."

"Err... okay; but what the hell are we going to do about

this mess? Dad will be home in less than half an hour."

Tapping a finger on his chin, he muttered, "Let me think." His eyes lit up. "Tell him you had to babysit the twin boys who live in number nine. I've often witnessed those kids making their house a right battleground."

I scowled at him so long that if a competition for scowling, I'd win hands down.

He smiled. "You know, Queen Victoria often had that same charming look."

Annoyed at his lackadaisical attitude, I screeched, "Shut up."

He began to pace back and forth. Items littering the floor didn't make it an easy trip.

After watching him almost trip twice, I spat, "If you can't offer something helpful Gabe, bloody well sit down!"

He stopped pacing and frowned at me. "First, we best get some ice on the lump decorating your head. Second, apart from the shattered shade on the Tiffany lamp, a smashed coffee table and a few dents here and there, it isn't all that bad."

I screeched, "For gawd's sake, Gabe, it looks as if a group of gigantic apes ransacked the place; don't you see the great big hole in the flipping wall?"

His eyes clouded with thought. "I may have a solution."

I waited, but not patiently. After a minute, I reminded him, "The clock is ticking."

"Wait here, I'll back soon." Before I could protest, he disappeared.

Hoping it was a nightmare, I closed my eyes and prayed I'd wake and find everything in place.

Gabe returned and plopped an ice bag on my head with such force I winced in pain. I prepared to return the favour by kicking him in the shins, but he vanished again. I cursed and gently applied the bag of ice to the egg growing on my head.

A most extraordinary sound made me forget my aching head. Snatching up a leg broken off a table, I prepared to do battle with Lucifer and walked to the kitchen. What I saw stole my breath. Gabe, gripping a halter attached to a full grown pony, was trying to pull the animal inside the room. The resistant pony bucked and kicked, knocking the back door off one of its hinges.

Unable to comprehend the scene unfolding before me, I slapped my face to make sure I wasn't asleep.

Gabe jerked on the rope hard and the pony stumbled into the kitchen, nearly knocking me down.

Gabe took a deep breath and looked at me. "Next to the area where you used to walk Bonnie, there's a pasture where a bunch of ponies live."

Attempting to prevent the pony eating the countertop took precedence over my response. The animal tried to bite me.

Gabriel tugged on the pony's halter and it forgot about dining on laminate. He rubbed the pony's head and the darn thing let him. Gabe then looked at me. "Don't you remember; two ponies escaped last year and were found eating the contents of some wheelie bin out front?"

Unable to utter a single syllable, I nodded.

"The pasture where the ponies graze borders the back of your property. Let us say someone accidentally left the pasture gate ajar and somehow this pony wandered into your garden and then into the house. Your attempts to get it out led to disastrous results."

A big grin spread across his face. "Well, what do you think?"

I screamed, "Are you insane?"

His grin died a sudden death. "I know it isn't the perfect

solution."

"You think!"

He shrugged his shoulders. "Do you have a better idea?"

"You're the guardian angel." I huffed.

"Then say you surprised a burglar and the ensuing struggle wrecked the living room."

"Oh that's a riot. I can see Mum dissolving into hysterics while Dad phones the local constable."

Scratching his head, he muttered, "Yeah, see what you mean."

I glared at him. He shrugged his shoulders.

Disgusted, I threw up my arms. "Guess I have no choice but to go along with your crazy arse plan."

Gabe led the pony into the living room where it decided to munch Mum's prized spider plant, and I couldn't have cared less.

The front door creaked open then closed and Dad strolled into the room. In all my lives, I'd never seen such horror on anyone's face.

Mouth gaped open he stared at the pony. "Jas..."

"Yes, Dad?"

He swallowed hard twice before managing to say, "Could you possibly enlighten me to what I'm witnessing?"

"Well as you see, Dad, there's a pony in our living room. I believe it came from the field in the back of our place. I must have left the back door open when I took a bath and it got inside."

His eyes remained transfixed on the animal that had devoured Mum's plant and started crunching the plastic pot. "So it decided to eat the entire living room including a wall and the coffee table I made?"

"Yeah, pretty much. I tried to get it out of the house but it knocked me down." I pointed to my head. "Got a nasty bump to prove it."

I thought he was going to blow a gasket and he did. "Oh my god! What the hell is your mother going to say? We best pack our stuff now because we'll be on the receiving end of her fury no matter what."

"Mum wanted to redecorate this room and..."

Dad's glare warned me to close my mouth immediately. I did.

Heavy silence formed, hung and lengthened. Finally, Dad strode over to the pony and cautiously took hold of its halter. He tugged on it and the pony followed him out of the living room. At the back door hanging from one hinge, Dad stopped and frowned at me. "The animal seems docile enough, Jasmine."

I puckered my brow. "Guess ponies don't like me?"

Dad shook his head and guided the pony through the doorway. He returned in about ten minutes looking annoyed. "The owner insists he wasn't negligent, claims a neighbourhood kid must have deliberately opened the gates."

I looked at the calamity Gabriel had created in the living room. "Yeah probably a couple of roaming, ruffians."

Dad heaved a huge sigh. "We should clean up the best we can before your Mum gets home from work tonight or she'll pass out."

I rushed around picking things up while Dad tried to repair broken furniture, the wall and the back door. The end results didn't make much difference. To prevent Mum from having a heart attack on the spot, Dad decided to call and warn her about the day's events. I heard her voice bellow from the landline as poor Dad promised her a new tiffany lamp. When he hung up, Dad informed me she planned to get off work early and come home. Claiming to have a headache, I made a beeline for my room.

When Mum showed up, her mothering instinct and the knot on my head saved me from a lengthy lecture about being responsible. She made me take a couple of aspirin, refilled the ice bag and ordered me to rest.

Lying in bed, thoughts of Malcolm and the after party rolled through my mind. With the movie premiere only two days away, I hoped things would go as planned. A trashed living room and the painful lump on my head indicated otherwise. Lucifer would do anything to stop me.

~~ Chapter Twenty Five ~~

Mum and Dad left Friday afternoon for their weekend getaway. The moment their car drove out of sight, I took a quick shower, then grabbed my phone and dialled Susan's number. She agreed to rush over and glam me up for the party. On my wild shopping spree Thursday, I'd purchased a black strapless dress with a corset style bodice. Red rosebuds with silver tipped petals trailed down the floor length skirt.

Susan soon arrived lugging a makeup case filled with her amazing concoctions. I squeezed into the body hugging gown and Susan laced up the corseted top for me. I slipped my feet into a pair of silver, strappy heels and tried to fasten the clasp of my new necklace with nervous fingers.

Susan heaved a sigh and took the necklace, placed it around my neck, then secured the clasp. She appraised my dress and nodded. "Very nice; now we need to tame those wild curls of yours."

I sat on the stool in front of my vanity table and watched her begin to straighten my hair. Light from the small table lamp made my necklace glitter. I stared at the tiny gold snake wrapped around the red apple dangling from the chain. The irony of the design had inspired me in purchasing the necklace.

The Garden of Eden beckoned my thoughts once more. God had asked only one thing. For us not to eat from the tree of truth, but weak and naïve I gave in to temptation. The guilt became almost unbearable at times. All of humankind would truly hate me if they knew my real identity.

Susan saying, "What's wrong, Jasmine?" jarred me. "Don't you like your hair?"

I blinked and told her. "Sorry; I was thinking about other stuff." I looked in the mirror. "Wow, my hair almost resembles the famous red carpet."

She smiled as she smoothed a wayward strand of my hair. "You haven't told me how things are going with Malcolm. Since you're not bragging, I'm guessing not as expected."

"It's been somewhat bumpy."

She laughed. "Aren't all relationships?"

I managed to half smile. "Well...we...uh...we did seem to have a special connection."

She raised an eyebrow. "And now?"

"I'm hoping tonight will settle things one way or another."

She frowned. "What does that mean?"

"Don't ask, please."

She shrugged. "Okay." Picking up a makeup brush, she said, "Let's highlight those beautiful green eyes of yours."

When she finished, I couldn't believe the transformation. My skin glowed with the richness of Irish cream liqueur and a soft terracotta colour covered my full lips. Expertly applied brown eye shadow, liner and mascara brought out gold specks in my eyes, making them appear luminous.

Giddy with happiness, I cried, "You've done it again!" and threw my arms around Susan. "How about me buying you lunch on Sunday as a thank you gift?"

She grinned. "On one condition."

"What's that?"

She started packing up her stuff, "Famous people will be at the party, right?"

I frowned. "I suppose."

Eyes sparkling, she said, "I want all the juicy details."

I giggled. "Of course."

She nodded. "Then lunch it is."

I escorted her to the door. She gave me a peck on the cheek and wished me luck. I promised to bring her a souvenir from the party and waved goodbye.

The mantle clock chimed seven times. I rushed up to my bedroom and grabbed my black glittery evening bag. Gabriel, who had agreed to be my chauffeur for the night, waited in the living room. Even though he reassured me Malcolm would fall at my feet like a lovesick puppy, I felt like a bundle of nerves.

Traffic in London moved at snail pace making me late for the party. I blew Gabriel a kiss and hurried from the car. The venue was Trinity House, a spectacular place that reminded me of when Malcolm took me to Paris. Booking the place for his party fit Malcolm's style. I ran up the stone steps, and showed the doorman my invitation. He nodded and opened the door for me.

Eighteenth century paintings highlighted the stunning décor of the grand reception room. Statues of benefactors, Captain Sandes and Captain Maples stood on either side of an ornate Georgian staircase. Women draped in high fashion and suave-looking men in tuxedoes filled the room. I scanned the crowd for Malcolm. There were too many people in the way. Feeling like a duck in a flock of swans, I begin weaving around people enjoying drinks and laughing. Several women raked their eyes over me and whispered something to their companions, who laughed.

A passing waiter offered me a glass of champagne. In need of liquid courage, I swigged down the contents of one glass, returned the empty, and grabbed another one. Sipping champagne, I scrutinized the area. A group of people stood like packed sardines near a window overlooking the gardens of Trinity Square. Someone in the centre of the group said something I couldn't hear and the sardines laughed. Looking divine like James blond, his hair sleeked back wearing a black tux and a white shirt, Malcolm walked from the adoring crowd.

His piecing eyes met mine. The world seemed to stop as we stared at each other. Then with a wry smile, he curved an arm around his companion, Lily Olson and pulling her close, kissed her passionately. The deliberate display shattered all of my hopes. Drawing a full breath became impossible and my knees threatened to give way.

Obviously, the conceited arse got his kicks crushing the dreams of naive fools like myself. I made a beeline for the exit. Somehow I held it together long enough to make it outside. Tears staining my cheeks, I leaned against a pillar and tried to catch my breath.

A voice sharp as a boning knife sliced the air. "It's your own stupid fault."

I looked up and found Malcolm glaring at me.

He snarled a half laugh. "Frankly, I don't know why I ever wasted my time on you. Much more attractive women than you throw themselves at me daily; ones I don't have to wine and dine. I've concluded you're not special, just another desperate loser."

Pent up anger inside me boiled over and I dug my nails into the palm of my hand. "You son of a bitch; I should have known better than to let my defences down! Why I ever thought you had one shred of decency is beyond me.

Pretending you and Lily had broken up was one of your many lies to just lure me into your bed!"

He smirked. "It was true at the time, but a man has needs."

"Clearly, like the Barbie twins at the hotel, if Lily is willing to be your sex toy, she has no self-respect."

"At least Lily isn't a stuck up bitch who thinks she's superior to me. There's a word for a woman like you; dickslayer."

Unable to bear the smirk on his face one second longer, my face flustered I ran down the steps and across the dimly lit street. Half blinded by tears, I nearly bowled over a couple on the sidewalk. The man cursed and told his companion, "She's probably drunk." The woman giggled. "Most likely."

A knot of nausea formed in my stomach and grew, filling my throat. I stumbled into a blind alleyway and fell to my knees. I heaved convulsively but nothing could get rid of the self-contempt brewing in my soul.

The shadow of angel wings fell across me. I wiped spittle from my mouth and looked up. Lucifer stood over me.

Terrified I scrambled to my feet, realising he blocked the only way out of the alley.

"I'm probably the last person, or should I say almighty being, you want to see. But I ask you to please consider a proposition that will ease your suffering."

The kindness in his tone took me aback, but I wasn't about to fall for that ploy again. I screamed, "Go to hell, you bastard."

"So you want to continue being punished for all eternity?"

"Let me pass!"

"Of course," he said, stepping aside.

I carefully edged past him and took off running.

Streaking to my side, he matched his pace with mine. "You could die and never be reborn again."

"Stop talking bullshit," I yelled. "You know that can't happen unless God grants me the privilege."

"Not exactly true."

I stopped and faced him. "What the bloody hell are you talking about? More importantly why would you want to help me?"

"You forget once upon a time, like you, I was one of God's favourites."

"Yeah, that time has long passed for you. Plus I'm pretty sure God no longer treasures my original mate or me now either. To be honest, he probably doesn't care less what happens to our souls."

A smile lit up his handsome face. "So in a way, we're all kindred spirits living out eternal damnation. Escape is impossible for me, but you hold the keys to your prison."

Painful multicoloured scraps of this life swirled through my mind. A graphic picture of Malcolm's cruel smile flashed. The prospect of another lifetime without the comfort of my soul mate was unbearable. What did I have to lose? I was already living in an ever renewing hell. I squinted up at Lucifer. "If I were to consider your offer, exactly what would I have to do?"

He held out a hand. "Come with me and I'll tell you."

"I... uh... I don't know."

He took a step towards me. I took one back.

"Do you honestly think God will ever forgive you?"

I placed my hand in his. To my surprise, his touch felt warm, comforting.

~~ *Chapter Twenty Six* ~~

Lucifer closed his hand over mine and twisted the same smug grin I remembered from long ago. I jerked my hand free and stared into the eyes of pure evil.

"What the hell am I thinking? Only a complete idiot would trust you for a second!"

His eyes boring into mine he shook his head. "You must have a masochistic personality because you clearly don't want your pain to end."

"Leave me alone, you monster. Any solution you offer is sure to only make matters worse."

He chuckled. "You misunderstand, my dear, the power to end your anguish lies in your hands and yours alone."

I glared at him. "Okay spit it out; so what will end this nightmare?"

After a cautious glance around, he leaned in close and whispered, "Suicide!"

The word stunned me. Did he speak the truth? Could self-destruction grant me freedom from a circle of never ending torment?

Someone abruptly pushed me aside. Gabe stared fiercely at Lucifer. "Keep away from her!"

"Oh shut up, Gabe," Lucifer sneered. "You don't scare me. Go play with some fluffy bunnies, you pansy."

Lucifer puffed out his chest and Gabe stepped closer to him. Fed up with life and quarrelling angels, I seized the opportunity to escape.

Wandering in a mental fog, I found myself standing on the Tower Bridge. Painful memories of many past lives flickered through my mind, as I stared down at the great River Thames. The cold wind swirling around me moaned a dark challenge.

Someone asking, "Are you alright dear?" startled me.

I swiped my eyes, turned and found a woman peering at me from a rolled down car window.

"I'm fine, thank you."

"Sure? Because you seem upset."

I gave her a fake smile. "I have a bit of a headache that's all."

She frowned. "Well can I give you a lift?"

"Thanks, but I'm waiting for a friend to pick me up."

"Oh, okay then, but mind the cars zipping past."

I smiled. "I will."

She nodded, rolled up her window, and slowly drove off.

Watching taillights of her car fade into the night made me feel so alone, abandoned. Even Gabe appearing did not ease my misery.

Concern etched his face. "Pay no attention to Lucifer. You and I will get through this together, just like we always do."

"Stop spouting useless dribble! You're not even human so don't pretend you comprehend my agony." The wounded look that crossed his face only fuelled my fury.

"You're not concerned about my welfare. The only thing you care about is defeating Lucifer. He wants to get even with God and guess what; I don't blame him. How many miserable lifetimes do I need to endure before God pardons me. I don't believe he ever will. I think this hellish torture will carry on until the end of all time!"

Gabe took a step towards me. I screamed, "Stay away from me, you freak," and gathering up my dress, I climbed onto the bridge railing.

"No; don't!" Gabriel yelled.

Sitting down on the railing, I yelled, "Shut up."

"Lucifer is trying to seize control of your mind, but you're stronger than he is, fight him. Never give up!"

I snorted in disgust. "Why? So I can exist as an empty shell for another sixty or seventy years in this life, then die and repeat the gut wrenching experience all over again?" I gripped the railing and scooted closer to the edge.

"Please don't," Gabriel cried.

Trying to block out his plea, I closed my eyes. My abiding guardian was like a brother to me, but without human emotion, he couldn't really understand my despair at the prospect of facing countless more lives.

"I'm doomed anyway," I told him. "Who knows what torture awaits me in my next life." With my legs dangling over the rail, I stared at the rushing water below.

Lucifer's offer perforated my mind, burrowing deeper and deeper into my brain like a parasite. According to him, committing suicide guaranteed me a cosy spot in Hades as his new plaything. What did I have to lose? I was already living in a revolving hell with God raining fire and brimstone on my head.

Manifesting beside me on the railing Lucifer's seductive voice blocked out Gabriel's frantic cries. "My dear," he whispered, "Gabriel never had yours or your soul mate's best interests at heart. He's simply God's soldier assigned to ensure you suffer for eternity, but you can end the punishment now. Your soul mate will never know his real identity in this life and be forced to relive the sorrow of his other lives."

He had a point. Without me roaming the earth, even if my original soul mate was born a million more times, he could enjoy each life unburdened by knowledge of our past sin. My suicide would set our eternal love free. But I needed to attend to one final detail first.

I glanced at Gabe. "Fetch my memory box."

He shouted, "No."

I stared at him in disbelief. "What! How dare you deny me a simple request as I contemplate death? Isn't that violating the rules?"

Gabe crossed his arms and shook his head.

I deliberately loosened my grip and glaring at him kicked off one of my shoes, watching as it plopped into the murky water.

Lucifer leaned closer. "Reveal the location of this box and I'll happily retrieve it for you."

"It's in..."

"Okay okay," Gabe yelled, "I'll get your box."

After he disappeared, Lucifer chuckled. "Now you're rid of him we can discuss things without being interrupted."

I hissed, "Shut up."

Lucifer's eyes widened. "That's the second time you've told me to shut up today; we are certainly going to have fun, my dear."

Gabe returned with the box. I told him, "Give it to me!"

"You can't balance on the railing and take the box. I'll only give it to you if you get down."

Wondering if he had some angel trick in mind, I scowled at him. An unexplainable longing to hold my precious treasure once again persuaded me to climb down off the railing.

Gabriel handed over the container. I opened the lid, removed the photos and flipped through them. Images on simple paper depicted the sum total of my many lives; lives filled with desperation. A picture captured my thoughts. Fingers trembling, I fished the photo of me taken just before WWII. What I suffered at the hands of the Nazis paled to the knowing Malcolm would never remember he was my Adam. Gazing at the photo unspeakable anger begins to churn inside me. God allowed this to happen. Lucifer had spoken the truth; God didn't care about me. Part of me wanted to kick and scream at the top of my lungs, but instead I felt deflated, as if all hope had been relinquished in my wronged soul.

Sobbing and cursing God, I hurled the pictures and the black leather box into the river. Watching the current carrying the mementos downstream, emptiness seized my soul, gathering up my dress, I climbed back onto the railing.

Gabe cried, "Surely you know if you jump, I'm going to save you!"

I laughed. "You're forbidden to interfere with someone's free will. If I wish to die, you must allow it!"

A chuckle erupted from Lucifer. "She's got you there, bro."

Gabriel ignored him, telling me, "God's essence runs through you. He is your saviour; draw on his strength to overcome your despair and defeat Lucifer."

"Don't you get it?" I shouted back. "God excommunicated me and my mate from his grace for all eternity. I feel nothing of him inside me."

"If God doesn't love you then why did he assign me to act as your guardian?"

"You're an idiot, Gabriel!" Lucifer yelled. "Have you learned nothing over the ages? All of this is a charade; a game God plays to make him appear merciful. In truth, assigning angels to humans stops both species from questioning his divineness. I can attest that's something he will not tolerate."

Suddenly everything I had wondered about fell into place. "So what you're saying is God uses Gabriel and the other angels to make it look like he'll never abandon any of his children?"

Lucifer smiled. "In a nutshell, yes."

Tears fill my eyes once more. "Well I'm no longer willing to be part of this sham." I stood and balanced on the railing.

Gabriel screeched, "He lies!"

Closing my eyes I leaped off the bridge.

~~ *Chapter Twenty Seven* ~~

I plunged into the shocking embrace of cold river water. Something large splashing into the water echoed and I vaguely heard Gabriel and Lucifer fighting, but I didn't care. With the chill of death spreading through me, I closed my eyes and abandoned my will to live.

As the rushing water carried me downstream, a bramble of confusion snagged my thoughts. Adoration for my soul mate had streaked across the ages with the sureness of Haley's comet. Surly, I'd been wrong. My mate's soul simply couldn't reside in someone as despicable as Malcolm Dice, but that mattered little now. All physical sensation drifted away and an eerie buzzing filled my head, before escalating into a welcoming crescendo. Darkness then encased me.

Suddenly, I found myself bathed in brilliant light. Where was I? Had Gabriel saved me? Shading my eyes with a hand, I scanned the area for Gabe, but found no sign of him or Lucifer.

I noticed a tall man standing in the distance. Dressed in a silky, dark blue suit and silver shoes, he began walking towards me. An aura of peaceful tranquility emanating from him struck a familiar chord. Mesmerized by the kaleidoscope of beautiful colours enveloping him, I stared at the man. Questions whirled through my mind and tears filled my eyes. Was the curse over? Had I finally earned forgiveness? What about my soul mate? Was he here also? I looked around. I then shockingly realised I was back in Eden.

Outside of the shimmering moon, the velvety black sky above me was void of stars, but a billion twinkling crystals filled the man's dark hair. God's long hair was the universe! The question I'd often pondered had been finally answered, beyond the stars was God. As he drew nearer, kindness shining in his golden eyes washed away all my fear and his touch filled my heart with happiness.

He tilted my chin up until our eyes met. "My sweet child, it's your life and I will respect your decision but there are things you should know. It's up to you how best to use this knowledge."

Hypnotized by his loving tone, I gazed up at him in awe.

He smiled. "Far too long you have believed I am the one punishing you and your soul mate. In truth, Lucifer is the one keeping both of you from abiding with me again."

I gasped in shock. "What do you mean, Father?"

"I made a terrible error when I created Lucifer who was the first angel I made. You see, I so craved a companion and invested too much of my own essence in him. Even the purest of souls can be corrupted with that amount of power. As unfortunately he grew envious and tried to seize control over heaven, forcing me to exile him. Desperate to exact revenge, he started a campaign to corrupt my earthly children. You and your soul mate were his first victims. I wanted to punish only him, but that would have made the other angels think I didn't value them. No, I had to be fair. So, with a heavy heart I cast both of my precious children from the Garden."

Confused, I told him, "I don't understand. If you didn't

want to continue punishing us, why didn't our souls return to Heaven when we died?"

"Desperate to fulfil his quest, Lucifer used a major quantity of the power I originally gave him to bind your souls to him."

I frowned. "But why didn't he just take our souls to his own kingdom?"

Cupping my hand in his, he kissed my fingers. "Back then, he couldn't condemn you both to Hell. Instead, he has used his limited power to trap both of you between Heaven and Hell, where you repeatedly die and are reborn."

I shook my head. "But I don't understand his ultimate aim."

God stared into my eyes. "He wants you to willingly commit a sin so egregious it'll damn you both to hell. There, he'll remove the trapped power within your souls and add it to his own." He paused to wipe away a lone tear running down my cheek. "I should have reversed Lucifer's hold on you both in the beginning, but I thought you should have an opportunity to redeem yourselves in a new life. Another mistake on my part. After your second death, I tried to lift the curse but Lucifer had already harvested many souls, thus greatly increasing his power. However, I manipulated events so the path of your soul mate crossed yours in each life. I also endowed you with the power of remembrance at the age of eighteen."

"Why didn't you also make Adam remember?"

He sighed. "Somehow Lucifer discovered my plan and blocked it, but I dictated if your mate truly fell in love with you in the next life, he'd remember your past together."

I frowned. "Oh; that explains many things."

He planted a soft kiss on my forehead. "What Lucifer didn't realise is how many times both of you would redeem yourselves. This is why claiming your souls are so important to him."

"Surely it's within your power to override Lucifer's curse."

"To break the curse, I'd have to annihilate Lucifer."

"Forgive me for asking you this, Father, but are you saying he is your equal?"

Sorrow etching his brow, he released my hand. "No, but fuelled by the evil infecting mankind he has grown very powerful. Waging war against him and his minions would wipe out this entire galaxy. I will not endanger so many innocent lives unless it becomes absolutely necessary."

"Then what are we to do?"

"Whenever you and your original mate reconnect, your souls become one, merging your strength. Together the two of you are unbeatable and Lucifer cannot harvest your souls."

His eyes met mine and then a feeling of sweet peace and everlasting love swept over me. "Now, my child, do what you must."

In a flash, I found myself back in the rushing river fighting for my breath. My strength renewed, I begin swimming towards the riverbank. Reaching my goal, I grasped the river bank reeds and pulled myself onto dry land. Exhausted, I collapsed on the grassy bank and sucked needed air into my lungs.

Someone called my name. I opened my eyes and found Gabriel staring down at me. River water dripping off his ruffled wing feathers, he asked, "Are you all right?"

I nodded. "Where's Lucifer?" A muffled cry of frustration pierced the night air, confirming Gabriel had managed to kick Lucifer back into hell; temporarily.

Gabriel snapped his fingers and his water-soaked feathers instantly dried.

I grinned at him. "A nice trick but could you do me a favour?"

Pulling me upright, he asked, "How can I be of service?"

"Can you sense where Malcolm is right now?"

"I'll try." Tilting his head, his eyes clouded over. After a moment, he said, "Malcolm and his date are preparing to leave the party."

I scrambled up the riverbank to the bridge and raced barefoot down the street.

Gabe flew to my side. "Where are you going?"

"I am going to get my soul mate back."

"Lucifer is pissed you changed your mind about committing suicide. He'll use all his power to stop that from happening."

"Gabriel?"

"Yes?"

"Please find Malcolm and prevent him from getting frisky with Lily Olson."

He said, "I will try my best," and disappeared.

When I arrived at the venue, majority of the partygoers were leaving, most of them quite inebriated. I searched the area for Malcolm without success. The doorman stared at me strangely still dripping wet, then informed me he'd already left.

Unsure of what my next move should be, I walked down the path and stood waiting for Gabriel to return. A sudden gust of wind rose up and swirled around me, wrapping me in a rising sense of dread. Cracks appeared in the path underneath my feet, then widened into a dark crevasse. Screaming, I clawed at crumbling concrete and mud as the earth swallowed me up.

~~ *Chapter Twenty Eight* ~~

I emerged from semi-consciousness and realised I was mired in a pool of what appeared to be coagulated blood. Horrified, I struggled to free myself but the effort caused me to sink deeper in the disgusting sludge. Neck deep in bloody ooze with increasing pressure against my chest, my vision blurred. With the fog of unconsciousness closing in, hideous images began to twist through my mind. A blood curdling scream echoed and I realised it came from me. Using the last of my fading willpower, I shoved the images from my mind. With the little strength I had left slipping away; I heard a voice ordering me to watch a hypnologic scene which formed in front of me.

A dreamlike, hazy movie began flickering before me. I watched Gabriel fly to Malcolm's penthouse, and cloaked in invisibility, enter the apartment. Malcolm, sitting on the sofa, drained the glass in his hand and reached for a half empty bottle of scotch on the coffee table. Refilling his glass, he tossed the whiskey down his throat, and poured another.

Gabriel's eyes widened and he muttered, "Damn you, Lucifer!" From the dismay on Gabe's face, I suspected he was just notified about my dire situation. The guidelines guardian angels operate under dictate Gabe can't reveal my true identity to Malcolm, so I'm shocked when he fully manifests in front of Malcolm. At the sight of a huge angel, Malcolm jumped to his feet. Looking as if he was going to crap himself and choking on whiskey, he coughed, spraying the liquid on to the sofa.

Gabriel glared at him. "First of all, dummy, you're not drunk. Second, yes I am a freaking angel! Lastly, get your skinny arse in gear or you're going to lose Jasmine forever."

Malcolm's face blanched and he muttered, "No bloody way is this happening!"

Gabe grinned. "You're slow on the uptake aren't you?"

Malcolm staggered backwards, tripping over a throw rug in the process and landing on the floor. Sprawled on his backside, he stared up at Gabe. "You've gotta be a hallucination or something. Some rowdy bloody bastard must've spiked my drink at the after party."

Gabriel shook his head. "Look, stupid, I'm God's messenger sent to open your eyes. Now get your act together because I need your help to save Jasmine from the Devil's clutches."

Malcolm, his eyes glued on Gabriel, got on his feet, and slurred, "This is seriously messed up. I clearly need a lie down." Dismissing Gabe with a wave of his arm, Malcolm weaved towards the staircase. "Go back to wherever you flipping came from, freak."

Shouting, "I don't have time to deal with your lack of belief," Gabe caught Malcolm up and transported him to the scorched plot of ground that had swallowed me.

Terrified, Malcolm cried, "Bloody mother of God; am I dead?"

Gabriel snapped, "You're not dead, you dolt! I told you that I needed your help to save Jasmine. This spot is where

Lucifer opened a portal to take her to Hell."

Malcolm quirked an eyebrow at him. "On the off chance I'm not delusional, let's get one thing straight; there's no way I'm letting you drag me down to the bowels of Hell. Besides, what do you expect me to do? Kick the evil emperor of hell in the nuts and poke out his eyes? In case you haven't noticed, I'm not the super being here, you are!"

"Because you're ignorant to some aspects of your psyche, you underestimate your importance and strength." Gabe spat.

"Cut out the new age mumbo jumbo and speak a language I understand."

"Okay; basically you have no idea of true identity. Is that simple enough, dimwit?"

Malcolm sighed and he rubbed his bleary eyes. "I don't like you one damn bit. Don't understand why God hasn't fired your sorry arse."

"Is that so?" Gabe snorted. "Well I can't stand your current alter ego of Malcolm Dice, but we don't have time for idle chit chat."

"Look here, I'm Malcolm Dice, not a fictional character in a movie you moron. All this talk about me having an alter ego is a load of codswallop"

"It's far too complex for someone with the intellect of a baboon to understand."

Malcolm glared at him and Gabe glared back. Silence built and lengthened.

Gabe heaved a sigh. "Guess it won't hurt to reveal that you've lived many other lives."

Malcolm snorted. "I don't believe the twaddle about reincarnation either."

"We can discuss that later. Jasmine needs you, so stop wasting precious time and give me permission to transport you to Hell with me."

Malcolm twisted a sarcastic grin. "Ah-ha! The almighty angel doesn't have Satan's power; otherwise he'd simply drag me down to hell."

Saying, "If you insist," Gabe grabbed the front of Malcolm's shirt and flew high in the air. Still clutching his captive who was screaming like a banshee, Gabriel executed a sharp u-turn and plummeted toward earth. Using his fist like a bullet Gabe pierced the portal to Lucifer's kingdom.

When their descent into the pit of hell ended, Gabe set Malcolm down.

Malcolm, his eyes unaccustomed to the darkness, groped for something to familiarize him with the surroundings. He jerked his hand back. "What the bloody hell was that?"

Gabriel chuckled. "Oh, nothing to worry about."

"Being in hell may give you the jollies, but I want outta here...Now!"

Gabriel seized his arm forcefully. "Be quiet, Mr Shag anything or we'll have a demon welcoming party."

"Demons?" Struggling to break free, Malcolm spat, "Great, I can't see anything and the place is patrolled by demons."

"Be grateful you can't see what surrounds you."

Gabe began dragging him down a corridor. "But don't worry, puny human, I can see everything."

A disembodied arm reached out from a slimy wall and tried to grab Malcolm. Malcolm squealed, "Something touched me."

Gabriel slapped the decaying arm and it sank back into the wall.

Nervously peering into the darkness, Malcolm said, "By the way, why can't I see?"

Gabriel chuckled. "Because, you're not dead, yet... dummy!"

Malcolm mumbled under his breath, "What a dickhead."

"I heard that," Gabe snapped. "Just so you'll know I have finely tuned hearing."

Malcolm smirked. "I was counting on it."

Gabriel made an abrupt stop and held up his hand. "Shh." Cocking his head, he said, "I can hear Jasmine."

His voice a harsh whisper, Malcolm asked, "What does the devil want with her? Exactly what the heck is this about?"

"Can't waste any time explaining; all you need to know is Lucifer snatching her is part of his ultimate plan."

After a moment, Gabe, with Malcolm in tow, continued down the corridor.

"So, Sasquatch," Malcolm said, "I assume you have a counter plan?"

"Nope, just going to see how it all pans out as we go."

"Freaking fantastic," Malcolm muttered.

In a barely audible whisper, he told Malcolm, "When we pass through the next veil you'll be able to see what is happening."

"What veil?"

"The veil concealing Lucifer's chamber. What lies on the other side defies the imagination, so it's imperative you control your thought processes. If Lucifer senses you're traumatized, he'll seize control of your mind and direct your actions... something he's done on many occasions."

Malcolm frowned. "What are you actually implying, I'm Satan's bitch?"

Gabe grinned. "More than you realise."

Malcolm gave him a filthy look.

Gabriel began glowing until a brilliant blue light surrounded them both. Malcolm squeezed his eyes shut against the sudden light. Gabriel shoved him through the static force field.

On the other side, Malcolm grabbed his head and winced in pain. "Shit, that felt weird."

Echoing wails of anguish made Malcolm quickly forget his pain. He stared wide eyed at deformed demons the size of rhinos. With dagger shaped horns protruding from their scaly skulls, blood dripped from their decaying teeth as they tore limbs from the still alive dammed and cast the appendages aside. They then begin devouring the internal organs of their screaming victims. Smaller cat like demons with glowing green eyes fought to capture a severed limb as their prize. The successful ones made slurping noises as they savoured the fresh meat. Malcolm, moving slowly, pressed against Gabriel.

"Don't let it affect you," Gabe whispered. "Switch off your mind; pretend it's not happening."

Malcolm nodded. His eyes fixed on a gruesome creature chomping a live head like a jawbreaker, he asked, "Why aren't they attacking me?"

"They can only see the dammed. You're not far from achieving that status."

"You're one twisted arsehole," Malcolm snarled.

Gripping Malcolm's arm, Gabe strode down the corridor smiling. "Coming from you I find that quite comical. Maybe being down here will make you grow some balls and awaken your better side."

Gabe stopped before an opening edged by flames. Malcolm tried to pull away but Gabriel tightened his grip and sneered, "Welcome to Lucifer's inner sanctum."

~~ *Chapter Twenty Nine* ~~

Adrift in a haze of confusion, I watched Gabriel and Malcolm striding towards the slush pit which trapped me.

Gabriel crouched by the pit. "Jasmine, can you hear me?"

Detached from reality, believing they were all part of the illusion swimming before my eyes, I whispered, "Oh, Gabe, I so wish you and Malcolm were here. I really do."

Gabe plunged his hands into the congealing blood. "We are real and we're going to get you out of here."

A chilling laugh sounded. "If I'd known visitors were popping by, I would have cleaned the place up first."

Gabriel jerked me from the pit and cradling me in his arms, he smiled at the embodiment of evil, standing behind Malcolm. "We're not staying, so go find some other entertainment!"

Lucifer folded his arms stared at Gabe. "I can understand you wanting a guided tour of my domain, Gabriel. I know from personal experience how boring it becomes fluttering amongst the heavenly clouds. So, my honoured guests please enjoy all the hospitality hell has to offer." He motioned to where demons were consuming the dammed. "What do you think about my lovely decorated foyer? I dubbed it limb-

limbo. It's an ever-changing masterpiece. You might say people are dying to gain entrance."

Gabe sneered, "You're an artist alright...an eternally dammed one."

The crackle of evil laughter echoed off the walls. "Why thank you, my brother. How kind of you to acknowledge my talent. Sadly my wall is missing two important pieces." He raked his eyes over me and then turned to Malcolm. "But by sheer good luck, or should I say stupidity, both of them are now in my domain."

Gabriel hissed, "Your stupidity is showing. You will gain nothing by killing them. Their souls will be reborn again, not trapped down here with you."

Lucifer's eyes widened. "If you believe that, my brother, then why are you here?"

Gabriel's arms tightened around me. "You believe you're as powerful as God, but we both know you aren't."

"How naively foolish you are," Lucifer told him. "My artistic hallway serves a higher purpose. A slow, agonizing torture extracts ultimate energy from corrupted souls and adds it to my power." His attention snapped back to me. "Even though her original sin was committed long ago, I thirst for her energy."

Lucifer directed a grin at Malcolm "Her mate here will make a yummy, bedtime snack."

Malcolm edged closer to Gabe.

"Good still outweighs the bad Lucifer," Gabe calmly declared, "and do not call me brother. You are nothing to me."

Lucifer's upper lip curled in disgust. "Need I remind you, dear brother, we both have the same father? Unfortunately, while you have dined on heavenly scrapes for centuries, I have enjoyed a buffet of earthly delights. All because our creator, gave his brainless, human pets free will."

Gabriel snorted. "You're nothing more than a doomed outcast feeding on the weak minded. God is the omniscient ruler of the whole universe."

Ignoring him, Lucifer turned full attention to Malcolm. "So, movie star, how does it feel to know I'm the guiding force behind your fame and wealth?"

Beads of sweat streaming down his brow, Malcolm stammered, "Really? Well cheers for that, mate."

Lucifer's cackle sliced the putrid air. "Your stupidity in this life is what attracted my attention. The moment you concluded you were superior to everyone else, it opened the door to your pathetic mind. Wallowing in the worship of your fans conquered your remaining humanity, thus letting me in to control you like a mindless puppet. As like others, when your brother needed you most, you treated him appallingly. While he drove his car onto the rail tracks, you were banging a fan in a filthy alleyway."

Lucifer winked at me. "Bet lover boy here didn't tell you that part, did he? But I must admit I enjoyed watching the girl on her knees servicing your boyfriend."

Malcolm struggled to respond but seemed too shook up to speak.

I glared at Lucifer as Gabe set me down. He pushed himself between Malcolm and Lucifer.

"I won't allow you to dump all the blame on Malcolm for his brother's death. You made James commit suicide."

"Yes and what a delightful time I had. Comparing himself with his famous sibling had diminished James' self confidence, so I simply pushed a few buttons, which sent him tumbling over the edge of insanity."

Lucifer sneered at Malcolm. "I'm surprised you didn't notice that your brother is a nice feature on my wall of despair."

A guttural scream ripped from Malcolm as he lunged for Lucifer. Gabriel, still holding on to me with one arm, pushed Malcolm back with the other.

Malcolm, his face distorted with rage, struggled to reach Lucifer. "You bloody reject of heaven, I'll find a way to hang your carcass on that flipping wall!"

Lucifer squealed gleefully. "Don't make threats you can't keep, monkey boy."

He then clapped his hands. "This little family reunion has been fine and dandy, but I am extremely busy. So at the risk of sounding rude, Gabriel, I insist you must leave now."

Gabriel's face was stern. "Not a problem, but they both are coming with me."

Lucifer rubbed his chin thoughtfully. "I figured you might try something daft, Gabriel, so my devoted employees will escort you out."

Three huge, slug like creatures with four arms emerged from the pit of sludge. High pitched screeches came from their mouths lined with multiple rows of razor sharp teeth. Moving with incredible speed, the first creature slapped Gabe upside the head, staggering him. Another wrapped a slimy appendage around my waist and lifted me into the air. The third captured Malcolm before Gabriel could recover his balance.

Gabe tried to fight the blood slug pinning him down, but his efforts proved futile.

Lucifer chuckled. "Bro you're on my turf now, so you best get your powerless arse out of here, before my pets crack open your head and devour your tiny brain."

Gabe continued his valiant struggle.

Lucifer waved his hand and an opening appeared in the ceiling of the underground kingdom. The Prince of Hell issued a command and the creature snatched Gabe up and flung him towards the opening. Similar to water spewing from a broken pipe, Gabe flew up through the portal and then the opening closed.

Lucifer issued a guttural order and the slug demons dragged us out into the hellish foyer. At the limbo wall, I fought to break free from my captor, but the thing used ropes of slime from its putrid mouth to begin entombing me in the wall. I couldn't see Malcolm in the pitch dark hallway, but the sound of his protests revealed the same was happening to him.

As the creature weaved its slimy web over me, I cried, "I'm sorry, Malcolm, this is all my fault."

Clearly fighting for freedom, he yelled, "No it's not. You made me feel things I'd never felt before. It frightened me when I began to fall in love with you, so I did my best to run you away. Please forgive me?"

Rising terror stole my response. A pair of hands belonging to a damned soul sealed within the wall closed around my arm. I made a fist, punched at the unseen, hitting something that felt like a half decayed face. A shriek of pain ripped from the face. Hands released me but other hands latched on and began pulling me deeper into the wall. I screamed.

"Jasmine," Malcolm yelled, "What's happening?"

Before I could reply, the slug demon looped a rope of sticky goo around my neck and slowly tightened the noose.

"Are you still with me, Jasmine?" Malcolm pleaded.

With the sound of Malcolm violently resisting his fate in the background, I surrendered to the velvety blessing of unconsciousness.

~~ Chapter Thirty ~~

Someone loosened the slime rope from my neck, allowing me to suck in much needed air. I opened my eyes, but in the darkness didn't know who was aiding me.

I slowly slipped down the wall and on to what felt like more solid ground. I sat slumped on the floor. A hand gently shook me. "Are you okay, Eve?"

As full consciousness dawned, I realised it was Malcolm's voice. But he used my original name which meant he had full knowledge of our shared past. My heart beating wildly, it took several attempts before I managed to hoarsely whisper, "Adam?"

He caressed my face. "Yes, my darling, I'm Adam again. I'm so sorry for being such a jerk in this lifetime."

Tears trickling down my cheeks, I threw my arms tight around him. "It's okay; all that matters is we're together." A sudden thought hit me. "But how is this possible? To have remembered, you obviously felt true love for me, but yet you're not in a coma?"

"I don't know. When I thought that I had lost you, memories surged throughout my mind. My strength renewed, I managed to free myself of the slime encasing me and then made my way through the darkness to where I last heard your voice. I ran my hands over the wall of bodies until I felt one warmer than the others. Praying it was you I clawed off the revolting gunk."

Cupping my face in his hands, he kissed me gently. "Thank God, my prayer was answered."

Kissing him back, bliss filled my soul. Until, a deafening screech pierced our happiness.

"Why do you insignificant maggots continue doing this to me?" Lucifer shouted. "My plan was bloody perfect, but you had to destroy all my hard work with that cursed love of yours. Now I might as well kill you both, then you will get to enjoy yet another tragic life."

The thought I'd have to find Adam all over again in another lifetime filled me with dread.

No! I could not, would not, be separated from my soul mate again. Righteous anger replaced my fear of Lucifer.

I asked Adam, "Do you trust me?"

"You know I do."

"Then trust me now. Someone told me the power of God exists within each human. To defeat Lucifer and save our souls, we must access that power." Clutching his hands, I said, "Concentrate!"

Adam's hands tightened on mine. Time seemed to stand still as we struggled to merge our thoughts. A faint glow formed around us and grew into a golden orb of pulsating light. The floor beneath our feet and the walls around us began shaking violently. Suddenly, a flash of blinding light spun through Hades. A horrific scream ripped from Lucifer.

In the next moment, Adam and I stood above ground. Gabriel, bathed in glorious light, appeared beside us. Lucifer manifested. His features twisted into a grotesque mask of anger, he glared at us with hate glowing in his red eyes.

"How the hell did you do that?" He pointed a trembling finger at Gabe. "Not even bird brain there can unlock the doors to my empire. Who told you the secret?"

I laughed. "Realising you have limited power can be very frustrating." Slowly enunciating each word, I added, "But you know that now."

Lucifer taking a step towards me almost fractured my bravado.

"Who told you the secret?" He demanded.

Adam squeezing my hand refortified my determination.

I screamed at evil personified. "You're a fool, Lucifer! Why do you think I changed my mind about committing suicide? God snatched me from the river into his presence. He revealed everything; including you were the one responsible for the centuries of misery Adam and I have endured. The knowledge God loves me gave me the strength to swim to the riverbank." Caught in a whirlwind of anger, I strode towards Lucifer until we stood face to face. "Get this, you evil bastard, even if Adam and I are reborn a million times, you will never possess our souls. They belong to our creator; God!"

Struck dumb, Lucifer stared at me; then his spine chilling laughter sounded, spraying rancid spittle on me. "Surely, my dear, you don't still believe in happy ever after. Sadly, I have some bad news for you."

In a fiery flash, Lucifer streaked past me and grabbed Adam. Yelling, "Adam, I hereby release your soul from my bind," he broke Adam's neck. Like a martinet without strings, the lifeless body of my soul mate slumped to the ground.

Screaming, I ran to where Adam lay and sobbing hysterically, I clutched his body against my chest.

Lucifer bent over me. "How pathetic you humans are. Tell

me, Eve, how enjoyable is your victory now? Will it sustain you in this life and the many to follow or will the permanent death of your mate leave you incomplete for all eternity?" His laughter echoed off the surrounding buildings. "Now this is what I call fun!"

Knowing only desolation lay ahead without Adam, grief consumed my mind. Gripping Adam's body even closer, the pain in my heart felt like it was going to detonate like a bomb and blow us all up. Suddenly I heard Gabe chuckle. I swung my head in his direction and saw he wore a big grin.

Lucifer giggled. "Gabriel, my dear brother, have you switched sides... or have you finally lost your marbles and become a holy nutcase? I hope it's the former, because I have a very special room reserved for you in my kingdom."

Ignoring the taunting remark, Gabriel walked to my side. Placing a hand on the top of my head, he said, "By the power of almighty God, I break the hold Lucifer has on your soul. From this day forward, you will never be reborn again, and when this life is over you will join Adam and a host of others waiting for you in heaven."

A blue glow encompassed my head and incredible warmth flowed through me, turning my tears of sorrow into ones of joy.

Lucifer screamed, "How is this damn possible?"

Gabe smiled. "Lucifer, overconfidence is why your schemes to overthrow God have and will always fail. When you set Adam free, where do you think the power in his soul went?"

Lucifer stared at him speechless for a moment then snarled, "This isn't over!"

Gabriel launched a supercharged fist against Lucifer's mouth, sending him flying backward. The king of the underworld landed on his arse with a mighty thud, causing a ring of putrid smoke to rise into the air. He laid there looking stunned.

"Fallen yet again, Lucifer?" Gabe asked.

Lucifer swiped at the blood trickling from his mouth.

Gabe smirked. "Don't want to seem impolite, bro, but it's time for you to go. So you best get off your backside and return to your delightful living quarters before friends of mine escort you there."

Lucifer slowly got onto his feet. He cast a look of utter contempt at me before disappearing.

Tears rolling down my cheek, I kissed Adam's cold lips. "We'll soon be together, my darling and no one will ever separate us again."

Gabriel, sadness etching his voice, laid a gentle hand on my shoulder. "Your screams have surely attracted attention and the authorities will soon on the way."

Caressing Adam's ashen face, I shook my head. "I don't care."

Gabriel spread his wings to cloak us with invisibility. "We need to make it look like Adam had an accident; otherwise the police might think you killed him." Gabe forcefully pried my hands from Adam and lifted my soul mate into his arms.

Overcome by grief, I couldn't move. Did I really want to live without my one and only true love? Peace the River Thames could offer beckoned me.

"Eve, get on your feet. Now." Gabe ordered.

Feeling numb, I managed to stand without my legs buckling.

Gabriel's brow furrowed. "A broken neck requires making it appear he accidentally tumbled down a flight of stairs, preferably somewhere with people who witness it happen."

Confused, I mumbled, "That's impossible."

"Not exactly," Gabe told me. "The steps in front of Trinity

House will be sufficient. At this time of night, several security guards should be on duty to serve as witnesses...that means I need to stage the accident properly. Keeping myself cloaked, I can make sure Adam is the only one seen. If I prop him up at the top of the stairs then let him go, he'll tumble..."

"No; I won't have his body abused!"

"What else can we do," Gabe asked, "tell the police Lucifer broke his neck?"

Fresh tears streaming down my face, I looked at my Adam lying so peacefully in Gabe's arms.

Tenderness framed Gabe voice as he said, "This body is only an empty shell; Adam is waiting for you on the other side. You must know that, don't you?"

I nodded.

He kissed my forehead. "Please don't watch, okay?"

I avoided looking towards Trinity House as Gabe took flight.

Time seemed to stretch endlessly as I waited for his return, but I sensed Adam's spirit and realised his soul was still linked to mine.

Gabe squeezing my shoulder startled me. "It's done. One of the guards witnessed the accident and phoned the authorities. He told them Malcolm Dice was drinking heavily at the party. They'll assume Malcolm left something at the venue and came back to retrieve the item. Drunk and unsteady on his feet, he must have slipped and fell, breaking his neck. I'm sure tests by the coroner will confirm Malcolm still had alcohol in his system."

The finality of my soul mate's death buckled my knees. Gabriel swept me up and carried me home. When I stumbled into the house in a daze, Mum and Dad assumed I was drunk and put me to bed.

The next morning every media outlet carried the news

that Malcolm Dice, famous movie star, had a tragic accident. Mum asked me if I had been with Malcolm at the after party. I told her some of the truth, that when I arrived at the party, I saw Malcolm kiss his former girlfriend, Lily Olson. We argued and I left. Dad asked where I'd been all night. I said that I spent the evening with two old friends.

A constant stream of news reports about Malcolm and tributes to him filled the next week, sending me deeper into despair. Gabriel never left my side for one minute.

At the funeral, I didn't join the crowd of mourners. Instead, I stood by a large oak tree and watched the proceedings from afar. A lump of guilt formed in my throat as I watched his poor parents sobbing. Lucifer's quest to claim my soul was the reason they'd lost both of their sons. Everything in me longed to tell them what really happened, but I knew they couldn't understand. The knowledge they would eventually learn the truth provided little comfort.

After everyone left, I stepped from behind the tree and Gabe escorted me to Malcolm's grave. I knelt by the gleaming black tombstone and ran my fingers across the name engraved in marble. It didn't register at first; then it hit me so hard that I gasped. The name on the headstone was Malcolm Adam Dice. Malcolm's middle name was Adam. Smiling, I leaned forward and kissed the earthly name of my dead soul mate.

Removing my apple and snake necklace, I draped it over the headstone. In my mind, the necklace not only symbolized my downfall from grace, but the promise I would join my soul mate in Heaven one day.

Staring at wilting roses covering the fresh grave, I pondered how best to spend my time in this life. Adam and I often discussed volunteering for aid work in Africa but we never did. Faith renewed, I was determined not to waste one moment in the precious life I'd been given. Aided by the counsel of my guardian angel and comforted by the spirit of Adam, I could be of some good service in the world.

The end